Readers love the Plenty, California series by TA MOORE

Bone to Pick

"TA Moore brings readers a solid, well written, suspenseful mystery in *Bone to Pick*. The plot is multi-layered and peppered with suspicious characters who had me fooled almost to the very end."

—The Novel Approach

"*Bone to Pick* is a great mystery that is sure to pull readers in from the beginning."

—Top 2 Bottom Reviews

"TA Moore is fast becoming a go to author for me, and I think this is another really enjoyable story."

—Joyfully Jay

Skin and Bone

"…this book checks all my boxes. I could not put it down."

—Love Bytes

"I would totally read the next book in the series given the quality of writing and emotional engagement I had with the first two books in the series."

—Gay Book Reviews

By TA MOORE

Every Other Weekend
Ghostwriter of Christmas Past
Liar, Liar
Take the Edge Off

BLOOD AND BONE
Dead Man Stalking

DIGGING UP BONES
Bone to Pick
Skin and Bone

ISLAND CLASSIFIEDS
Wanted – Bad Boyfriend

PLENTY, CALIFORNIA
Swipe
Bone to Pick
Skin and Bone

WOLF WINTER
Dog Days
Stone the Crows

Published by DREAMSPINNER PRESS
www.dreamspinnerpress.com

SWIPE

TA MOORE

Published by
DREAMSPINNER PRESS

5032 Capital Circle SW, Suite 2, PMB# 279, Tallahassee, FL 32305-7886 USA
www.dreamspinnerpress.com

Swipe
© 2019 TA Moore

Cover Art
© 2019 Kanaxa
Cover content is for illustrative purposes only and any person depicted on the cover is a model.

Trade Paperback ISBN: 978-1-64405-615-8
Digital ISBN: 978-1-64405-614-1
Library of Congress Control Number: 2019947714
Trade Paperback published December 2019
v. 1.0

Printed in the United States of America

This paper meets the requirements of
ANSI/NISO Z39.48-1992 (Permanence of Paper).

CHAPTER ONE

TWELVE-HOUR SHIFT in the ER—seventeen patients, three biters, and eight cups of subpar waiting room coffee. However you did the math, that was a long day. Tag frowned at his reflection in the fly-specked mirror as he looped the black silk tie around his neck. Unfortunately it wasn't over yet.

Music—the unchallenging strains of familiar classical airs barely a step up from elevator Muzak—filtered up through the floor as he fumbled with his collar. Back in med school, nose deep in cricothyroidotomies and venous cannulation, he'd imagined himself at the cutting edge of neurological research at this stage in his career. Instead he was struggling with a bow tie before he went out to pick his colleagues' pockets for grant money.

Four years ago he imagined he'd be happily married and settled down with a dog or possibly even a kid by now. Instead he was unhappily separated, and all his friends, the ones he still had since he left New York and moved to Plenty, CA three years ago, thought he needed to go and fuck someone new—as though something that lasted five years could really be over in two months.

Fold back, pinch the end, and through the loop....

The bow tie looked like a dog had tied it and then chewed on it. Tag gave one lopsided loop a halfhearted tug in an attempt to straighten it. Instead it just unraveled. *To hell with it.* He pulled the strip of silk loose from his collar and tossed it back into his locker. Emergency room doctors were supposed to be the bad boys of medicine. Tag unbuttoned the top two buttons on his collar and tugged it loose around his throat. There. That was on-brand.

Tag lifted the black tuxedo jacket off the hanger and shrugged it on. He'd bought it before the hospital's big charity ball ten years ago, when he was a first-year medical resident. It seemed like a ridiculous expense at the time, but if nothing else, it motivated him to stay in shape. The waistband of the trousers was only a shade too tight—too many night shifts, too much Chinese takeout—but the fabric of the jacket still caught satisfyingly across the width of his shoulders.

It would do.

He raked his fingers through his hair, pushed the day's frustrations to the back of his brain, and headed downstairs. The lobby had been decorated with swags of brand-red fabric and glossy white balloons, and long trestle tables were scattered around and laden with one-bite morsels to keep the donors content and talking.

Surgeons in evening wear, rented tuxes in black and floor-length gowns in the recommended muted jewel tones, chatted with businessmen and lawyers over glasses of midprice champagne. Cardio and neurology mostly, Tag noticed. They always had it easiest. Rich people worried about heart attacks and strokes before anything else.

ER was down the list. People never thought accidents would happen to them until they did.

Tag tucked a hand in his pocket, grabbed a glass of wine from a passing waiter, and headed out to worry some rich people. Car crashes, aneurysms, the unpleasant parasites you could bring home from visiting summer homes in exotic locales. Brains were sexy, but emergency medicine had variety on its side.

Half an hour later he had worked his way through a quarter of the room and tapped out his ability to laugh at borderline offensive humor. He leaned against a pillar, wine swapped for a glass of ice water, and waited to see if hotel heiress Hetty Alderdice's anecdote about her trip to London would veer dubiously into race, gender, or ability. When it didn't, he chuckled with polite relief.

"I actually had a patient who was in London last month," he remarked as the laughter faded. Positioned at Alderdice's elbow, Ned Blake, Tag's best friend and pediatric oncology's finest, rolled his eyes at the five-year-old story and then turned to grab another glass of champagne from a waiter's tray. "Well, London and Madagascar. When she got sick, she blamed Madagascar, but actually she'd gotten rat-bite fever from a—"

"Tag," Ned interrupted just as he hit his rhythm. "Here. You'll need this."

He shoved the flute into Tag's hand. Straw-colored fizz slopped over the rim and trickled stickily over Tag's fingers. Tag cursed and fumbled for a second, both hands full as the champagne dribbled onto his polished shoes.

"I'm fine, Ned," he protested as he looked around for somewhere to offload the unwanted drink. "I've had a—"

Shit.

Tag stumbled over his own tongue as he finally saw what, or who, had made Ned think he needed a drink. His ex was here. Of course he was. Psychology needed funding too, and Kieran had always enjoyed these meat markets. Although Tag doubted the pretty boy on Kieran's arm was here to compete for department funding.

"Son of a bitch," Tag said. His heart crawled up into the back of his throat, the pulse of it loud in his ears, and his chest cramped painfully around where it had been.

"Is something wrong?" Alderdice asked as she raised a perfectly manicured eyebrow. She turned to follow the direction of Tag's gaze across the crowded ballroom. She hazarded a guess. "Did someone… fall?"

"No. Nope. Nothing like that," Ned said. He patted Alderdice's shoulder to distract her and waved his hand at random toward one of the milling doctors. "Let me introduce you to… Bill. Dr. Havers. He's got some wonderful stories."

Ned grimaced at Tag, the expression either an apology or an injunction to behave, as he dragged a slightly baffled but cooperative Alderdice over to the hospital's lead pathologist, who did, to be fair, have wonderful stories that not many people wanted to hear.

"He's a nurse in my department," one of the cardiologists in the group provided cheerfully as they turned to check Kieran out. He popped a cube of cheese in his mouth and added as he chewed, "Apparently they got caught fucking in Dr. Pierce's office by that ER guy he was dating."

Accurate enough, although Tag hadn't realized the guy was a cardiology nurse. All he knew was that he had a tacky tattoo of a winged heart on his ass and was, in Kieran's words, "Exciting, like you used to be."

The cardiologist's companion untangled her arms from her shawl so she could jab him in the ribs with a sharp elbow. "Shut up," she hissed through still red lips.

"What?" the cardiologist protested as he rubbed his ribs. "It's what I heard, that's—"

Fuck it. Tag drained the glass of champagne in one unsatisfying draft, handed off the water to a confused lawyer, and stalked out. He managed not to look back to see if Kieran had noticed his departure, but he wanted to. In fact, it was only after he grabbed his bag, called for a driver from the hospital's car service to come get him, and went out into the street to wait for it in the rain that some breathless little part of him gave up on the idea that Kieran would chase after him.

God knew why. He never had before. "If you want to storm out," he always said, "you get to crawl back too." There had been days, weeks, when their relationship was caught in limbo between the fight and Tag's apology.

Now it was Kieran who had—royally—fucked up, and he showed no signs he wanted to apologize.

The indignation that had driven Tag out of the hospital flared again, hot as cinnamon in the back of his throat. He leaned back against a light and let the rain soak him as he waited for the cab. For the last two months, he'd been *fucking* reasonable, held his tongue, and swallowed his anger, accepted his own "role" in what happened because he wanted to hang on to that last rickety bridge back to where they'd been.

Meanwhile Kieran had just moved on.

"Bad boy of medicine," he muttered aloud with scathing self-contempt as he pulled his iPhone out of his pocket. "More like a scorned wife from the fifties, crying in my fucking gin. To hell with it."

There were fifteen unread messages stacked up, but he ignored them. It was probably just Ned, eager for assurance that Tag hadn't done something stupid like kill himself or key Kieran's pride-and-Porsche.

Tag flicked through the phone until he got to the app, the one he was definitely not ever going to use but hadn't deleted either.

"Like Tinder," Ned had explained as he downloaded it, as though Tag had been in a relationship since 1983, not just the last few years. "Only with more cocks."

Online had never been Tag's scene, to be fair. He'd always preferred to find his hookups the old-fashioned way—sweaty bars and dangerous glances, setups from friends, a fuck-it kiss to see what happened. Tonight he didn't want a chase or, God forbid, a challenge. He'd already lost once, come in a hobbled second to a hot young tattooed thing, and he didn't want to put his dinged ego through any more rejection.

No. Guaranteed preapproved satisfaction, that's what he needed.

"Okay," Tag muttered as he tapped the app to open it. "Let's see how fucking exciting someone new can be."

Ned had set up the profile for *HotDoc* with a two-year-old pic of him on holiday, scavenged from the depths of his phone. It wasn't that far off what he looked like now—happier, but his hair was worse. It would do for an online date. It was probably at least as accurate as everyone else's photo.

All Tag had to do was find the right green box to tap. He impatiently flicked through the options. It wasn't like he actually cared, or had to care. That was the point. He didn't need a connection. That was the last thing he wanted.

Maybe that was what made him stop on one headless-torso shot. Broad shoulders and lean hips, worn jeans that sagged carelessly low over the pubic bone. The expanse of tanned skin on show was decorated with stark, tribal lines of ink—a blank hot slate.

A car service sedan pulled up to the curb and waited expectantly. Tag had never been so grateful for the opportunity to misuse the hospital's "don't drink and drive" policy.

Tag hesitated in the chat window, thumbs poised over the keyboard. How much advice had he heard over the years? Hell, how much advice had he *given*, smug in his castle of committed relationship?

Just be yourself. That was always a favorite.

The cabbie rolled the window down. "Dr. Hayes?" she checked as she stuck her head out, one hand up to ward off the rain. "Everything okay?"

"Sure," Tag said. He quickly patted over the screen as he crossed the pavement. "Sorry, just finishing this."

"Where d'ya want to go?" the driver asked as Tag got in. The back of the car—near midnight on a wet Friday—smelled of cheap perfume and damp. The driver reached up to adjust the rearview mirror, her eyes tired behind smudged glasses. "Home? Club? Can't stay here. It's no parking."

"Just... go," Tag said as he waved his hand absently down the road. "I'll have the address in a minute."

The driver shrugged and pulled away from the curb. Tag leaned back against the leather seat and stared at what he'd typed but hadn't yet sent. He didn't know what he was waiting for. Second thoughts? To suddenly be thrown back in time to when he was the hot young thing people wanted to fuck in an office?

In the absence of either of those options, he hit send. The message flicked onto the screen, bright green in the dark.

Wanna fuck?

"YOU SURE about this?" the cab driver—Susan from San Diego, who'd been an accountant before her firm went belly-up and now had an upside-down mortgage and two side hustles to keep it going—asked as she pulled up in front of the bar. She kept the engine running as the rain hammered down on the car in heavy, unrelenting sheets. "This isn't a part of town where you see people in tuxes."

No kidding.

When they moved to Plenty, Kieran spent hours on Google to narrow down the "best" place for them to live. Gated community or hipster enclave had been a real dark-moment-of-the-soul decision for him. The Heights were one of the places that turned up consistently at the top of the "Worst Places to Live in Plenty." It hit the trifecta of high crime rates, low property values, and poor infrastructure.

At the time Tag was skeptical. He'd been an ER doctor in New York, for fuck's sake. There were shifts where all he did was dig out bullets and sew up knife wounds. The rough side of some hippy California town would hardly give him pause.

Apparently three years in Kieran's hipster enclave had kind of blunted Tag's edge. The boarded-up windows of abandoned houses, the scrawls of angry, overlapped graffiti, and the row of black primer bikes lined up under the half-lit neon light of the Sheep's Shirt bar all made his stomach tighten with suburban anxiety.

That was the guy who got dumped, Tag thought dourly. He stiffened his spine and handed the hospital's account slip through the seats to Susan.

"I know what I'm doing," he said.

Susan pursed her lips in disapproval but took the slip.

"It's your funeral," she said portentously as Tag climbed out of the car. He slammed the door behind him and watched, already drenched again, as the car pulled away. Water dripped down the back of Tag's neck, under his shirt, and he wondered if he should call Ned.

In case I turn up skinned, dismembered, and missing a cock, the guy who did it is called FightJunkie *and has abs you could climb like a ladder.*

Tag snorted and wiped his hand over his wet face to flick away the water. Under the circumstances, he thought he'd rather his last hours remain a mystery instead of a cautionary tale about internet safety.

The door to the bar slammed open, and two big men shoved out a heavyset man in stained denim and a ragged T-shirt.

"Sober up and fuck off, Boone," one of them yelled before they slammed the door again. Boone staggered around, gave the bar a very dignified finger, and then headed around the side of the building. He paused on his way past Tag to give him a squinty look of suspicion.

"Fuck *you*," he slurred, underlined with a jabbed finger, and then lurched away.

After a second Tag checked the directions in chat. They hadn't changed, so he swore under his breath and headed around the side of the bar. A rusty set of stairs was stapled to the side of the building. It creaked under Tag's weight as he headed to the second floor. Country music and the sounds of a rowdy good time pulsed through the cracked siding of the bar and vibrated under Tag's feet.

Number 25A.

This was, it occurred to Tag as he knocked on the door, fucking ridiculous. What the hell was he about, soaked to the bone on a booty call in the Heights like some horny teenager? He'd had enough contempt for Kieran's on-call fuck, but that was just careless. This verged on pathetic.

He took a step back and down when he misjudged the small landing as the door opened. The excuse he was about to make was lined up on the end of his tongue, the old doctor-on-call get-out-of-jail-free card. Then he saw the man who'd opened the door, and the words dried up on a wash of quick, uncomplicated lust. The thought of sex—after two months of angry, hopeful celibacy—had been a low-grade itch in his balls all the way over here. Now it flared to life, hot and eager, and scorched quickly through his hesitation.

"Sonofabitch," the man drawled as he leaned against the doorframe, tattooed torso just as bare and ripped as in his photo. Light-brown hair stuck up in messy curls around a lean, sharply carved face that would have been handsome even without the ridiculously sensual full mouth framed by a scruff of day-old, gilt-pale stubble. The tilt of humor to that mouth carved a deep line in his cheek as its owner returned the favor and slowly looked Tag up and down. He raised his eyebrows. "You taking me to prom, Doc?"

Just because he was hot didn't suddenly make this a good idea. Tag had seen enough good-looking bastards wheel their victims in and out of the ER. Psychosexual killers could have curls and skin the color of fresh honey.

He knew that. But standing on a narrow metal landing, soaked to the skin with Johnny Cash in the background, it seemed worth the risk.

"I had something else in mind," Tag said thickly as he leaned in. He scruffed the back of the other man's neck, the prickle of fresh-cut hair against his fingertips, and pulled him into a kiss. Heat crawled under his skin, an eager rush of lust that arrowed down to jostle his already hard cock. The lush mouth curled into a smirk under his.

"Good," the blond muttered around Tag's tongue. He hooked his fingers into the waistband of Tag's trousers and tugged him through the door. "Cause I've got fuck all to wear."

CHAPTER TWO

BASS HADN'T actually expected Doc the Grindr hookup to turn up at his door. If the location hadn't put him off, he figured the rain would do the job. He'd just used the tease of it, the blunt lust of "wanna fuck," and the picture of the dark-haired man who looked sardonic even in sunshine and shades, to make jerking off a bit more interesting.

The last six months—broke, back home, and bored as fuck—had left his usual go-to fantasies a bit worn out from overuse.

Not that he was going to object now that Prince Charming, with his wet tuxedo and sweet, cider-sharp mouth, had knocked on the door. He dragged the tall drenched man out of the rain and into the apartment, mouths pressed together in scraped kisses and eager, curious hands on, in, and over their bodies. Bass's cock rubbed impatiently against his jeans, already primed for *someone* to touch it. He pushed his hands up under Doc's shirt, wet silk tangled around his fingers, and grazed his hands over bare, cold skin. The raw gasp that clawed up out of Doc's throat, a shock of need, was gratifyingly immediate.

Bass bit Doc's lower lip—he had thin, firm lips that probably looked stern under other circumstances—and then let it scrape out of his teeth as he leaned back. "Shut the door," he ordered.

Doc swallowed raggedly and licked his bruised lip. He reached back and fumbled blindly at the edge of the door until he shoved it over. The click of the lock tightened in Bass's balls like a promise.

"You still want to fuck?" Bass asked as he shoved Doc against the door. He pressed against him, wet fabric a thin layer between their skins, and felt the hard nudge of Doc's answer against his hip. "Then we should set some ground rules. I'm in charge. You do what I say."

Doc swallowed and leaned his head back. His dark eyes were dazed with lust as Bass touched him, and it took him a moment to focus.

"If you knew me," Doc said, his voice low and rough like the growl of a well-tuned bike, "you'd know that doesn't sound like me."

Bass shrugged and pressed a hard kiss against the hinge of Doc's jaw. "That's the point, ain't it?" he said. "I don't know you. You don't know me. So tonight you can be whatever I want you to be."

"Uh-huh," Doc said skeptically. He ran his hands up Bass's arms to grip his biceps. "And what do I get out of that?"

"Whatever I do for you… to you… Doc," Bass said as he worked a trail of wet, bitten kisses down Doc's throat to the bony jut of his collarbone under his shirt. "Nobody has to know."

Doc swallowed audibly, and Bass felt the gulp as it moved past his lips. He tightened his hands around Bass's arms, ready to push him away, and then he relaxed.

"So what do you want me to do?" Doc asked.

Bass had planned to see where lust took him, but… off the top of his head? He licked the bruised stain he'd left on Doc's skin and stepped back. He folded his lower lip between his teeth, the pinch of pain a brief, sweet itch as he looked Doc up and down. Even drenched, his cock an unmistakable bulge against his fitted black trousers, the man looked expensive. Bass reached out and pleated the lapel of Doc's jacket between his fingers. The fabric caught against the calluses on his fingers.

"This? Keep it on," he said. His voice thickened at the thought, a catch of lust in the back of his throat. Apparently he had a thing for well-dressed men. Who knew? "You actually look like you might *be* a doctor."

Doc raised a dark, straight eyebrow. "That's because I am," he said. "Doctor—"

That was not what Bass wanted out of tonight. He used the handful of jacket to drag Doc away from the door and into a "shut up" kiss. Doc growled into Bass's mouth in a flash of temper but didn't try to pull back. He tangled his hand into Bass's hair and pulled him closer so he could deepen the kiss. With lips and tongue still chilled from the rain, Doc explored Bass's mouth almost desperately. He curled his hand around Bass's hip and dragged him closer until Bass's cock rubbed against the hard line of his thigh.

Pleasure ran through Bass's marrow and pulled his skin tight. There had been a fuck of a lot of reality the last few months—engine grime under his nails, the shabby friendships he needed to barter into opportunities, broken noses under his knuckles for the hundred bucks they owed the club. He wanted the lie of this, the hot doctor on his knees for some rough trade, without any of the details that would make him wonder if this was a good idea.

"You obviously haven't done this before," he said as he broke the kiss. "I don't need your name or your job, and if you tell me where you live, I'd probably rob you."

A flash of dark humor creased Doc's face. "Too late for that," he muttered. "And I need a name."

Bass drew back. "Don't get attached, Doc. Trust me, it'll end badly."

"Fightjunkie," Doc said as he tugged Bass's head to the side so he could kiss the hollow under his ear—all teeth and eager mouth. "It doesn't roll off the tongue."

Yeah, he could have a point about that. The night Bass made his profile, he had a hangover and broken knuckles and was as sick of himself as everyone else got. Eventually. It seemed appropriate enough, and it certainly hadn't slowed down the steady stream of dick pics.

"Bass," he said after a pause. It was just a nickname, after all, no more his legal name than his app handle. The only difference was it sounded less aggressively fucked-up. Bass felt a shiver run down his spine as Doc mouthed the name against his throat. "You?"

Doc let go of Bass's hair and ran his hand down his back, along the tight lines of muscle and under the waistband of his jeans. He stroked the curve of Bass's ass, and the rain's chill had finally faded. His skin felt hot where it touched Bass.

"I thought you didn't need my name," Doc teased.

He didn't. Want, though? Kinda, just to even the playing field now that Doc knew his.

"I thought I told you to do what you're told?"

"Tell me, then," Doc said. His voice caught in his throat, a dark thrill mixed with stiff uncertainty. He really wasn't used to being told what to do. "What do you want me to do?"

For a moment Bass almost spent the chit on Doc's name. But that would have been a waste when there were so many other things he wanted to do. Besides, if Bass still wanted to know when they were done? If Doc wouldn't tell him whatever he wanted, he'd have really lost his touch.

Instead he smirked and twisted his hands in the wet silk of Doc's shirt and tugged him in tightly against his body. He pressed a quick, hard kiss against the pulse that fluttered in Doc's neck.

"Whatever I want," he whispered against the wet skin. Then he gave Doc a shove.

The fine white shirt ripped open, and the mother-of-pearl buttons, torn from their moorings, pinged onto the floor. Doc stumbled backward and sprawled over the couch, all long legs and a vaguely aggrieved expression. Bass tugged a packet of lube out of his pocket before he unfastened his jeans and pushed them down over his hips. His cock nudged up toward his stomach, tight and eager as he kicked the tangled denim from under his feet. Bass tossed the foil packet onto the coffee table and then wrapped his fingers around his erection. He stroked the length of it and then squeezed. The quick discomfort in the shaft mellowed to liquid pleasure by the time it reached his balls.

"Take your pants off, Doc."

Doc obediently hitched his hips up off the couch as he fumbled with his trousers, his attention fixed on Bass. He finally managed to undo the buttons and impatiently shove the pants down toward his knees. That left him with a pair of fitted black briefs, his cock a hard ridge under the tight fabric. Doc palmed his erection through the cotton and rubbed it roughly.

Bass didn't know why that was hot as fuck. It just was. Maybe because Doc didn't look away as he did it. His eyes, so dark they looked black, stayed focused on Bass as Doc bit his lip and tugged his cock with impatient fingers.

"You missing something important to be here?" Bass asked. He pumped his hand along the hard shaft of his cock as he walked over to the couch. Doc licked his lips and squirmed, his palm pressed against his cock as he glanced from the hard jut of Bass's wet cock up to his face as though he couldn't decide what made him go hard quicker. "Jilted some lady at the altar? Ditched an award ceremony?"

Doc snorted. "Last girl who thought I was a good bet as a husband was Marcie Green. We were five, and she married my Action Man instead," he said. He set his jaw for a second with a flash of something dark that cut through the haze of lust, and his voice hardened. "Never work with your ex. Mine brought his new boyfriend, who he fucked behind my back, to a fundraiser. I wasn't in the mood to stomach it."

"He hotter than me?" Bass asked as crawled onto the couch, one knee braced between Doc's sprawled thighs.

"Who?"

Bass pulled Doc's hands away from his cock—he ignored the low noise of protest Doc made—and pinned them against the couch. He leaned down until he could feel Doc's breath, warm and uneven from arousal, against his mouth.

"Either of them," he said.

"No," Doc answered immediately, his voice harsh with thoughtless honesty. Regret caught up with him a second later as he grimaced guiltily and tilted his head back. His throat worked as he tried to swallow what he'd just said, as though that would mean it weren't true. "That's not—"

This time Bass kissed him just to shut him up. He didn't much care if Doc wasn't over his pencil-neck ex, but that didn't mean he wanted to waste any time on it. After a startled second Doc stretched up into the kiss, his mouth wet and aggressive as he chased the kiss back over Bass's lips. He strained against Bass's grip on his arms, the tendons in his wrists tight against his fingers.

"Learn to shut up when you're winning," Bass told him with one last scraped bite to Doc's lips. He lowered himself onto the long sprawl of the other man's body, his cock pressed up against the flat plane of his tight stomach. The pressure dragged a low, ragged noise out of Doc's throat as he squirmed under Bass. "I'm hot, and I'm going to fuck you. Enjoy."

"Oh, because there's nothing in it for you," Doc said, a hint of something between dry and bitter in his voice. "Just doing me out of charity?"

"I was bored," Bass said. He thrust against Doc's stomach, precome and sweat slick as his cock slid between their bodies. "And you clean up good."

Doc laughed. It squinted his eyes and creased his cheeks with a flash of dark humor that made Bass's mouth go dry. Like Doc's voice, his tux, and the hard, practicality of his body, it hit a bunch of buttons Bass didn't know he had.

"Maybe I should change my profile pic," he said.

Bass smirked as he looked down at Doc's face. His hair was wet and unruly, his lips reddened, and there were spit-wet bruises on his collarbones. The holiday photo he had now was hot enough, if a bit cheesy, but if he'd looked like this when Bass opened his profile? Bass would have gone to him... even in the rain.

Despite that thought, gravelly resistance swelled in Bass's chest at the prospect. He didn't want to spend too much time on why, but he didn't like the idea.

He pushed himself against Doc's stomach again with a hard thrust that ground his cock against smooth skin and rough hair. Pleasure tightened in his balls and the backs of his thighs, an impatient ache for more. Under him Doc choked out a curse between his teeth and arched into the contact.

"Shut up," Bass told him genially, "and let me fuck you."

He let go of Doc's wrists and kissed his way down his body, from his bruised collarbone to his lean chest. His pink nipples tightened, puckered into tight buds as Bass scraped his teeth and tongue over them. Doc groaned and tangled his fingers in Bass's hair, his breathing ragged and muscles tight as he struggled for control.

There was a scar under his ribs, a folded dip of flesh ridged with old stitch marks and almost lost in the bony shadow. The skin was tight under Bass's tongue, slick where it had knit back together, and Doc hissed uncomfortably when he lingered.

Bass left it and squirmed lower. The taste of his own come was sharp and musky against his tongue as he bit kisses down Doc's stomach, the dark trail of hair matted and sticky under his tongue until he reached the thin barrier of black cotton.

"Fuck," Doc groaned thickly as Bass mouthed at the ridge of his cock through his briefs. Spit soaked the fabric as Bass worked his way from the tight curve of his balls to the precome-sticky head. He braced his arm across Doc's hips to pin him down as he sucked with wet, messy enthusiasm at the heavy rise of flesh. "You're gonna kill me."

Bass chuckled around a mouthful of cotton and cock. "I thought you were a doctor," he said. "Blue balls never killed anyone."

"Great," Doc said breathlessly. "I'll finally get to make medical precedent."

Bass hooked his fingers in the waistband of Doc's briefs and pulled them down. The elastic caught on the curve of his cock and then sprang free. Shiny with spit, it was average length but thick and flushed with blood. Bass licked a wet swipe from root to head and then shifted back onto his knees.

His cock nudged wetly against his stomach as he sat back. Bass ran his hands up Doc's thighs, muscles pulled long and tight under the skin, to his knees so he could push them up. He grabbed the lube from the table and ripped it open with his teeth. It gave off a sharp, chemical scent of watermelon as he squeezed it onto his fingers.

Doc shifted and hitched his hips off the couch so Bass could push his gel-slick fingers into him. His head fell back, the line of it pulled tight under bruised skin and stubble. He pushed his hips forward against the penetrating fingers as Bass worked his tight ass wide and open. His cock bounced against his stomach in ragged time with his heartbeat, skin slick with come.

"So your ex was a bottom?" Bass asked as he pushed his fingers deeper until they grazed the firm, smooth bump of nerve-rich flesh.

A laugh and a groan tangled in Doc's throat as his thighs trembled. "I take it you're not?"

Bass brushed a kiss over Doc's knee—all bone and a dozen faded childhood scars—and pressed down on the same spot again, a little harder this time. Doc swore, the words shredded between gritted teeth as he clenched around Bass's fingers.

"What gave you that idea?" Bass asked smugly as he slid his hand free.

It took a second for Doc to get his breath back. When he did, the "condom" he gasped out wasn't exactly what Bass wanted to hear. With one hand he groped at his jacket as he propped himself up on his elbow.

"I've got a clean bill of health," Bass said as he wrapped slippery fingers around Doc's cock. He dragged his thumb over the head and smirked at the whimper he coaxed out of Doc's throat. "I don't usually bother with a jacket."

"I do," Doc said as he extended the condom, pinched between two of his fingers. "Always."

Bass could have argued, but he didn't see the point. It would take longer than it would to just put the condom on, and either way, he'd get laid. He grumbled his assent and pulled the wrapper open so he could shake out the round of latex.

"Even with your ex, Doc?" he jabbed as he rolled the latex down over his cock. It stretched, tight and shiny around the shaft. "Every time?"

Doc sat up, his long, lean body folded awkwardly in half, and cupped Bass's face in his hands. The kiss was quick and deep, as though Doc liked the taste of himself on Bass's tongue.

"I treated six patients with Hep A last month. My last needle stick was from a meth addict with a staph infection. Came up clear, but it was a worry," Doc said. He moved his hands to Bass's shoulders and then down his arms, fingers light against inked lines as he talked. "And my ex is a doctor too. So yeah. Now are you going to fuck me or not?"

An old pinch of insecurity caught Bass off guard at that bit of information. He shrugged it off. The ex might have a medical license, but Bass was still hotter. For this? Hot was all that mattered. He adjusted his position and tugged Doc into his lap, his long legs still tangled in suit pants and wrapped around Bass's waist.

"I can do that," Bass said, his cock pressed into the warm, slick crease of Doc's ass. "You sure you want me to, Doc?"

"No," Doc said sardonically. His voice was frayed at the edges with frustration, but his cock was rigid as he rubbed against the hard planes of Bass's stomach. "I just thought I'd lecture you on safe sex."

Bass bit his shoulder. The sweat was salty against his lips as he lingered over the spot. "Just wanted to be sure."

He reached between their bodies and grabbed his erection in one hand. The condom was lube slick under his fingers as he pushed against Doc's ass, and the ring of muscle was tight as it stretched around the blunt head of his cock. For a second it seemed as though he couldn't go any further. His cock was too thick where his fingers had slid so easily. The sweet pressure ached down his shaft and settled tight and hot into his thighs.

Doc gripped his arms, dug his long fingers into the old ink, and pressed down. The muscles in his stomach flexed, clenched under the skin, as his ass stretched around Bass's cock. It was still tight enough to make Bass chew on the inside of his cheek, the unspent lust in his muscles twitchy and desperate.

He wanted—*needed*—to be balls deep inside Doc, his cock squeezed hard by hot flesh as he fucked Doc into the couch. Sweat itched at the nape of his neck and matted into the curls and between his asscheeks as he hung on to control by a thread. Bass ran his hands up under Doc's jacket, the ruined shirt twisted around his hand, and explored the long lines of tensed muscle and the sharp jut of shoulder blades. He licked salty kisses along Doc's throat and across his chest, careless of any stains he left with lips and teeth on his pale skin.

Doc said he was single. If he wasn't… that wasn't Bass's problem.

Doc squeezed Bass's shoulders as he thrust his hips down. His ass flexed with each stroke, a tight grip that worked its way down to the base of Bass's cock. Pressure built in Bass's balls, a knot of electric heat that spilled back into his ass and itched in his thighs until it drove him to move. He rocked his hips up and hooked his thumbs over Doc's sharp hipbones to take control.

"God," Doc groaned as he wrapped his arms around Bass's shoulders. He brushed his hands over Bass's back and pressed warm, tickled kisses against his throat. "That's… fuck, Bass. Yes."

His cock slid between their stomachs with every thrust, and his ass pressed down against Bass's thighs. Doc breathed raggedly as he stroked faster, and the long muscles in his thighs trembled with effort.

Bass gave up on control. He gripped Doc's lean ass in both hands to steady him and tipped them both over. Doc sprawled out on his back, and Bass, cock still buried in his ass, braced himself on top of him.

"Son of a bitch," Doc gasped and dug his fingers into Bass's shoulders as the move drove Bass's cock deeper.

"Always," Bass promised with a smirk as he stole a sweaty kiss against Doc's bitten lips. "God, you're hot, Doc."

He thrust into Doc with long, steady strokes that made him groan. The expensive silk jacket was stained and wrinkled under their bodies. Bass pulled out until only the head of his cock was still inside and then buried himself again. The tangle of sensation tightened in his balls and twisted in on itself like an overstretched elastic band. He gripped Doc's shoulders and thrust again. Each stroke dragged a hitched noise of pleasure from Doc.

Doc came first with a spill of wet come that smeared between their bodies and the tight clench of his ass around Bass's cock.

The band finally snapped, and Bass thrust roughly against Doc as he came. Release washed through his nerves like champagne. He lay limply on top of the wiry, half-dressed body for a second, his mouth pressed against the damp hollow of Doc's throat as he mouthed hopefully inaudible lies.

He'd always been a post-come promiser. It made him sentimental.

Doc stroked his sweaty hair back from his face and brushed a kiss against his ear. He didn't squirm out from under Bass or check the time. Apparently he really was new to hookups. Bass let it go. He was kinda comfortable, considering how many sharp lines Doc had to his body.

Eventually he had to sit back and strip the wet condom off his softened cock. He tied the end and gave Doc's sprawled body a once-over. One of his arms was tucked under his head, and his hair was damp with sweat instead of rain. The ex was an idiot. Doc wasn't the prettiest man Bass had ever had, but he had something.

Bass cleared his throat.

"The point of a hookup is you don't hang around for breakfast, Doc."

Doc arched an eyebrow without actually opening an eye. "Would I get a breakfast?"

"Nope."

"Well, then…." Doc sat up with a wince for overworked muscles and extracted himself from under Bass. Once he was up, he made a try at presentable. He hitched up his trousers, tucked in his shirt, and buttoned his creased jacket. His shirt still flashed a 70s' vee of chest, and he still looked well-fucked. Bass didn't object, but he supposed whatever MILFs infested Doc's fancy suburb might. "Any chance I could get an Uber to come down here?"

Bass smirked as he lay back on the couch, naked and spent, and watched Doc try to do something with his post-sex hair. There had never been a lot of moments where he could just be… done, especially not since he got back to Plenty. The life he lived demanded he stay on guard. So he enjoyed the rare times he didn't have to be, even if the moment didn't mean anything.

"It's the Heights," he said. "We need to get out to go and work for you rich folks. We've got Uber, Doc."

Doc nodded and looked around for his phone. He found it on the floor. As he picked it up and swiped in his code, he said, "Tag."

Bass tilted his head.

"My name," Doc said. "Taggart. Tag."

Bass scratched his stomach, which was still sticky with come. "I like Doc," he said. Some old vestige of hospitality poked at him. "If you can't get a cab and don't mind a ride on a bike…."

"I don't," Doc said dryly as he glanced up long enough to flash a crooked smile. "My ass might."

CHAPTER THREE

IT WAS Saturday. Tag didn't have to be at work until later. The baby in the flat upstairs didn't care. It wanted one of the short list of things a baby wanted, and it was going to scream until it got them an hour before Tag had to get up or not.

Tag groggily dragged a pillow over his head and folded his arms over it. He tried to hang on to the last indulgent dregs of sleep despite the warbled screech that pierced the walls. It didn't work.

"Jesus," he muttered finally as he blindly shoved the pillow aside. He yawned into the mattress hard enough to make his jaw creak and rubbed his hand over his eyes. After a second he rubbed his eyes again and rolled over. Usually by this point he'd be pissed off and want to yell at the kid's mother to actually parent the brat.

Hadn't so far, mostly because it would be a dick move, and less flatteringly because it wouldn't do much good. The mom, Maria, was barely more than a kid herself and obviously worked all hours and odd shifts to support them. From the few meetings they'd had on the stairs as Maria dragged her thrift-shop baby carriage in off the street, she didn't speak much English. And while Tag could ask "Where does it hurt?" in seven languages, that scraped the barrel of his knowledge of Ukrainian.

This morning he didn't just feel resentfully tolerant. Another hour of sleep wouldn't have gone amiss, but babies were going to baby.

Something was different. It took him a second to realize what. Despite the eardrum-spike wail of discontent from above, the hard mattress that came with the prefurnished flat, and the fact that he was *in* a prefurnished short-term apartment, he felt... sore, self-satisfied, and like he should be—but wasn't quite—ashamed of himself. And good.

His ears got a rest as the baby finally got whatever it wanted. Tag stretched out on the cheap sheets and grinned at the crumpled disaster of his tux tossed over the dresser. His stomach muscles were tender, and there was a pleasant ache between his hips. The memory of rough kisses and rougher hands made his cock stir with lazy interest, but it had to make do with his hand, loosely cuffed around the half-hard shaft. He rubbed his thumb along the ridged vein to the head, and a shudder of pleasure flicked down his cock and into his balls.

When was the last time he woke up with a hangover from a night's misbehavior? It had never been his normal—medical books and antisocial shift patterns had put a crimp in any plans he'd had for a life of debauchery—but he'd still had some memorable nights.

Two months. At *least* two months. Even when his and Kieran's relationship wasn't on a collision course with a hot nurse and his ass tattoo? It had been a while since the sight of each other naked had kicked them in the gut with bewildered lust.

Although… Tag hadn't lied last night. Bass was hotter.

Tag shifted uncomfortably on the sheets as that settled. Guilt was a funny thing. Last night he'd staggered home with his shirt glued to his chest by a more-or-less stranger's come, and he hadn't felt a twinge. A stray thought about who he thought was prettier, and he felt like a cheater.

Fuck that. Tag kicked the sheets down to the bottom of the bed and braced his bare foot against the mattress. He chewed on the inside of his lip and pumped his fist along his cock as lazy interest sharpened to lust.

He tilted his head back against the too-thin pillows and closed his eyes. The memories of last night, still sharp edged and in high definition, rose easily to the surface of his mind—salty-sweetness of warm golden skin under his tongue, black lines of ink drawn tightly over hard muscles, and the rasped encouragement of a low, harsh-edged voice against his jaw.

Tag lifted his hips off the bed and tightened his fingers around his cock. His breath was quick and harsh, and it hissed raggedly between his teeth as he strained toward the finish line. He could feel the plucked string of nerve endings that ran from the nape of his neck all the way down to his balls.

He licked his lips and tasted sweat caught in the scruff of overnight stubble. His mind skipped a handful of pages in the play-by-play of his fantasy and dropped him straight into hands clenched around his hips and a cock buried in his ass. He twisted his hand around his cock impatiently and came with a groan, the spill of come wet and sticky between his knuckles.

The tension leaked out of him and left him boneless, more relaxed on the unfamiliar bed than he'd been since he moved in. He exhaled slowly, wiped his hand on his stomach, and just lay there as he enjoyed the quiet inside his own head.

For all of a minute. Then his actual alarm went off.

Tag took a deep breath and sighed it out through loose lips. It was still a better morning than most lately. He spent a second more in contemplation of it, and then the angry guitar riff of Metallica set the baby off again.

Maria yelled something Tag couldn't quite make out and hammered on the floor with what sounded like a brush. He groaned but gave in to the inevitable and scrambled out of bed. His phone was on the dresser—out of reach, since otherwise he could never ignore the snooze option—and he grabbed it with one hand to silence "Whiskey in the Jar."

Fifty-two unread messages. Two from Fightjunkie.

Tag caught a grin at the corner of his mouth and bit it back. It could be a bill for damage to the couch. Fuck, it could be some sort of app feedback. That could be… ego bruising. He hovered his thumb over the notification for a moment and then bit the bullet and tapped the screen.

An icon spun as his phone downloaded a picture. The text beneath it read *Could have been your one chance to ride me!?*

The twitch of immediate arousal ached in Tag's spent cock like pins and needles in the oversensitized flesh. He chewed absently on the inside of his lip as he waited for the image to flash onto the screen. His eyes were drawn to the spread thighs, denim pulled tight and faded over heavy muscles as though they were the focal point of the picture, and then down to the worn leather seat the thighs straddled and the matte black of a gas tank.

Tag snorted at his own thirst. He'd gotten laid *and* jerked off, yet he was still dry mouthed over a pair of spread thighs? Some things didn't change. He'd always been uselessly horny when he was single.

Should have said that was on the table before my ass got ridden, he sent back.

He got a leering smiley back, and he grinned as he tossed the phone onto the unmade bed. The rest could wait. He had to get back to normal—deal with the crappy water pressure in the apartment and apologize to the director of surgery for the way he'd left the fundraiser—but not yet.

It could wait until he had breakfast… or at least a shower.

THE GOOD thing about emergency medicine, other than all the lives saved, obviously, was that it didn't give your mind time to wander… or give you time to check your phone.

It had been over a week since Tag had hooked up with some random hot guy on an app and six days since they started to text.

Or, if he was gonna be honest, sext. The occasional video and one raspy voice message where Bass gave Tag a raw-edged play-by-play of exactly what role he played in Bass's fantasies—a really well-dressed and well-fucked role.

That was fine sprawled on Tag's bed at night, cheap sheets around his thighs and his hand around his cock, but last night he'd spent hours with his attention divided between old reruns and the flicker of those three little dots on his phone. Had Bass read his message? Too much? Not enough? Was he going to say something or not?

With his social life temporarily embarrassed for other options, it was easy to get a bit too invested. Luckily his company was still in demand at work. It got his mind out of the digital gutter.

Tag pressed down on either side of the cyclist's trachea. His blue-gloved fingers sank into the swollen bruised-plum skin, and the man gargled something thick and confused through a mouthful of torn flesh and broken teeth. He thrashed on the stained sheets and clawed at Tag's face as the tubes from his IV tangled around his arm.

"Hold him down," Tag ordered an intern, "before he rips that port out. Again."

The woman flushed as she realized she was on deck and bolted forward to pin the man's shoulders. Bloodshot eyes rolled in his bruised sockets as the man hitched and spat through his broken throat.

Tag pressed the scalpel to the man's throat and sliced. It was the third he'd done that day—two peanut allergies and a full-sized Lego brick in a teenager's throat—and he'd lost count of how many during his career. He remembered the first one—side of the road when he was a medical student, a bike messenger crushed between two cars, and the dizzy realization he was actually cutting a person's throat—and he'd probably remember the last. This guy he'd forget by Friday, God and medical complications willing. The scalpel pierced the membrane in a neat, clean-edged line, and he poked in a blue-gloved finger to work it open.

A nurse handed him a length of tube, and he threaded it into the patient's windpipe. He blew two quick puffs of air into it and then leaned back for a second to wait for the ragged hitch as the patient started to breathe on his own.

"We have avulsion injuries to both arms and legs, head trauma, facial fractures, dental trauma, and genital injuries." Tag rattled off the collection of injuries, voice pitched to carry over the noise of the ER as he taped the tube in place.

He glanced around as he talked, on autopilot as he mentally triaged the other casualties from the incident. Take a cycling club, an SUV, and a designer who'd had too many mimosas at brunch, and what you got were lacerations, fractures, and an hysterical driver who wanted someone to tell him it wasn't her fault. One woman had a head injury and a dislocated knee, but Mr. Jason Morrow here was the worst.

Tag switched his attention back to his patient. He pulled away the shredded T-shirt to reveal black bruises and a purple stain that spread out over his stomach. "Internal injuries, from the location, probably impact with the handlebars. We need him in surgery now."

Tag stepped back as the nurses pushed the patient toward the left. He stripped off his bloody gloves, balled them, and tossed them into the garbage. The backs of his hands itched from the neoprene. It was a mild allergy. All it ever came to was an itch. One bad shift he'd gotten hives, but that was an exception. Most of the time an antihistamine was all he needed to function, but he had, between one thing and Bass, forgotten last night.

"Ennis," he said, voice pitched to carry over the sobs and barked orders. "What do you need?"

She looked up from the compound fracture she was trying to stabilize until they could get her patient to X-ray. Blood was splashed over the visor she had slotted over her glasses.

"I've got this," she said. "Just send someone down to keep the families informed."

Tag caught the intern's eye. "You," he said. She blanched and opened her mouth to protest, but he ignored the squeak of dismay. "We're doing our best for their loved ones. As soon as we're able, we'll give them more. Commit to nothing. Promise nothing. Do *not* speak to anyone from the press. If the cops want something, send them to Ennis. Got it?" He didn't wait for an answer. "Good. Get on with it."

The intern looked scared, but she'd get over it. Tag left her to it as he jogged after the stretcher. It was the third hour of his shift, and so far he'd had three overdoses, a suicidal teen, a meth head with a nasty staph infection, a major trauma, and almost no time to think about the last sext he'd sent Bass.

Otherwise known as.... He'd obsessed over it every second that he hadn't actively had his fingers inside someone. He'd tried to work out what the hell he thought he was doing while he had a piss, and he wondered if scrubs would get the same reaction as the tux while he grabbed a cup of tepid coffee from the vending machine and watched nondairy creamer half dissolve on the gray-brown surface.

Not that it mattered. The point of a one-night stand was.... Well, it was in the name. Hour-long sweaty fantasies aside, neither of them had actually suggested a replay of their hookup, although Tag was pretty sure they both knew he'd be up for it.

So the key was obviously to stay busier. Tag elbowed his brain out of its own way as he caught up with the stretcher.

"Drop a line to Plastics too, once we have him prepped for surgery," he told the nurse, Harris, as they reached the elevators. A sidestep put him in front of the doors, and he jabbed his finger against the button. "He's going to need skin grafts on those abrasions, particularly his thighs and flank if he's to retain normal motion."

"He was here the other night, you know," Harris said as he fastidiously checked the IV. He clucked his tongue sympathetically as he looked down at the patient. "Some hotshot lawyer up in San Diego. I met him up in pediatrics when he got the big tour of the wards. I bet he didn't think he'd be back here like this."

"Probably not," Tag said absently.

"Yeah, but you never know, do you," Harris pointed out with a sage shake of his head. "One minute everything is in order, and the next thing someone comes into your life and just changes it. Forever."

Tag avoided his reflection in the chrome doors of the elevator. It wasn't that he hadn't heard Harris or recognized the... similarity of the idea, but it was hardly the same thing. Last week had been—really good, admittedly—sex, not a DUI that could have killed him. Since they used protection, that would only change Tag's life if Bass had a bedbug infestation.

Tag was still here—an expat New Yorker who'd lost the house, the car, and even the cat he didn't like in an acrimonious breakup. Nothing had changed.

The doors finally slid open.

"God works in mysterious ways," Harris said solemnly as he shoved the stretcher into the elevator. "Good and bad."

"He was hit by a drunk in a Volvo," Tag said dryly as he stepped into the car, "not a whale. Let's not get carried away, huh?"

Harris shrugged but shut up and pressed the button for the theater. As the elevator doors closed, Tag couldn't avoid a brief glance at his own fingerprint-smudged image on the way past. Their eyes met for a second before Tag dragged his attention away, but the tall, scruffy man with blood on his scrubs begged the question....

What *would* it take to change his life?

BY THE time the patient got to Recovery, he was short a spleen, had a Foley catheter for the next few weeks, and more surgeries in the pipeline. In some specialties that would be a cause for concern, but trauma had a lower bar for what counted as a successful surgery.

Still alive? Good job.

That wasn't the news that Plenty's finest wanted to hear. Deputy Tancredi scribbled down Tag's brisk answer and tucked her notebook into her belt.

"Do you have any idea when I can speak to him?" she asked as she kept pace with Tag through the ER waiting room.

"Sorry," Tag said as he stopped to check on a well-dressed woman who'd spilled coffee on her pencil skirt. "None. He had major surgery and significant trauma, Deputy. Until he comes around from the anesthetic, I can't tell you anything about when or if he can talk to you. Ma'am, can you follow my finger?"

The woman laughed uncomfortably and wiped at her stained skirt with a handful of napkins. "It's just the hiccups," she protested, interrupted midsentence by a startled squawk of noise. Her cheeks flushed. "I've had them since last night, and—"

Tag held up a finger in front of her face and moved it from side to side. Her eyes jerked as she tried to track it.

"Any dizziness?" Tag asked. "Headache?"

She shook her head to the first question and laughed around another hiccup at the second. "I have three kids, a deadbeat ex, and a full-time job," she said. "I *always* have a headache."

Tag took the coffee off her, what was left of it, with a quick apology. He set it aside, took both her hands in his, and lifted them up in front of her.

"Hold them still?" he asked.

"Honest, I just need something for my hiccups," she said as her left arm sank unsteadily down. "I don't want to be a problem."

Tag nodded. "How about we get someone to check that out?" he asked as he stood up. A shrill whistle caught one of the interns' attention, and he got the woman, still full of protests about the hiccups she now wanted to believe in, into a wheelchair and on her way to a neurological exam.

"Must be odd," Tancredi said as he turned back to her. "Always on the lookout for these subtle diagnostic telltales about your barista's brain tumor or the postal worker's staph infection."

The word *subtle* made Tag snort. "Trauma medicine isn't that delicate," he said. "The diagnostic test for a compound fracture is 'Does their bone stick out of their leg?' In her case, the first diagnostic tell was that she was in an ER. So I knew there was something wrong with her. Most people out in the world, I work on the assumption they're doing okay."

Tancredi chuckled and scratched her eyebrow. "Way to burst my *House* bubble, Dr. Hayes." She pulled a card out of her pocket and held it out, her name and number neat on the white surface under the San Diego Sheriff's Department crest. "If anything changes with Mr. Morrow? Call me."

He took the card and tucked it into his pocket. "I'll pass it on to the nurse's station," he said as he checked his wrist. "By the time he comes around, I'll have handed him over to the next shift."

Tancredi shrugged her understanding and stuck out her hand to grip his. "Thank you anyhow, Dr. Hayes, I appreciate the help. Anything on this patient, okay, just keep me updated."

One quick businesslike shake, and then she was done. Tag frowned after the deputy as she left through the sliding doors of the ER and wondered why she was so insistent. It was a cut-and-dried DUI. The yummy mummy had admitted as much even as she tried to bargain down her mimosa indulgence… unless she changed her story once her lawyer got to her, or a rich spouse made a few calls and put some weight on someone to make the accident look a bit more mutual fault. It happened.

Tag made a mental note to remind the nursing staff of the borders of their responsibility between the patient and the police.

His stomach picked that moment to gurgle sourly behind his ribs. Lunch had been a bite of reheated noodles two hours ago, before a Code Blue interrupted him. Breakfast was yesterday. His bloodstream was, at any given moment, 70 percent coffee, but his stomach still needed something to soak that up.

"Later," Tag promised it as he headed across the ER toward the food truck that would hopefully still be outside. The cyclist wouldn't wake up for a couple of hours. Tancredi's request wouldn't be pressing until then.

It took him twenty minutes to get to the door, his scrubs a beacon for everyone in the ER too desperate to wait for their turn. A meth addict with a pit of an ulcer under his tongue huffed sour breath into Tag's face, a frantic young mother's baby had "meningitis" that turned out to be a heat rash, and a student nurse was in a panic about a nicked vein in a homeless man's arm, and his blood was in the nurse's hair.

The food trucks changed out weekly, ordered by some agreement the vendors had made between themselves. Today it was pizza, sold by the slice and served up by a genial old man who had silver dreads and a heavy hand with the toppings.

Tag ordered a slice, grabbed a can of seltzer to go with it, and paid. He slouched against the side of the truck while his order was prepared and finally let himself pull his phone out of his pocket. Three messages from Bass—*What gets your cock so hard it hurts?* at noon and then two question marks spaced an hour apart.

Heat flushed up the back of Tag's neck, as though anyone who looked at him could tell what he'd just read. He shifted to the side, out of the food truck server's view, and tapped out a quick answer.

Or tried to. His brain spluttered out a dozen toothless stereotypes— bad boys, motorcycles, big cocks—and he deleted them all after a second look at how trite they read. Give him medical jargon any day.

A finger poked him in the side. "Don't text the ex," Ned warned. "Trust me. My ex-wife kept them all and had the ones where I begged framed at the divorce party."

Tag fumbled an attempt to close the app and nearly dropped the phone. He caught it and shoved it into his pocket, dry-mouthed and flustered at being caught. He supposed he hadn't actually done anything inappropriate… unless someone scrolled back.

"You're aware your ex was a very cruel woman," Tag pointed out dryly.

"With a very good lawyer. Yes, I remember every time I write my alimony check," Ned said as he stepped up to the counter. "Ham and pineapple, please? Two slices."

He paid, waved off the offer of change, and turned to look at Tag. Sympathy creased a familiar line across his forehead as he nudged his glasses up his nose. "Look, it was shitty of Kieran to turn up with Freddie at the charity ball. I told him that, but… well, done is done. Now that they're…." He paused, nose wrinkled as he thought of how he was going to put it. "Out. Well, it's different isn't it? Freddie isn't the dirty mistress anymore, and, ah, you're going to see them around. So maybe it's time to just accept it?"

The one thing you couldn't do in a breakup was ask your friends to pick sides. Most of them would anyhow, so why waste your time? The rest you just had to get used to the awkward timeshare and the fact that they knew the name of the hot nurse with the tattooed ass.

"You think I should go on a double date?" he asked wryly.

"No, of course not," Ned said. He scratched his head and shoved his hands into his trousers, his white coat tucked back behind his elbows. "Or maybe. One day. For now start to iron it out with him? Stay in the same room?"

"There's nothing left to iron," Tag said. The depressing thing was that was true. Five years, and it had taken a fifteen-minute fight to divvy everything up. The music was on the cloud, Tag couldn't afford the rent on the hipster ecolodge by the shore, and all Tag's clothes fit into one admittedly large suitcase. It was who got the Netflix account that took the longest to settle. The server leaned over the counter with a slice of pizza on a cardboard wedge. It was hot against Tag's palm as he took it, the cheese liquid and greasy as it dribbled over the edges of the flatbread triangle. "It's fine. Seeing them gave me the push I needed."

Ned gave him that encouraging smile that said he didn't actually believe Tag but appreciated the effort it took to lie. He took his pizza from the server and picked up one of the pieces to bite the end off it. "It isn't easy. I know that. When Elsie asked for a divorce, it still took a while to really… get that it was already a done deal for her while I was trying to bail out the boat. Hence the framed texts."

"Like I said, I'm already there," Tag said. He juggled the pizza from one hand to the other as he fished his phone out of his pocket. "By the way, thanks for signing me up to that app."

"Really?" Ned mumbled through a mouthful of pizza. He covered his lips with his hand as he asked, "You, ah, putting yourself out there?"

"You could say that."

Tag tapped the message one-handed as he fell in behind Ned on their way back into the hospital. Luckily it was short and, now he'd thought about it, easy enough. What turned him on? He typed the answer.

You.

CHAPTER FOUR

IT DIDN'T matter whose shit it was, the minute it hit the fan, everyone got their share of it.

"What the fuck!" Bass yelled as he gunned the van through the salvage yard. Behind them, enraged Albanians boiled out of the supposedly empty warehouse like armed bastard ants. A big gray-haired man pulled a fuck-off gun out of the waistband of his jeans and fired after them. A bullet pinged off the roof of the van, and the next one punched out the back window in a spray of safety glass. "I thought they weren't supposed to be here."

"They fucking weren't. The Cossacks double-crossed us instead. Goddamn Russians, can't trust them to stay bought," Sonny yelled back at him. He slid around the back of the van as Bass took a hard left, sideswiped a junked Chevy, and scraped along a stacked pile of crushed cars with a raw metal-on-metal screech. "Watch where you're going, asshole."

Bass veered away from the crushed cubes and hit a pothole deep enough to make the suspension crack. He clenched his hands around the steering wheel and threw a quick, risky glare over his shoulder at Sonny.

"You want me to slow down?" he asked.

Sonny braced himself against the side of the van. "Just get us out of here," he spat as he pulled off the balaclava. His lip was split, blood smeared over the salt-and-pepper stubble on his chin, and a bruise had puffed up around his eye. The Albanians had obviously not been glad to see him. "Before they—*fucking hell*!"

Sonny threw his arms up over his face as Bass swung his attention back to the road ahead of him. It was about as clear as any road in the maze of junk and junkers. Then he caught a glimpse of movement out of the corner of his eye, just before the big black Jeep crashed into the side of the van.

"Shiiiiit," Bass swore between clenched teeth as the door crumpled in toward him. The window broke, cracks spiderwebbed from one side to the other, and the seat belt cut into his shoulder as he was thrown to the side. Pain flared in his chest, a hot jab across his collarbone and head. He fought with the wheel as the van was shoved toward the wall of stacked cars on the other side. The steering had locked.

"Do something," Sonny yelled.

"Trying to," Bass said through gritted teeth as he reached over to grab the handgun from the passenger seat.

He broke the window with his elbow, and chunks of glass scattered over the polished black hood of the SUV as he aimed the gun at the dark-haired man behind the wheel of the Jeep. A distinctive three-pronged scar raked down the left side of his face from cheekbone to jaw. His deep-set eyes widened as he saw the gun pointed at his forehead.

Bass tightened his finger on the trigger and, at the last second, jerked his arm to the side. The bullet shattered the windshield, and the scarred driver braked at the same second. He yanked the steering wheel, and the SUV scraped to the side. It gave Bass just enough room to squeeze the van through the gap.

Two of the Albanians had gotten to the gate and padlocked it shut. They were stationed in front of it with crowbars. Bass skinned his lips back from his teeth in an adrenaline-sharp grin, hit the gas, and drove for the gates. The red needle of the speedometer juddered from twenty toward eighty, and Bass kept his foot on the pedal.

The two men in front of the gate held their ground longer than he would have. Twenty feet. Twelve feet. Their nerve broke at six feet, and they flung themselves out of the way. The van didn't bump over anything, so Bass assumed they made it. He didn't have time to check as the van bust through the gates and blew them off their hinges.

"You crazy bastard," Sonny muttered from behind him.

Bass just laughed. Adrenaline was a better high than whiskey and the hangover easier to ride out. He drove over the bent frame of one of the gates in the road and screeched around the corner. The Albanians tried to follow in their glossy matched SUVS, but Bass had too much of a head start on them. He left them in the dust of the badly lit alleys and dead-end streets.

"Fuck," Sonny muttered.

Bass pulled off his balaclava. His hair was plastered to his head with sweat, and the back of his neck itched with it. He tossed it and the gun into the passenger seat. "What?"

When he didn't get an answer, he reached up to angle the rearview mirror until he could see into the back of the van. Sonny was slumped gracelessly in the back, his legs sprawled out in front of him. A screwdriver jutted out of his thigh like the world's worst-timed erection. Blood welled up around the injury and puddled under him on the bare metal.

That was the other thing about shit. There was always more of it to go around.

SONNY LAY on the pool table, propped up on his elbow, and sucked on a bottle of whiskey. The screwdriver was still jammed into his leg, which was roughly bandaged with a couple of T-shirts someone had grabbed from the back office. He groaned and swore between gulps of liquor, and the worn green baize was smeared with mud where he'd kicked it in frustrated pain.

"What the hell happened?" Shepherd growled. He grabbed the collar of Bass's cut, the heavy vest they'd given him when they gave him his shot at membership, and shoved him back against the bar. Under other circumstances Bass wouldn't have minded the position. The president of Corpse Brothers Motorcycle Club was a big fair-haired man with broad shoulders and a nasty streak—just Bass's type. Unfortunately he'd never been into being roughed up, and far as he knew, Shepherd liked chicks with big tits and loose morals. He was also an asshole.

Shepherd hauled him up onto his toes and got into his face. "It was supposed to be an easy job. Clean and simple. In and out."

Bass glared back at him. He did good glare. He'd learned it from the best. "Yeah, well, that's what I was told too," he said coldly. "Instead we got there and found a dozen fucking Albanian gangsters already tooled up and pissed. So maybe I ain't the one you need to talk to."

He shoved Shepherd roughly away from him, and Shepherd fell back a heavy booted step, clenched his scarred hands into fists, and narrowed his pale eyes. The potential for violence fizzed in the air.

Bass wiped his mouth on the back of his wrist and waited warily for the first punch to be thrown. He'd only be back in town a couple of months. Old friends, old charges, and old debts had gotten him a few jobs with the Brothers, but he wasn't one of them, not yet. If Shepherd's lead on the Albanians' schedule had come from inside the club, it was easier to put a demonstrative beat-down on the hired help. Bad Info Brother would get the message, but there'd be no grudges within the chapter.

Not that Bass planned to curl up and take the kicking. He might want an in with the Brothers, but he'd never heard of a punching bag who got patched into a club. He balanced his weight on the balls of his feet and cracked his neck as he waited. He flicked his eyes from Shepherd to the other bikers sprawled around the bar as they waited for their cue.

"Fuck sake," Sonny spat as he pushed himself halfway into a sitting position. "Pissed off as those Albanians were when we walked in? Someone ripped us both off, Shep. Again. This time the only reason we know that is cause Sebastiani is a crazy bastard and got us out of there. Quick fucking with him and get me patched the hell up."

It took a second, but Shepherd finally grunted reluctant acknowledgment. He rubbed his knuckle along his unshaven jaw and nodded slowly.

"Fair enough," he said. "No hard feelings, Sebastiani, but you've been away for a long time. I don't know if I can trust you yet."

Bass stared at him coldly for a second longer and then let it slide away as he grinned and shrugged. He spread his hands in a disarming gesture.

"No harm, no foul," he said easily. "I'm here to do a job, Shepherd, not get an invite to your backyard barbeque. Just pay what you owe me, and we'll call it square. I won't even charge you extra for the rough stuff."

There was a pause as everyone in the bar waited for Shepherd to react before they committed themselves. In the end Shepherd chuckled harshly and grabbed the back of Bass's neck in a callused hand. He gave him a friendly shake, although there was still something flinty in his eyes.

"Your job was to pick up my shipment, Sebastiani," he pointed out. "Drugs or guns, whatever the Albanians are running. Since I don't have my package and you wrecked my goddamn van, I figure that right now, you owe me. Quite a bit."

Bass scowled but held his tongue. He'd been tapped to drive the van and watch Sonny's back—scutwork for the club's designated loser and the new guy. As far as he was concerned, he'd driven there and he'd driven back, so he was owed his money. Unfortunately one of the few drawbacks to a life of crime was that contract negotiations could be… touchy. There was a fine line between being a pushover and landing in a shallow grave with a bullet in your brain.

With a dozen of Plenty's biggest assholes ready to kick his ass for fun and money if he crossed that line, Bass planned to play it safe.

"You could at least front me a beer," he said.

Shepherd thought about being pissed but decided to be amused instead. "Help yourself," he said. "And sit tight. I might need you for something yet."

It wasn't the time—or the man—to point out that Bass might have somewhere else to be. Besides, Grindr dates came with a 50 percent chance you'd get stood up for a better offer. He went behind the bar and helped himself to a shot of rotgut whiskey from an expensive bottle. He tossed it back in one. The raw liquor was hot as it hit his stomach, and he grabbed a beer to wash it down.

The amber bottle dangled from his long fingers, old road rash scarred over the backs of his hands, as he leaned on the bar. Ville, who'd put in a good word for him when he got back to Plenty, gave it a minute and then came over.

"You need to learn to mind your manners," Ville said quietly. He caught the beer that Bass slid over the bar. "If you want in the Brothers, you need Shepherd to like you."

Bass lifted the bottle to his mouth. "Who says I want in?" he said, mostly just to be contrary. He glanced around the room at the gaunt gray-and-white banshee face of the Corpse Brothers' logo on every back, with the rockers stitched above and below. As a prospect Bass had the logo stitched on his cut, but if he wanted to be a full Brother, he needed the third patch. And he did want it. It made sense to join the Brothers. Even crooks liked to work for a salary. Still…. He took a draft of cold hops and then wiped his mouth on his sleeve. "I've never been a joiner."

"Yeah, I remember that," Ville said with a chuckle as he flicked the cap off his beer. They'd grown up together in the same shit part of town. Bass had fucked off out of the Heights the first chance—well, second— he got, but Ville had stayed and gone into the family business. "It would have made your life easier back then, will now too. It doesn't hurt to have people to watch your back."

Bass let a sly smile curve his mouth. "I have plenty of people that like to watch my ass."

That got him the old uncomfortable look from Ville. The side-eye that he was fine with Bass being gay but wished he wouldn't talk about it so much. For his own good, of course, because other people might not be so… tolerant.

Fuck tolerance. If Bass wanted to fit in, he'd have a job where he wore a suit and a tie. Or since kids with a GED from juvie didn't often get into white-shoe law firms, one where he clocked in and got overtime. Maybe he'd have a little house he could lose to the bank and a debt with interest he paid down on once a week, either with most of his pay or a run of broken bones from the loan shark's heavies.

Just like his dad.

Naw, not for him. He'd rather play the heavy than the doormat.

Ville washed his discomfort away with a swig of beer. "Seriously, though, if you want to me to put a word in—"

A guttural screech of pain from Sonny interrupted him. While they talked, Shepherd had recruited Fat Boone to pin Sonny's shoulders down on the pool table. Shepherd had taken the legs, one knee braced against Sonny's jailhouse ripped thigh as he gripped the bloody yellow plastic handle of the screwdriver and twisted.

"Get off," Sonny howled as he writhed under Fat Boone's weight. "Sonofabitch! You're gonna kill me, you bastard!"

Shepherd grunted and let go. He wiped his bloody hand on his leg as he stepped back.

"It's jammed right in there," he said. "We'd need a chisel to get it out—"

"Fuck off," Sonny blurted as he squirmed away from Boone's grip. He fumbled the bottle up to his mouth and poured whiskey down his throat, gagging around the burn of it. "Get the hell off me. I need a doctor. Take me to the hospital."

Shepherd took the bottle from Sonny. He wiped the mouth on his T-shirt and took a drink.

"Little problem there," he said. "Doc's been inside after that business in New Mexico, and you got…. How many active warrants on you, Sonny?"

Sonny swore and hammered his fist against the baize in a frustrated tattoo. "Fine. Whatever. But do something. You can't leave me like this. I'm in fucking agony."

He dropped back onto the baize with a thud and breathed raggedly through his open mouth. Shepherd and Boone looked at each other, the raised eyebrow and shrug the communication of people who'd known each other a long time and didn't have any current ideas. It was Ville who broke the silence.

"Here," he said as he turned to look at Bass. "Didn't you say that guy last week was a doctor? The one you... um...."

"Fucked?" Bass asked.

Ville flushed a dull, blotchy red from under his cheekbones all the way up to his eyebrows. He shot a quick uncomfortable glance at Shepherd and cleared the back of his throat.

"Yeah, whatever," he said. "Can you get him here? He could patch Sonny up."

Bass hesitated as he thought of Doc, with his clever hands and willing mouth. It had just been a sweaty fuck and a few hazy fantasies traded over the phone. It hadn't meant anything, but if he did this? The minute he made that call, it would be splashed with the same shit as the rest of his life in Plenty.

It might be worth it, though. Shepherd was the sort of man who couldn't wait to forget a good turn, but never someone he could use. If Bass made his problem go away, it would be better than Ville's introduction. He'd been in town for a couple of months now, and the occasional junkyard car chase wasn't going to scratch his itch for trouble much longer.

"Can you do that?" Shepherd broke into his thoughts. "Get a doctor down here?"

Bass pushed himself off the bar and pulled his phone out of his pocket. All told, whatever he had with Doc probably rounded up to a few hours of hot sex and a couple of pages of jerk-off material. An in with the Brothers, on the other hand, that could change Bass's life.

Bass stripped his Henley over his head and tossed it over behind the bar. He stretched his arms behind him to loosen the ache of his wrenched shoulder, where a black-and-purple stain bruised into his chest. Then he smirked at Shepherd.

"Give me ten minutes in a well-lit room," he said confidently as he hooked his thumb into the waistband of his jeans. It slid low over his lean hips, a flash of hipbone and ink over the frayed denim. "I can talk him into going anywhere I want him."

He grabbed his beer from the bar and took it with him as he sauntered toward the Men's room. He just hoped Doc had been telling the truth about being a doctor—that or he was ready to really commit to the lie.

CHAPTER FIVE

DROPLETS OF honey-colored liquid beaded against Bass's taut, inked stomach and dribbled down over the bare skin of his groin. A scuffed-up hand, knuckles bruised and split, wiped the liquid away as Bass reached down to—just off camera—palm his cock. The touch made his stomach muscles tighten, a sharp twitch under beer-damp skin, and Tag imagined the ragged hitch of Bass's voice as though he'd asked the question instead of typed it.

Thirsty?

Oh fuck yes. Tag's mouth was so dry his tongue stuck to the roof of it as he tried to swallow. Heat flushed through him in a wave that started at his balls and ended at his ears. He coughed to clear his throat.

"What?" Beattie, the charge nurse on duty, asked as she looked up from the computer. "If it's the tests for Bay Six, I already double-checked with Maguire. He's looking for zebras."

Tag reached for his coffee. "His patient, his zebras," he said with a shrug. A drink of the coffee reminded him it was cold and always bitter, and he grimaced as he set it back down. "Until the chief of surgery finds out. When did my shift end again?"

Beattie sniffed without looking up from the computer and pointed her finger at the papers spread out in front of Tag. "Two hours ago and as soon as you finish those charts."

"Done." Tag scrawled his initials over the last chart, gathered them up, and handed them to her. He texted *Parched* back to Bass as he rolled his neck from one side to the other to make the vertebra pop. "Tell Maguire his patient had an allergic reaction to whatever they cut his spice with. His balls are itchy because he's tripping balls."

"You sound sure."

Tag shrugged. "He was in last year for the same thing. Ennis saw him. I remembered when I saw his chart. See you next shift, Beattie."

She rolled her eyes and clacked at the computer as she called up the files. "Not if I get a better offer," she said. Then she tutted her tongue against her teeth. "Not that it's happened yet."

Tag checked his phone. The location pin had already been dropped under his last text—same place as last time. Excitement itched along his spine and refused to be blasé about the invitation. He could pretend to be jaded when he got there, but he wasn't going to fool himself. It wasn't that he had any illusions—or only a few, which he knew would bite him eventually—but it was still nice.

Nice to be wanted.

Nice to be a horny idiot.

Nice to be in... fatuated. See? No illusions.

"Yeah. I can't say the same," Tag said with a smirk. "You just have to put yourself out there. Get out of the hospital."

Beattie looked up at him, her eyes narrowed behind funky glasses. "Run," she told him. There might have been some humor behind the dry warning... or not. Either way, Tag was already on his way out.

He grabbed his stuff from the locker room, slung his jacket over his shoulder, and whistled absently to himself as he took the elevator down. One of the cardio residents got in when the doors opened on his ward and gave Tag a curious look.

"Good news?" he asked as he hit the button for the basement.

"Not really," Tag said. "Just glad to be getting out of here."

He looked up just in time to catch the dubious face the resident made. "Really?" he asked. "I mean, I always heard you were married to the job, Dr. Hayes."

It wasn't a question. That was a good thing since Tag found himself lost for words. He'd always had a life outside the hospital—a boyfriend, some friends, his sister and the kids he sent obligatory holiday money to. Once a month he grabbed a pickup game of basketball at the court opposite the hospital.

On the other hand... when had he last been more excited to leave the hospital than arrive?

The elevator pinged as it reached the lobby, and the doors opened to let Tag out. He blinked at them for a second and then tried to shrug off his suddenly pensive mood. Tonight wasn't the night to resolve his work/life balance.

"Night, Dr. Hayes," the resident said chirpily. "Don't do anything I wouldn't do."

"No, it's more something I wouldn't do," Tag said.

He walked away from the resident's baffled face as the doors swiped shut in front of his nose.

A BOTTLE crunched under the wheels of the old Mustang as Tag pulled into The Sheep's Clothing parking lot. He winced and took the first empty spot he could find, next to a battered yellow Jimmy with mud caked like makeup on the windshield.

The engine coughed as he took his foot off the gas, and it died before he had a chance to touch the keys. That was probably fine.

Tag glanced at himself in the rearview mirror and absently brushed his hand through his dark hair to flatten it down. That didn't work. It just stuck out in different directions than before. He gave up and twisted around to get his bag from the back seat. The click of the door made him jump as someone opened it.

"Shit," he yelped.

Bass leaned down, one arm slung along the top of the door, and raised an eyebrow at him.

"What's the matter?" he teased. "You got a guilty conscience, Doc?"

"Actually no," Tag said. He dragged the bag between the seats and slung it over his shoulder as he got out of the car. "You just startled me."

Bass wrapped a hand around the nape of Tag's neck, his fingers warm and sweaty, and pulled him down into a kiss. Stubble scraped against Tag's lips, and Bass's mouth tasted like beer and salt. Tag ran his hand down Bass's back, over the long, toned muscles under the thin T-shirt, and into the dip of his lean waist.

"What?" Bass asked as he leaned back. His grin was wickedly careless and caught under Tag's ribs like a hook. "Were you expecting someone else?"

Tag pulled him closer, the line of their bodies half-hidden behind the Mustang's open door, and teased a light kiss against the corner of Bass's lush mouth. "No," he said. "Not tonight, anyhow."

"So you can manage to fit me in?" Bass asked as he reached around to grab Tag's ass. He squeezed roughly and nudged his knee between Tag's thighs. Tag had to grab the side of the door for balance, desire hot under his skin and in the back of his throat. It would be easy to sprawl back into the car, the gear stick in his ribs and Bass's weight on top of him. Stupid as fuck, but easy. Bass bit a kiss into his throat. "Good to know."

"It was tight, but…." Tag's voice trailed off into a breathless moan as Bass scraped his teeth along his collarbone. A laugh tickled against damp skin, and then Bass exhaled, his chin tucked into Tag's shoulder and his hands tight where they gripped him. Tag absently ran his hand upstroked Bass's back, and he could feel the tension in the hard lines of muscle. "What?"

Bass gave a low, rough chuckle and stepped back with a shrug. He hooked his finger in the V-neck of Tag's scrubs and tugged him away from the car.

"So you really are a doctor?" he asked.

"I told you I was," Tag said. He shoved the door shut behind him and clicked the button on his remote. The flicker of the lights highlighted the scrawled graffiti on the side of the bar. Black paint roughed out a mask of empty eyes and gaped, fanged mouth, and then it faded back into the dark as the bulb dimmed. Nerves itched at the back of Tag's neck, but he tried to ignore them. "Not going up to your place?"

"Not yet," Bass said. He let go of Tag's collar and turned around, one arm slung companionably over his shoulders. "Come have a drink first."

Bass tightened his fingers on Tag's arm as he dragged Tag across the lot toward the bar. A bright yellow sign plastered crookedly in the window announced that the bar had been closed for "Health and Public Safety." It was dated three days ago, but the closure didn't seem to have slowed business any. Music pounded against the walls, and voices were raised to hear over the guitar riffs. A bottle smashed inside, and someone cursed in a ragged voice.

"What's going on?" Tag asked as he balked.

"Just trust me," Bass said, his voice suddenly low and intent. "Play along. It'll be fine."

He glanced over his shoulder at the road for a second and then pushed Tag through the door into the bar. The smell of alcohol and old blood hit the back of Tag's throat as he inhaled. Bloody rags lay on the floor, and a pallid, sweaty man was laid out on a table, one hitched leg roughly bandaged with old T-shirts and towels. Two mean-looking men in leather and denim held him by the shoulders as they tried to pry a blood-smeared pool ball out of his hand before he could break any more of the bottles in the bar. A dozen other men were slouched at the bar, arms around skimpily dressed women with rat-tailed hair and their attention on Tag.

A kick of adrenaline made Tag's blood fizz in his ears. He took a step back, but Bass grabbed his elbow.

"Trust me," Bass reminded him under his breath as he shoved him into the room. "It'll be okay."

"Go fuck yourself," Tag hissed back.

Bass sighed ruefully. "Figured I would be."

One of the other men in the bar jumped up to lock the door behind them with a sharp click. It made Tag flinch, and he swallowed hard. His mouth was dry, but not for the usual reasons.

Bass pulled him to a halt in front of the table and pitched his voice to carry to the rest of the bar. His voice sounded rougher, cockier, and he reached up to scruff a hand through Tag's hair. "See, Shepherd? I told you I could get him to follow me anywhere."

The big fair-haired man finally wrenched the slimy cue ball out of the bloody man's fingers. He tossed it idly in his hand, the hard slap of weighted ivory against callused skin distinct enough to cut through "Let the Bodies Hit the Floor," and stared at Tag with narrowed eyes. Deep wrinkles fanned back from the corners in a web worked into his skin by sun and wind.

"I know you," Shepherd—Tag assumed—said slowly. He pointed a finger at Tag's face. "Where do I know you from, Doc?"

Tag yanked his arm out of Bass's grip and throttled the urge to correct Shepherd with his name. This guy did not need to know his real name. Doc would do.

"Prostate exam?" he asked, his voice tight in the back of his throat.

For a second the option of violence hung in the air as everyone waited for Shepherd's reaction. Calculation flickered through the big man's eyes as he weighed his response. Practicality won out over brutality, and he laughed, his grin nowhere near his pale eyes.

"Check out this bastard," he said as he glanced over the pool table to the heavyset man on the other side. "He's got balls the size of church bells."

The man on the table groaned and pushed his knuckles against his forehead. "I don't care if he drags 'em around on a fucking cart," he slurred. "I'm in fucking agony here, you bastards."

Bass put his hand between Tag's shoulders and gave him a push forward. "What do you think, Doc? Have a look and see if you can patch Sonny here up?"

The cue ball spun up into the air and smacked back into Shepherd's hand. It was obviously not a request. Tag swallowed hard, wiped his hands on his scrubs, and stepped up to the table. The green surface under Sonny's hips was soaked through with blood. Tag carefully peeled the sodden towels back to uncover a dirty screwdriver jammed deeply into a bloody thigh. The metal looked to be buried at least half the length of the shaft into his leg, and when Tag gingerly pressed the flesh around the wound, it was hard and swollen.

Sonny howled a stream of "fucks" forced through clenched teeth and squirmed in place.

"He needs to go to the hospital," Tag said as he stepped back.

Toss. Smack.

"See, Doc, that ain't gonna happen," Shepherd said. "Sonny here, he doesn't like hospitals."

"Does he like having two legs?" Tag asked. "Because if we don't get him to hospital, that could change."

Shepherd wound back and threw the cue-ball at the wall. It hissed back at Tag's head as Bass yanked him out of the way, and it smashed through the window with a crash. A moment later a car alarm went off outside, the shrill drone out of time with the steady flash of the headlights through the window.

"Fuck sake, Shep—" Bass spat, but he was ignored.

"You've misunderstood me, Doc. Either you fix Sonny up, or I fix your face so the next time you try to pick up a pretty boy, they puke on you," Shepherd said, the affable mask still in place. "Understood?"

Tag did. He took a deep breath and shoved all the unhelpful stuff—the ball-clenching fear, the angry humiliation, the sour feeling of helplessness—down into the pit of his stomach. It wasn't the first time he'd been threatened. People in trauma situations were either at their best or at their worst, and it probably wouldn't be the last time.

The *stupidest*, but not the last.

He pulled his keys out of his pocket and tossed them to the heavyset biker. The guy grabbed them out of midair and glared at Tag.

"I'll need the first aid kit out of the trunk of my car," Tag said as he tried to work out his wish list for a makeshift surgical theater. "A bottle of whiskey, six feet of rope, and someone's belt."

Shepherd folded his arms and gave a slight nod of assent. "Go on, Boone. Get him what he needs."

THE BELT was thick leather but supple enough from the owner's body heat to fold easily around Tag's hand. He held it in front of Sonny's mouth.

"Bite on this," he said.

Sonny pulled his head back. "You ain't fucking me," he grumbled.

"It's going to hurt like hell," Tag told him. "This will stop you biting through your tongue or breaking your teeth. It's up to you."

It took a second, but Sonny grudgingly opened his mouth. Tag shoved in the wad of leather and waited for Sonny to set his teeth in it. Then he grabbed the bottle of whiskey, resisted the brief temptation to take a swig, and poured it over his hands. It stung in the raw patches between his fingers and where he'd scratched his knuckles earlier. He hissed in a breath and shook the stray drops of liquor off his fingers.

Bass handed him a pair of sterile gloves and draped the limp blue neoprene over his fingers. "I got you into this, I'll get you out," he promised quietly. "Trust me."

Tag took the gloves but otherwise ignored him. He plucked a scalpel out of his kit and turned back to his patient. The leg of Sonny's jeans had already been cut away and peeled back to reveal his swollen thigh and the solid jut of the screwdriver. It had stopped bleeding for now, but that wouldn't last.

Despite what Shepherd had diagnosed, Tag didn't think the screwdriver had pierced the femur. Instead it was just swollen muscle that wouldn't release its grip on the dirty metal. Tag touched the drum-tight thigh, and despite the sweat that lashed off Sonny, the muscle was cold.

Compartment syndrome. More common with a crushing injury, but a penetrating object in the right place could cause it too. Tag had seen it once before, around a bit of rebar that had gone through a man's forearm.

"Get the fuck on with it," Sonny slurred around his leather bite guard.

Tag exhaled and sliced the knife along Sonny's thigh in a single smooth motion. One of the bikers gagged and looked away. The others jeered and slapped him across the back of his head for his weak stomach.

Under the superficial calm, part of Tag's brain was frantic with what a bad idea this was. He probably wouldn't lose his license, since it was exigent circumstances, but he'd be suspended during an investigation. Everyone would find out what an idiot he'd been. Worst of all, he could have a death on his conscience by the end of the hour. While all that churned through his head, his hand stayed steady and his fingers light on the knife as he sliced deeper into Sonny's leg.

He had to release the pressure he needed to get to the fascia, not just the surface layers of skin, and do it quickly enough so his patient didn't bleed out on the table. Maybe Sonny deserved it—he had reason to avoid the police, if nothing else—but that wasn't Tag's call. He packed the wound with gauze as he worked to release the muscle.

"When I tell you to…," he said without looking up. The back of his neck hurt, and the old scar under his ribs itched and ached. "Pull the screwdriver straight up and out. Carefully."

It was Bass who grabbed the bloody yellow handle. Tag licked his lips, sliced deeper, and squashed the urge to be grateful.

"Now," he said as he braced both hands against Sonny's thigh. The skin felt hot under his fingers again.

Bass gave the screwdriver a sharp yank, and it slid wetly out of Sonny's leg. Fresh dark blood welled like syrup out of the hole. Tag took a second to rub the back of his wrist over his eyebrow, the sharp, metallic scent of blood thick on his fingers, and then he grabbed the bottle of iodine he'd saved to rinse the wound with.

With luck it wouldn't get infected.

"I need to reiterate this," Tag said as traded his scalpel for a needle and surgical thread. His hands were still steady, and he made neat little stitches in black rows that his old teachers couldn't have taken issue with. "He needs to go to the hospital. I've done my best, but this is a serious trauma. He's lost a lot of blood, and there's a significant chance of infection. He needs supervision, rehab, antibiotics, and painkillers—"

Sonny's head lolled to the side, his parted mouth dry and the sliver of eye visible under his lids wet and shiny. His breathing was unsteady, but it was hard to tell if that was from the surgery or the depressive influence of liquor.

"You need to shut up and get on with patching Sonny up," Shepherd said. He picked up a shot glass of whiskey and smiled thinly at Tag from behind it. "I bet you'll do the best job of your life, Doc. Because if this doesn't go well for Sonny, it won't go well for you."

Tag grimaced. "I'm not saying threats aren't effective," he said without looking up from his work. "But a top-of-the-line surgical suite, staplers, and an anesthesiologist would make for a better job."

He used Kessler stitches on the muscle, black lines against the dense fibers, and sopped up the blood when it got in his way. Sweat itched on the side of his face, and he paused to wipe it on his shoulder before he started to pull the skin back together over the raw meat of Sonny's leg.

It was a mess. Even if it healed well, Sonny was going to end up with a nasty scar, and the situation still offended Tag on a professional level. He'd tear apart a resident who did work like this, not that anyone who would pass judgment was going to see this… hopefully.

He tied off the last stitch and straightened up. The small of his back ached dully with the movement, and his neck popped like knuckles as he craned his head from one side to the other. He grabbed the whiskey and soaked a gauze pad to wipe most of the blood off Sonny's leg. His hand started to shake midwipe as the habitual steadiness of surgery was no longer needed.

"He'll need to change the dressing regularly and clean the wound each time," Tag said. "The stitches will dissolve on their own, but if he sees any swelling, redness, or the pain gets worse, he needs to go to a hospital. Toss him in a car and head down to a clinic over the border if you have to, but I mean it. If he gets an infection, he could lose his leg, and that's the best-case scenario. He could lose mobility, his eyesight. The infection could spread to his—"

"What do you care, Doc?" one of the bikers, the one with the weak stomach and Van Dyke beard, said with a sneer. "You ain't doing this out of the goodness of your heart."

Bass gave him a shove. "Shut up, Ville." He got a snarl and a shove back, a stiff-armed blow to the shoulder that made him stagger. The quick, vicious look Bass gave the other man caught Tag off guard.

"I've killed people," Tag admitted. "I didn't work fast enough, I missed something, things just didn't come together in time. They're all on me. If Sonny dies, it won't be because of anything I did or because I didn't give you all the information you needed to keep him alive."

He stripped the bloody gloves off his hands and balled them up to toss them on the table with the rest of the bloody refuse from the operation. Then he grabbed the whiskey and took a slug straight from the bottle.

It was cheap whiskey in a good bottle, harsh smoke and turpentine notes that made his sinuses sting. But the burn of it—the "two more of me and we won't care" reassurance—as it caught on the back of his throat and ran down into his stomach was just right. Tag wiped his mouth on the back of his sleeve and looked at Shepherd.

"I've done what I can for him," he said harshly. Then he took another swig since a DUI seemed like the least of his worries tonight. "Can I go? Or not."

"You can go," Bass said in a quiet, edged voice. He gave Shepherd a hard look. "Can't he?"

CHAPTER SIX

"NICE CAR," Bass said. He leaned back against the long fire-engine-red hood of the Mustang and crossed his arms. "Gotta say, I figured you more for Jags than muscle cars."

Tag shot him a bleak look. "I guess there are things neither of us knew about the other," he said harshly, but he didn't break stride. He paced the length of the car and then back again as he took deep, unsteady breaths of the cool night air. There was blood on his scrubs and sweat stains under his arms and around his collar.

It was oddly hot.... *All* of it. The steady hand, the confidence as he opened Sonny's leg down to the bone and fucked around in there like he knew what he was doing, and the rangy, restless energy of him now that all that adrenaline was off the leash.

From experience Bass knew that the sex right then would be amazing. He'd been there often enough, his veins itchy with suddenly aimless energy that needed to be pointed somewhere. Of course it wasn't going to happen. Under the circumstances, a fight was more likely. Although he did, briefly, consider just shoving Tag up against the car and kissing him. Whiskey and anger sharp in their mouths and the gradual surrender of Tag's lean, responsive body as Bass bent him over a car hood—

Tag interrupted Bass's fantasy as he stopped midpace in front of the car. He stood for a second, jaw set and eyes closed. Then he gagged and bolted over to puke into the weeds at the edge of the lot. Bass looked away, his attention focused on the scuffed toe of his boot until Tag stopped retching.

"Son of a bitch," Tag muttered, his voice clogged and raw. He was doubled over, hands braced on his knees, and his head hung between his shoulders. For a second, Bass thought he just meant... generally. Then Tag spat, wiped his mouth on the back of his wrist, and spat the words out between his teeth. "You son of a bitch."

"I got Shepherd to cut you loose, didn't I?" Bass protested, the defensive prickle automatic even when he was in the wrong. "I had your back."

Tag pushed himself upright. "Sure," he said bitterly as he stalked back. "You're a fucking prince. Get off my car."

"Look, Sonny needed help," Bass said. He didn't know why. What he did was the sort of shit you couldn't come back from, and he knew that when he honeytrapped the text. His mouth apparently hadn't gotten the memo, and it just wanted to justify itself. "If I hadn't called you, then Shepherd would have ripped that screwdriver out with a crowbar and got Sonny a whore to distract him as he bled out. You'd rather that happen than I ask you for help?"

"You didn't ask," Tag pointed out. He stalked by Bass and prepared to get into the car. "That's the point. Get off my car."

It was a fair point, but Bass reached out and slammed the Mustang's door shut. He held out his arms when Tag glared at him.

"Go on, then."

"What?"

"Hit me," Bass said. He stuck out his chin as a target. "Take your best shot, and I won't even duck."

Tag choked out a laugh that he scrubbed off his mouth with an impatient pass of his hand. He shook his head and jerked the door open again.

"You think that will make me feel better? What? I split your lip and we're even? Break your jaw and I owe you one?" he asked. "No hard feelings?"

Bass met his gaze. "I deserve it," he admitted.

"Yeah," Tag said quietly. "You do. But there's two problems with that. If I break my knuckles, I'll be benched for a couple of months, and you aren't worth it."

The sting of that caught Bass by surprise. It made him sneer and bristle in reaction.

"Not what you said before," he said, even though he knew he should shut up. The hole he'd dug was deep enough. "You thought I was worth it when you drove down here on a promise of some ass."

Just when you thought it couldn't get any worse, Bass thought with a grimace at the taste that sentence left on his tongue, he went and opened his mouth.

Tag shook his head and folded himself down into the bucket seat of the Mustang. The engine spluttered and coughed as he fought with the ignition. It finally caught with a hiccuped growl that Bass could feel through his hips.

"Stay away from me," Tag said.

He threw the car into reverse and hit the gas. Bass had to jump clear of the car to avoid being rolled under the wheels. He shoved his hand through his hair, and knotted curls caught around his fingers as he watched Tag's taillights drive away.

"Shit," he muttered. "Should have just kissed him. Couldn't have worked out any worse."

At least then Tag might have punched him. It would have made Bass feel a bit better, if nothing else.

Fuck it. Bass swallowed the scratch of regret in the back of his throat and pushed Tag out of his mind. He wasn't the first guy Bass had fucked over, and he wouldn't be the last. It was probably for the best that he got out now, before Bass pulled him in any deeper.

A wry smile tucked the corners of Bass's mouth as he headed back into the clubhouse. Hell, if he looked at it that way, he'd done Tag a favor. Bass shouldered open the door of the bar and ducked inside. The sweaty mug of body heat and leather greeted him, and he kicked the door shut behind him.

"Well, I ain't getting fucked tonight," he said.

Boone's laugh was a coarse blurt of sound as he tossed a garbage bag at one of the younger bikers to clean up the mess. "Don't look at me," he said and reached back to slap one hefty cheek. "Your cock ain't big enough to reach my hole. Fuck, get Sonny to set you up once he's conscious. He's the one who owes you, and he won't be much good for anything else till that leg heals."

Ville looked uncomfortable at the laughter that eddied around the bar, but he brought Bass another beer. "You did good," he muttered to him. "Shepherd's pleased. If you keep your head down, keep on his good side—"

Bass plucked the bottle out of Ville's hand and walked away midsentence. A couple of the brothers slapped his back as he crossed the bar, and Mick cracked his hand across Bass's ass with a roar of laughter. Bass tipped his beer over the asshole's head and left him to splutter through his drenched beard while he joined Shepherd's table.

Shepherd sat back, arm cocked over the back of the chair, and sipped his whiskey.

Bass dragged out a chair, spun it around, and straddled it as he sat down. "So am I in or not?"

Shepherd picked at something in his teeth with a bruised thumbnail and glanced around the bar as he judged the mood of the room. "Is that the only reason you helped? To get on my good side?"

Bass snorted. "What? You thought I did it because of my unrequited love for Sonny? He's not my type."

Shepherd chuckled and poured a second glass of whiskey. An odd, cold smile twisted his mouth.

"What do you say, boys?" he asked, his gruff voice raised to carry over the noise. "You think Sebastiani here has what it takes to be our brother? Anyone gonna vouch for him?"

Ville didn't. It was Boone who shrugged. "Why the hell not," he said. "It ain't like he's new blood. He grew up around here, stole his first car down the road, and got in his first drunken brawl on the street outside. If he hadn't been sent off to juvie in fuckin' Nebraska, he'd probably be a brother already. I'll back him."

"I'll second him," Mick said as he wrung foam out of his beard. "I figure none of you bastards would put their *actual* ass on the line to get me out of the shit."

Shepherd pushed the glass over the table. "I'm good with it."

There it was. Finally.

Bass picked up the glass and slammed back the shot to whoops and cheers. He smacked the glass back down on the table and grinned, sharp and hard edged, at Shepherd.

"I won't let you down," he told Shepherd.

"You better not," Shepherd said genially as he got up. He clapped his rough-knuckled hand on Bass's shoulder and squeezed down with hard fingers. The pressure made Bass's collarbone creak, and he clenched his teeth against the dull pulse of pain. Shepherd leaned down and winked at him. "Because you'll only do it once."

Point made, he let go of Bass's shoulder and clapped his hands. "Fuck it. Prop Sonny up in the corner and crack out some more bottles. Time to celebrate! Tomorrow we get even."

Dragged up out of the chair by eager hands, Bass was bounced around the group as his new brothers hugged, slapped his shoulders, and punched him. Mick pulled him into a headlock, fist tucked under his jaw and sweaty armpit pressed against his cheek, and baptized him with a warm beer.

Bass blinked the liquid out of his eyes as he grinned and leaned into the friendly slaps. When he finally pulled himself free, Shepherd handed him the third patch for his cut. He gripped the stiff fabric in his hand, the edges sharp against his fingers as he grinned at the other bikers.

A full member of the club. One of the Corpse Brothers. This was the reason he'd put his tail between his legs and slunk back to Plenty in the first place. It made everything he'd done to get here worth it.

Right?

"FUCK." BASS dropped the breaker bar as he barked his knuckles for the third time. It clattered against the floor as he pulled his hand out of the locked engine and shook it. His knuckles were bloody, he had a blister on the heel of his hand, and the old Chevy's engine was still locked.

He kicked the tire in frustration. The car ignored him, probably because it was deader than a dodo.

The car wasn't the problem. It was *a* problem, since Fat Boone's aunt hadn't replaced the oil since the Bush administration, but not what had Bass on edge. It had been near enough a month since he got patched in, the badges still stiff where Mick's old lady sewed them on for him, and all he'd done was play mechanic and sit on his ass in the clubhouse.

It wasn't exactly what he expected. Worst of all, now that he was officially one of Shepherd's crew, no one in town would scratch his itch for a pointless brawl. His other itches… well, he could scratch those, but his heart wasn't in it.

Bass had always gotten bored easily—at school, at work, most of his relationships. After a while it just started to feel like each day was a replay of the last, and he got the urge to kick the whole shitshow over. It never ended well, but that hadn't stopped him yet.

He grabbed a chipped mug from the metal sink and poured himself a cup of black, six-hour-brewed coffee he sweetened with condensed milk from a pierced can. The hit of syrupy sweetness somehow made the coffee taste more bitter, and the aftertaste snuck up on you and hung on in there once the sugar was gone.

Bass drank it anyhow as he stared blindly at Shepherd's office and weighed his options.

"Don't," Ville said.

"What?" Bass asked as he glanced over. The Porsche was up on blocks, with the logo pried free, the doors unhinged, and the engine lifted in a heavy-duty sling. Give it another hour, and the car would be spare parts on the net—what Shepherd's contact hadn't already put dibs on—and all the original owner would get was an insurance payout.

Ville wiped his hands down his stomach and scowled. "Fuck this up just to see what would happen."

Bass made a face and drained the last of the coffee. Apparently Ville was *still* pissed off that his help hadn't been needed to get Bass into the Chapter.

"It's a coffee break." Bass upended the cup and shook the last sticky drops of liquid onto the concrete floor. "Don't read too much into it."

"I know what you're like," Ville said. "It's the same as when we were kids. You get a good thing going, and you decide to put your foot through it. Not this time. Keep your head down and your nose clean. Shepherd will let you know when he has something for you to do."

"One way to do things," Bass agreed blandly.

Ville made a disgusted sound in the back of his throat and pointedly turned his back to yell at one of the other mechanics to mind what he was doing. Bass left him to it. Eventually he'd get over this too.

The two of them were friends when they were kids, dragged up in one of Plenty's half-dead blue-collar neighborhoods. Their parents had snuck in just under the bar for the dream of self-improvement, with mortgages they'd pay off one day and plans for their kids to go to college. Their kids aspired to the gutter. In Plenty, crime had more prospects than middle management.

They fell out of touch when Bass got shipped out to a juvie in Nebraska, and there wasn't any reason to relight the connection while Bass was in New York or Denver. But now that he was back, Bass appreciated Ville's willingness to give him a hand up in the local scene.

He just didn't have fifteen years to waste on slow and steady until Shepherd voted him because he'd been a prospect long enough that it got awkward. The long game was for people who had patience.

"I kind of figured there'd be more to do than suck up to Fat Boone's family," he said to no one in particular, although he knew Ville would listen. "Especially after what happened at the junkyard."

Ville grabbed a welder's mask and pulled it on over his head. "You got a problem with how Shepherd does things, you bring it up to Shepherd."

He ignited the torch with a hiss and a shower of sparks. Bass scratched the back of his neck.

"Maybe I will," he said as he added his cup to the pile in the sink. "Shepherd always did appreciate the straightforward approach. But you should know that better than me."

That was the thing about old friends. It didn't matter how many years it had been; you still knew how to pull their strings. Bass left Ville to gnaw on that and headed back to the Chevy. One last try to unlock the pistons, otherwise he was going to have to rebuild the whole engine to get Fat Boone's aunt back on the road.

Bass kicked the breaker bar out from under the car and grabbed it to get back to work. He'd just ducked back under the hood when someone shrieked behind him. The raw panic in the noise hooked Bass by the spine and jerked him like a fish. He banged his head on the hood of the car—a starburst of surprise pain that made him squint—as he bolted upright and turned around.

One of Shepherd's mechanics, a wiry man with thin ginger hair and a sour, hound-dog loose face, writhed on the floor. Blood smeared the ground under him and drenched his gray overalls as it poured out of what was left of his hand.

"Son of a bitch," Ville yelped as he staggered backward. Thank fuck he had enough presence of mind to switch off the torch. The flame fluttered out and left a blue afterimage scorched over Bass's retina where he'd looked at it. Ville shoved his helmet up. His swarthy face had that grayish tinge it always did when he panicked. "Where the *fuck* are his fingers?"

"On the floor," Bass said.

He shucked the top half of his overalls as he scrambled over the shop floor to the wailing mechanic. The two severed fingers lay on the floor at the side of the car. One of them had a wart on the knuckle and the other a black bruise under the thick nail. It should have been horrifying, but they looked more like cheap horror-flick props than flesh and bone.

Bass pulled an oil-stained cloth out of his pocket and picked up the loose digits. They were lighter than he expected and still warm. He thrust the cloth at one of the other mechanics, who recoiled from the bundle.

"Take it," Bass snapped. "Get some ice from the bar, and maybe they can reattach them."

Disgust twisted the man's face, but he did what he was told. While he ran over to the clubhouse, Bass pulled off his shirt and wrapped it roughly around the bloody remnants of—fuck, George's? Greg's?—hand. He had to lift the little finger, which hung by a gory thread of skin, fat, and a shred of sinew, into place before he wrapped the cotton around it.

"What are you doing?" Ville asked. He sounded like he was about to puke.

"I'm going to take George here to the ER," Bass said. "Because I gotta tell you, Doc's still not taking my calls. So unless you want to try and glue George's ass-scratching finger back on—"

Ville hesitated, mouth set in a grimace, but George tried to scramble to his feet. "It's Grant," he corrected in a thick, ragged voice. George had been close. "And get me to the hospital. I want my fingers back."

Bass pulled him to his feet and wedged his shoulder under Grant's arm. His body felt cool, almost clammy as he leaned against Bass's shoulder. Blood had already soaked through the makeshift bandage and splattered the ground with round, red drops that grew bigger each time.

"Ville, you drive," Bass said. "I'll sit in back with Grant."

The prospect of something to do made Ville look relieved. He mumbled assent and dashed into the office to grab his keys from the hook. Meanwhile Bass gripped Grant's wrist and held it up over heart level.

"It'll be okay," he said. "They have some good doctors at Plenty Hospital."

Probably. Bass had only met one, but Tag had been good in bed, and Sonny's leg hadn't fallen off.

Bass supposed there was a chance Tag might be on duty tonight. Bass supposed it would be pretty sick to see a coworker's chopped-off fingers as an excuse for a meet cute again, but... he hadn't cut them off, and if Tag happened to be at the hospital too, that was hardly Bass's fault.

The whole honeytrapping Tag to a bar so he could be threatened into a possibly illegal surgery, that was on Bass. But he was in the clear on Grant's fingers.

"Got 'em!" Ville finally burst out of the office, keys in hand and a tarp thrown over his shoulder. He gave the greasy-pale Grant a dubious look. "Will he be okay?"

"I fucked a doctor. It doesn't make me one," Bass said. He shifted Grant's weight onto Ville's shoulder. "Get him in the car. I'll go see what's keeping the fingers."

The answer to that was that everyone in the bar had wanted a look at them before they went in the ice. Bass fished one out of Mick's beer, tossed it with the other into the pint glass of ice like a macabre shrimp cocktail, and took it out to the car.

By the time they got to the hospital, the ice had melted and the fingers had started to look wizened. The exposed meat was pale, and the skin had started to curl back from the bone. The nurse raised her eyebrows as she lifted the pint and watched the fingers spin.

"Don't worry," Bass said. "They're not mine."

He was treated to a dry look from Nurse—based on her name tag—Beattie. "That's a relief," she said. "Seeing as you aren't freckled or redheaded. Who do they—"

The answer stumbled in through the sliding doors, slung over Ville's shoulder.

"Asked and answered," Beattie said. She handed the glass to a passing nurse with a barked order to get it on ice. Then she called for Dr. Ennis.

The short woman in wrinkled scrubs who answered was unflappable in the face of bloody stumps, and, probably, based on her confidence that she could reattach Grant's fingers, good at her job. Definitely not Tag, though.

It shouldn't have mattered. The off chance that Tag would be on duty and open to apologies in the form of a hookup in the on-call room was as much a fantasy as anything they'd sexted. Bass knew that. He was cocky, not an idiot.

But as fantasies went, it was a good one. Bass was surprised at how hard it was to let it go. He helped himself to a handful of mints from the nurses' station and watched a junkie handcuffed to a wheelchair try to convince his nurse he'd been attacked by a bear.

"Don't worry, your… friend?" Beattie said as she came back.

Bass shrugged and tossed another mint in his mouth. "Coworker at a new job."

"Good," she said dryly as she picked up a chart. "I'd hate to see you off your food."

He grinned at her and crunched the mint between his back teeth. The candy cracked into peppermint shrapnel.

"He'll be going into surgery soon," she said. "If you want to wait, there's—"

"Actually," Bass said. "I have a friend who works here, and I thought he'd be here tonight, but I can't get him to answer his phone."

Beattie scrawled something on the chart. "Sucks to be you."

"Tag," Bass said. "Taggart. He asked me to get him a quote to fix up that Mustang of his, but... I didn't have a chance this week."

That made Beattie roll her eyes. "Ugh, that car," she said as she initialed another chart. "My husband got one like that when he had a midlife crisis. I told him to take it back and find a waitress instead, because divorce would be cheaper than keeping that thing on the road."

It wasn't hard to grin at that. She was not wrong.

"So." Bass leaned on the counter and gave her his best smile. The one that didn't fool anyone about him being bad news but was wicked enough they didn't care. "Is he here tonight?"

Beattie finished with the charts and capped her pen with a sharp click. "Hopefully not. He's on a blind date with my nephew, and if they end the night here, something has gone very wrong." She pulled her phone out of her pocket and checked the screen. The corners of her mouth turned up in a smug little smirk. "Apparently it's going well so far, so I doubt we'll see Tag before his shift tomorrow. But if you want to leave the quote here, I can pass it on."

The mint wasn't strong enough to mask the sudden sour taste in the back of Bass's throat, but he ignored it.

"Don't bother," Bass said. He pushed himself off the station with a shrug. "I want to talk him through it so he gets how much work that thing needs. I'll catch him again."

"Start with whatever is wrong with the exhaust," Beattie suggested. She stepped out from behind the station, her rubber soles loud on the floor. "You did a good job today with those fingers. With any luck you'll have saved Mr. Molloy the use of his hand."

At least, Bass supposed, someone would get some good news today. He stepped away from the station at the same time Beattie did, and they nearly tripped each other up.

"Sorry," she said.

"My fault," Bass said as he tucked her phone into the back of his jeans. "Don't know where my own feet are."

CHAPTER SEVEN

THE BEER was expensive, the food was mediocre, and under normal circumstances, Tag wouldn't be caught dead at the PlentyFull Food Festival. It turned out that dating in California wasn't that different from New York, although in New York, it would have been a friend-of-a-friend's art exhibition Tag would have had to endure.

"… you know my aunt, of course, and my dad's a pediatrician," Joe said as they walked between the food stalls. Chutneys and jams were piled in multicolored jars on tables, a selection open for humans and ants alike to sample. Wheels of cheese were displayed, dissected, and the slices wrapped in wax paper by white-aproned farmers. It was so sweet it made Tag's teeth hurt a bit. "So I thought about medicine, but… I wanted a life."

He laughed at his own joke. It cut a little too close to home for Tag to really appreciate it—his realization he didn't have a life was 50 percent of why he was here—but he chuckled anyhow.

"Not sure lawyers have better hours," Tag said. "Although possibly less bodily fluids are involved."

A high school girl with ridiculously glossy hair and the sort of smile that interned at Disney over the summer bounced out from between the stalls. She thrust a tray under Joe's nose.

"Pig trotter sushi?" she chirped.

"Now here's where you might be surprised," Joe said as he gamely took one of the rolls. "So few bodily fluids. Almost none."

This time Tag's laugh was genuine. "*Almost* none?"

Joe nodded and popped the cured pork and seasoned rice rolls into his mouth. He chewed twice and then washed the mouthful away with a gulp of beer.

"An incident involving a coat closet, an open bar, and a senior partner spoiled the streak," he admitted after he cleared his throat. "Before that the last incident was with an abrasive executor who spat on me."

Tag snorted. "I could win this," he said. "But then no one would want to kiss me ever again."

It had been a long time since Tag had flirted with anyone. The whole "Wanna fuck" thing with Bass didn't count, even before it turned out to be a con. So he didn't know if that line would read as cute or corny.

From Joe's slow smile, it just about scraped cute. "Oh," Joe said as he leaned in and slung his arm over Tag's shoulder. "I wouldn't worry about that."

It took an uncomfortable second too long before Tag clumsily returned the gesture with an arm around Joe's waist. It felt odd, stiff. He didn't know how Joe moved, and they didn't fit together comfortably, but the other option was to shove him into a cheese stall. So he left his arm where it was and stopped to watch a pumpkin-carving competition behind a low picket fence. Orange pulp and wet seeds piled up on the straw as a local deputy and two teenagers stabbed at the large fruits.

Tag took a drink of his beer as he watched the pumpkin bits fly. The server at the beer tent had recommended it based on its notes of tropical fruit, bread, and custard… and presumably because it was worth $20 a plastic pint glass. So Tag tried to savor the hops as it slid over his tongue, but it might as well have been a can of Bud Lite. It wasn't that the beer didn't live up to the hype—it tasted like an alcoholic bread pudding—the date was just worse than Tag had expected.

He should have known it was a mistake to let Beattie set him up. He hadn't known his blind date was her nephew, but it was still a bad idea.

When he said he wanted to start dating again, he didn't exactly mean dinner dates with ambitious young lawyers who made awkward jokes. Jesus, was Tag old enough that he had to worry if Joe was *too* young? That was new.

He'd planned for a string of ego-boosting one-night stands and memorable bad dates—the sort that left you stranded in LA with no passport and a bunch of luxury purchases he'd never see racked up on his credit card. Then his bad judgment with Bass would be just one in a series of terrible decisions he made this year instead of the stupidest thing he'd ever done.

Joe was cute enough, nice enough, and he definitely didn't deserve to be Tag's rebound from being ditched with prejudice—twice.

"So," Joe said as he glanced sidelong at Tag. "You want to check out the pet chickens? Or would you rather go and get some coffee? I've got an Italian press at—"

Someone in the crowd slapped Tag's ass. He jumped in surprise, a *fuck* caught behind his teeth, and spun around to glare at....

Bass. His hair was cropped short, darker at the roots where the sun hadn't had a chance to fade it right, and his face was clean-shaven for the first time since Tag... didn't know him, really.

"Fuck." It got away from Tag after all.

"You're a hard man to track down, Doc," Bass said as he tucked his hands into his back pockets and his T-shirt pulled tight over his shoulders. He raised his eyebrows. "Did you get my texts?"

"I got them," Tag said stiffly. "What about them?"

"Okay," Bass said as he looked away from Tag. "That's fair enough."

Tag had done his research—too late, but better that than never—and the Corpse Brothers MC were not the genial bears on tricked-out Hondas who sometimes rolled through Plenty on a road trip up the coast to Disney. They were violent, dangerous criminals into drugs, car theft, trafficking. Basically if you wanted to move something illegal, they were your bikers.

So he wanted to be angry at Bass for using him, even if Tag had made it so damn easy, who could have resisted? He definitely should have been scared. Shepherd had been accused of a lot more than throwing a cue ball thrown at someone's head.

What Tag shouldn't have felt was happy to see Bass. It was just a bit, but it was still so stupid it hurt. Luckily he was angry enough to let that cover for him.

"What the hell are you doing here?" Tag asked shortly. A more important question occurred to him as paranoia scratched at his brain. "And how did you know where to find me?"

His mind raced as he tried to remember if Bass had any access to his phone that first night. Not that he'd need it. Tag had downloaded, opened, and played everything Bass had sent him before what happened at the bar. If Bass had put some sort of exploit into one of them, it could have copied any data he wanted from Tag's phone.

"Calm down," Bass said. He glanced over his shoulder toward the deputy, who had briefly stopped work on his pumpkin to look over at them. "I saw you at the beer tent. It just took me a while to catch up."

Tag snorted. He didn't believe a word of it. Of course, from Bass's careless shrug, he didn't expect him to. The explanation just left Tag with no reason to call the deputy over.

"Sorry," Joe said as he put a hand on Taggart's shoulder. The touch made Tag start in surprise. He'd actually managed to forget Joe was there, or least push him to the back of his mind. "Is this your ex?"

"No," Tag and Bass said at the same time. Irritation made Tag clench his jaw. He was the one who'd been fucked over, the one who hadn't read… most… of the texts, so he should get to be the one to go "Hell no" to the idea they'd been in a relationship.

He glared at Bass.

"It's not important," Tag said to Joe. "I just didn't expect to see him. Here."

"He slapped you on the ass," Joe pointed out, his eyes narrowed suspiciously.

The reminder made Tag shift, the memory of heat a tingle under the skin of his backside. He cleared his throat.

"He's not my ex, but he is—"

"His mechanic," Bass said smoothly. He thrust out a bruised, scraped-up hand to Joe and grinned as they shook. "Doc's just trying to avoid admitting that cherry-red pile of rust he calls a car belongs on the scrap heap."

Tag clenched his teeth. He wasn't the sort of guy who bristled over insults to his car as though it were an extension of his penis. The Mustang had spent the last five years under a tarp in the back of the garage because it *was* a piece of crap. He'd threatened to get rid of it every public holiday.

That didn't mean that Bass got to bad-mouth his car.

"Maybe I just need a better mechanic," he said through gritted teeth.

"Nobody else has complained."

There was something suggestive in the rough, dark note to Bass's statement. Heat flushed up from Tag's stomach, and this wasn't a fight he needed to have with his imaginary mechanic.

"Anyhow, this can wait," he said abruptly. "Joe, why don't we get out of here. Leave Bass to enjoy the fair on his own."

Joe still looked skeptical, but Tag dragged him away. He glanced over his shoulder once as the wove through the crowd, and he told himself he wasn't at all disappointed that Bass hadn't followed him. He tossed his empty plastic cup in a sack of trash as they passed it on the path.

"So," Joe said very casually. "Your mechanic slaps your ass?"

"In case you haven't noticed, he's a bit of a dick," Tag said tensely.

Except that wasn't entirely fair, not to Joe, anyhow. He was a lawyer, so he didn't need Bass and his... associates... even peripherally involved in his life. Especially when Joe wasn't someone Tag could see himself with—not right now, when all Tag wanted was cheap, nasty sex to soothe his ego, and probably not ever.

There was nothing wrong with Joe, but someone who'd decided not to be a doctor because they wanted a work/life balance? That was someone who didn't need to date a trauma surgeon.

"It was complicated," he admitted as they reached the edge of the park. Tag scratched his eyebrow and tried to think of the right way to put it. He sighed. "Actually, no, it was simple. Right now I think I'm the one who's complicated. And you're not."

"You mean I'm boring?" Joe said bluntly.

"I mean you're nice."

"Same thing."

"Not to me," Tag said. "I'm just not ready for a relationship that might work out. That's way too much pressure. I'd just screw it up so that at least I'd be the one in control when it fell apart."

This time.

Joe started to shrug but then stopped himself and ran his hand through his hair. "Look, this isn't.... This was a first date. No pressure. No commitment. So walk away if you want. I won't spend the night in tears. But sabotaging something before it can fail is kind of exactly what you're doing now."

That was... hard to argue with, and so were the light-hazel eyes that gazed soulfully at Tag as Joe waited for his answer.

"I know," Tag admitted with a wry twist of his mouth. "And I can see the hours weren't the only reason you became a lawyer. But like you said, it'll hurt less if I do it now. And your aunt can't be too pissed at me."

After a second, Joe shook his head in defeat. "Your choice," he said as he dipped his hand into his pocket for his phone. "Your loss."

"Absolutely," Tag agreed. "Trust me. This is a lucky escape for you. Look, I can give you a lift back to—"

Joe snorted. "Your complicated asshole of a mechanic just said your car was a death trap," he said as he tapped and swiped the screen. "I think I'll call an Uber. Have a good life, Taggart. Don't be complicated too long."

Good advice, Tag supposed. He should probably take it, but he doubted he would. In his experience, no one ever did. People ate what they shouldn't, went where it was stupid, and followed their hearts right into hell.

Or in Tag's case, he supposed bitterly, his cock.

"I'll try," he said. "If I sort myself out, maybe—"

Joe looked up from his phone and twisted his mouth into a dubious line.

"I don't think so," he said. "You're a handsome guy, and from what I've heard, a good surgeon, but I watched my mom wait for a doctor for fifteen years before she finally left. It's not for me. So if you can't sort yourself out before my Uber gets here? It's goodbye."

There was a pause. Like the unexpected arm around the waist earlier, it left Tag at a disadvantage as he tried to work out how his answer was supposed to fit into the conversation. The Uber, who must have just dropped someone off around the corner, turned up before Tag worked out what to say.

His silence was probably answer enough. Joe gave him a tight smile and a shrug. "It probably wouldn't have worked anyhow," he said, an edge of sarcasm to his voice. "Why risk it, right?"

Tag watched him get into the SUV and then waited for the big silver car to drive away. Once it was out of sight, he scrubbed his hands roughly over his face and wondered if he could convince Beattie on Monday that this had been the right thing to do.

He doubted it.

Shit. Tag sighed and decided he needed a drink—a real drink, something cheap enough he could get drunk without savoring every mouthful. The sort of bottle he had back in the apartment.

He turned and headed to where he'd parked his car. Whiskey wasn't the answer to everything. He'd seen enough drunks roll through the ER who thought it might be. But it did help make you forget about the question.

He saw the red curve of the Mustang first—death trap or not, Tag enjoyed what a beautiful car it was—and the sprawl of unwelcome biker on the hood a second too late to retreat. Tag faltered midstep, caught himself, and exhaled heavily as he tried to drag his eyes away from the stretched-tight stomach muscles and the careless dangle of heavy boots over the tarmac.

There was something unguarded about Bass in that moment, with his arms folded behind his head and his face relaxed. It didn't change anything, but it did mix an unwelcome splash of tenderness into the usual backwash of lust.

Tag cleared his dry throat. "How many times do I have to tell you to fuck off?"

Bass turned his head toward Tag and peeled open one eye. "I could say until you sounded like you meant it," he said slowly. "But we'd be here all night then.... Not that I'd mind."

He waggled his eyebrows suggestively at Tag as he sat up. The mix of anger and lust that hit Tag left him with his fists clenched and his mouth dry. His stomach was in knots, twisted around every shitty thing that had happened for the last few months.

"What do you want?" he asked.

He expected another smart-ass remark. Instead Bass didn't say anything for a moment as he slid off the hood of the Mustang. "An apology."

Tag spluttered in indignant disbelief. "Are you kidding me? I could have lost my license. I could have been killed and dumped in a shallow grave."

"I wouldn't have let that happen," Bass interrupted firmly as he stepped up onto the pavement. "C'mon, Doc. You know that I wouldn't."

Tag snorted. "Of course I don't," he said. "I don't know you. We fucked once. I've seen a couple of pictures of your hard-on."

"Don't forget the videos," Bass said lightly.

Tag ignored him and plowed on. "You want an *apology?* You should be glad I didn't go to the police and turn you in."

"I am. It wouldn't have done you any good, but I still appreciate it," Bass said. He took a deep breath and exhaled sharply. Then he admitted, "*I* wanted to say sorry, Doc. It was a shit move to drag you into what was going on... but Shepherd's not someone you can say no to if he asks you to do something. I *am* sorry. That's it. That's all I wanted."

Bass stuck his hands in his pockets and waited. His mouth was canted up at the corner, already rueful in anticipation of Tag's reaction. He looked like he meant it, that it was a genuine apology. Of course he seemed to mean it when he told Tag he wanted to hook up that night.

Still, Tag wanted to fall for it. On paper Joe Beattie, the lawyer, was everything Tag wanted—professional, reasonable, the sort of man you could adopt a kid or a dog with—but it was Bass, with the old scar high on his cheekbone and the rough, affectionate edge he put on *Doc* who made Tag trip over his own tongue.

Maybe that was how Kieran felt about his hot nurse. Tag was surprised at the dry note of the thought, which had none of the old frothy bitterness to it.

Tag scratched his ribs through his T-shirt. The problem was that people didn't change, and second chances always bit you in the ass eventually. Just because he wanted to believe something didn't mean he could.

"Okay," he said. "You wanted to say sorry. Now you have. So are we done?"

It wasn't the reaction Bass expected. He narrowed his pale eyes and shifted his weight. His heavy boots scuffed against the concrete as he did.

"We could be," Bass said. "Or not?"

Tag snorted as he yanked open the door. "One of the other bikers get stabbed? I don't need this in my life, Bass. Just—" He twisted the key in the ignition as he talked. The engine growled to life, the revs low and strained, and then it coughed hard enough to rattle the whole frame of the car. Tag grimaced and pumped the gas, but the engine just wheezed and died. He smacked his palm against the steering wheel. "Son of a bitch."

The engine ticked unrepentantly to itself under the hood, and the smell of burned newspaper and mildew leaked into the car through the vents. Bass draped himself over the open door, and his arms dangled down over the glass. Fresh ink chained his wrist—literally. Black and gray lines picked out a bracelet of thick links over his skin.

"Need a lift?" he asked.

Tag looked up and took in the satisfied cant to Bass's mouth. He narrowed his eyes. "Did you do something to my car?"

Bass just snorted. "You think a lot of yourself," he said. Tag clenched and tried the engine again. This time it barely turned over. Bass waited for the grate of it to rattle back into silence. His smirk widened into a grin that actually reached his eyes. "I didn't need to do anything. Your crankshaft is broken, and from that smell, your clutch is on its last legs. I actually am a mechanic, remember? Come on. Let me give you a lift."

"I'll get a cab."

Bass looked exasperated. He reached in, grabbed the keys before Tag could get them, and jingled them from his fingers as he held them out of reach.

"If I want to know where you live, Dr. Hayes, I can find out," he said dryly. Then his voice dropped to a suggestive rasp. "Besides, I still owe you a ride, Doc. Remember?"

Tag had deleted the picture from that first night, but it didn't make any difference. His memory conjured it back up in detail, from the threadbare seams of the jeans to the way Bass's lean thighs straddled the black leather saddle, and his balls tightened in Pavlovian response.

It was still a bad idea.

"All right," Tag said. "But that's it. After tonight, you stay away from me."

Bass gave him that slow, confident smile as he stepped back from the car. He tossed the keys to Tag, who caught them out of the air.

"If you're sure that's what you want," Bass said. "You won't see me again."

Tag groaned under his breath and got out of the car. This time, he told himself as he slapped the door, he really would have to sell it and get something more practical—hybrid instead of a car with a bottomless fuel tank.

"It's not about what I want," Tag said. "It's what I need."

Bass bit his lower lip and glanced around. Then he stepped forward and twisted Tag's T-shirt around his fist. Tag yelped as he was shoved back against the car, metal cold against his back and hips, and Bass pressed his knuckles against his chest. He had time to be surprised, but before he could work his way up to alarmed, Bass leaned in until his mouth was so close Tag could feel his breath.

"I think we both remember what you need," he breathed out, his voice low and tight with control. "And it involves me."

It would have been easy to blame it on Bass, on his cockiness and the knuckles pressed against Tag's chest. He wasn't to blame for his own bad choices at all. But it was Tag who wrapped his hand around the back of Bass's neck to pull him closer, and *his* lips that closed the distance between them. The kiss was slow and lazy, spiced with a hint of teeth and old anger.

"See?" Bass said as he finally leaned back. A smile tugged at the corner of his mouth for a moment and then slipped away. His face settled into serious lines as he reached up and cupped his hand around the back of Tag's neck. "I meant what I said, Doc. You don't need to be scared of Shepherd."

He clearly meant to be reassuring, but Shepherd wasn't what worried Tag. In the moment, he'd been scared, sure. He wasn't an idiot. The leader of the local MC had thrown a pool ball at Tag's head, after all.

But last week a teenage girl had gotten dosed with LSD at a party and tried to hit him with a bottle because she thought he was a lizard. Before that a drunk driver tried to choke him out with an IV stand because he wanted to get out of there before the police arrested him. Whenever he took a deep breath, he could feel the scar tissue under his ribs catch. After a while stuff like that got left at the door.

Shepherd wasn't the one Tag couldn't get out of his head.

"You know, we came to Plenty to get away from this sort of thing," Tag said. "Violence, dangerous men, property prices."

Bass laughed and pulled Tag back off the car. "You picked the wrong town, then," he said as he casually tucked his hand into the back pocket of Tag's jeans and led him across the road. A matte-black bike was parked under a streetlight in front of an open-late coffee shop. "Plenty's always been a hole. Trust me, I grew up here. Come on. I'll drive you home. And I promise I'll leave you at the door… if that's what you want."

Tag licked his lips. They were warm and wet, with a hint of the fruit-cider sweetness from the expensive hops.

Right now the last thing he wanted was for Bass to leave. Maybe by the time they got home, he'd have reminded himself why that was a bad idea.

CHAPTER EIGHT

THIS WASN'T going to end well. If they took the time to think about it, one of them—Tag, since Bass didn't give a fuck beyond the ache in his balls—would call a halt to it. So by unspoken mutual agreement, they kept themselves occupied so there was no chance to think.

There was just the growl of the parked motorcycle under them, impatient hands that dragged up T-shirts and tugged at jeans, and messy kisses bitten over each other's lips. Bass tore the collar of Tag's T-shirt as he dragged it down his chest. His fingers left sweat stains and dust worked into the pale cotton, and the faint smell of pretty-boy cologne that had stuck to the fabric was lost.

The shadows of abandoned buildings, windows boarded shut and graffiti layered in scabbed smears up to the second floor, lay over them. On the nearby building site, yellow police tape was strung through the chain-link fence and flapped in the breeze.

Tag leaned back, one arm braced against the saddle as Bass pressed hard, wet kisses into his throat and along his collarbone. His mouth left wet, red stains on Tag's skin, ready to bruise, and this time he deliberately strayed high enough that it wouldn't be hidden by a shirt. The next office drone in pressed chinos who thought Tag needed someone to fuck would be able to see he didn't.

The flash of possessiveness, sharp and bitter under his tongue, caught Bass off guard. He hesitated for a second, his mouth pressed against damp skin, but the cold trickle of fear along his spine made him put it out of his mind. Bass wasn't the sort of guy who *had* things. He didn't live the sort of life where it was possible. There was his bike, the clothes on his back, and the boots he'd finally worn in. Everything else— the rented fleapit he lived in, the thrift-shop furniture, and the half-empty bottle of whiskey on his bedside table—could be tossed in the trash. If he got a heads-up and an hour to work, he could clear out of somewhere as though he'd never been there at all.

Boyfriends, even fuckbuddies, were harder to get rid of than a dog-eared copy of *The Advocate.* They talked more, and they remembered the cigarettes you smoked and the money card you sent a friend in prison.

Last thing he needed was this—his apology, his fresh-hatched dislike of light floral colognes, the weight in his balls—to mean something. So it didn't. It wouldn't.

And fuck whatever part of his brain snorted at that.

"What is it?" Tag ran his fingers through Bass's curls and cupped his fingers around the back of his skull. Elegant doctor's hands that had cut open Sonny's leg as calmly as though it were a slab of underdone roast beef. Bass found that hot. He'd probably have to talk that over with a shrink one day. Tag's voice was as ragged and uneven as the breath that hitched in his chest each time Bass slid his lips over wet skin. "Realized we're gonna get murdered?"

"You didn't complain when we stopped." Bass mouthed the tight nub of Tag's nipple through his T-shirt and then sucked on the wet cotton. He glanced up at Tag as he bit down on the sensitive skin, just hard enough to make him gasp. "Or did my cock in your hand distract you?"

It had distracted the fuck out of Bass. He'd been jerked off on the bike before—properly, not just groped through his jeans. But this was Tag's breath warm against the nape of his neck and his fingers squeezed over the bulge of Bass's cock. He'd nearly driven into the abandoned building site instead of stopping in front of it.

Tag flushed. The color started at his collarbone and crawled up to his ears—a little embarrassment, but mostly desire. Any hint of good sense in his eyes was shuttered as he chewed on his lower lip—his tell, maybe for poker, but definitely where his cock was involved—and dragged Bass up for a kiss. He traced the curve of Bass's lips with his tongue in a tickled caress that sent a quiver all the down his spine to his cock. He imagined it around his cock instead, the flick of Tag's tongue against the underside of his shaft, and Bass's balls tightened. He ran his hand up Tag's thigh, across the hard muscle and warm skin under the thin denim, and leaned into the kiss.

He darted his tongue between Tag's lips and explored the slick, wet inside of his mouth and the smooth line of his teeth. Tag groaned. The sound was tangled between their mouths as he slid his hand under the collar of Bass's shirt, stroked the taut bands of muscle, and traced his fingers along the sharp hook of his shoulder blades.

"Who else have you fucked, Doc?" Bass asked as he caught Tag's lower lip between his teeth and tugged on it gently. "A guilty hand job with your ex in his car? Picked up some other tight-assed stranger from the internet? Bet they weren't as good as me."

He had no right to complain. Even before Bass fucked it up, their thing hadn't involved any sort of expectation that they wouldn't fuck around. He still wanted to hear it, to feel the sharp goad of jealousy as he reminded Tag exactly why he'd come running when Bass called him.

He didn't get jealous. Envious sometimes, he supposed, when he saw one of his exes as they settled in with something real with someone else. Or maybe that was more... regret. Resignation. Something bittersweet and then gone, spent in a sweaty ass or spilled over his own sheets and some new porn.

But he'd felt jealous, felt an unexpected scrape at the nape of his neck when he saw Tag lean into the pretty-boy date's side, laugh at something he said, and look like they fit. It wasn't going to change anything, but the adrenaline jolt of it persisted. He kind of liked it, in a masochistic way. It was half exactly what he deserved, and half challenge to make Tag forget all about his pretty boy... again.

"That's none of your—" Tag's voice cut off on a gasp as Bass slid a hand between their bodies and grabbed his junk.

The dark denim was stiffer, newer, than Bass's old, worn-down-to-thread-and-cotton jeans. New enough that Bass indulged his new kink with the notion that Tag had bought them just for his date, and he felt the sticky, jealous burn flare again. Tag squirmed under the rough-handed grope, dug his fingers into Bass's back hard enough to leave a mark, and whimpered. Bass squeezed the hard bulge, the zipper rough against his palm, and smirked as Tag bit down on his lower lip and dropped his head back.

"What was that?" Bass asked, the words murmured against Tag's damp throat. "I didn't hear you. How many?"

He kneaded Tag's erection again, the denim folded around his fingers just as Tag opened his mouth to answer. This time he didn't even get out the "none of" before he choked on a moan. His arm gave way, and he went down onto his elbow, body sprawled over the saddle.

"—*fucking* business," Tag finally managed to get out. "Asshole."

Bass couldn't disagree with that. Hell, Tag didn't know the half of it.... Never would either unless the shit really hit the fan one of these days. He shrugged and pushed Tag's shirt up his chest so he could undo his jeans, button and zipper parted to reveal a vee of pale skin and a narrow trail of dark hair.

"Tell me, did you jerk off to my pictures?" he asked as he followed the line of hair from Tag's belly button down to his still denim-pinned cock. "Even after what I did?"

Tag closed his eyes and bit his tongue, the tip of it trapped firmly between his teeth. He squirmed against the bike as Bass stroked his cock, hand shoved down into Tag's jeans.

"Admit it, and I'll give you something better to think about when you jerk it," Bass prodded. Precome slicked his fingers, wet and sticky as he rubbed it back along Tag's shaft. As he worked, Tag moaned and arched his hips off the saddle, his stomach muscles drawn long and tight under his wrinkled shirt.

"I deleted them," Tag said finally. "Didn't... exactly... want to think about you."

Insecurity dug cold little fingers into the nape of Bass's neck. He knew what he was, what he had to be for his life to work, but he was a good fuck. He got who he wanted for a night on sweaty sheets—or wherever—or an hour out of the day as he bent them over a desk or shoved them against a wall. That was what he had to offer, and usually that was enough.

It obviously was now. He had Tag's cock hard and slick in his hand, his body tight as a wire from *want* as he leaned back. Bass was still under his skin. That was what mattered, not whether or not he'd deleted a couple of pictures.

Except it felt like it meant something.

"Well, then I guess I need to remind you what it looks like," Bass said as he leaned back. "In case you got me confused with someone else."

The snug fit of his jeans across his erection had passed pleasant pressure to discomfort a while back. He popped his buttons and hitched up his hips to push his jeans down over his hips. The curve of his cock twitched up toward his stomach, the skin flushed and tight. He wrapped his fingers around the head and pulled down, syrupy pleasure warm in his balls as he squeezed.

Tag watched him touch himself with lust-dazed near-black eyes, as though he couldn't look away. He reached for his own cock but then let his hand drop onto his thigh instead. "I hit delete," he said after a wet swallow before he could get the words out. "Not my head. I remember what you look like, Bass."

"Hotter than your ex?"

Tag finally dragged his eyes away from Bass's one-cock show. "Bad decisions always look the best, and you're a bad decision made flesh."

Bass supposed he deserved that. It still stung, but it wasn't untrue… or unfair. Hell, even he could tell this whole ride was a bad idea on Tag's part… although he kinda hoped Tag hadn't realized quite how bad. Since it had come up.

"You sure you want to make this bad decision?" Bass asked as he let go of his cock. The ache of it pulsed between his legs, but the night was young. And if he couldn't find *someone* to fuck or fight—or both—in all of Plenty…. Well, then the town had changed more than he thought, but blue balls had never killed anyone. "I'll still get you home."

Tag rolled his eyes and pushed himself upright.

"I thought it was what I needed, not what I wanted," he said as he wrapped his hand around Bass's cock. His fingers were soft, uncallused and well moisturized, and his grip was confident as he slowly stroked his fist up and down.

"You know what I mean." It was Bass's turn for his voice to creak in his throat, not quite a crack, but only barely. He clenched his jaw against the hot ache that pulled at his balls and stomach. "I'm hotter than your ex, but you're never gonna take me out to dinner to prove it to him."

"Good. He'd have me committed," Tag muttered with a grimace of old, faded irritation. Like it was the fight version of the tired "You had to have been there" couple's joke. It might also qualify as actually unfair, even after everything Bass had done.

"Because I'm not a doctor?" Bass mocked harshly. He caught Tag's chin in his fingers and tilted his head back so the moonlight picked out the flush of lust on his cheekbones and in his dazed eyes. "Or because you want Heights trash to fuck you so bad?"

Something bleak twisted Tag's mouth for a second. "Because… five years," he said. "And old scars, old promises. Some things predate you and your hot ass."

It wasn't an answer, but fuck it. Bass slanted a hard kiss over Tag's tipped-back mouth. He'd take the "hot ass" remark and stick with that.

Then he pushed Tag back and swung his leg, awkward with his cock out and his jeans shoved down to his hips, off the bike.

"Lean forward," he told Tag as he stepped back. Glass crunched under his heavy boots. "Hang on to the handlebars."

They stared at each other for a second, and then Tag did as he was told. Cotton stretched over his shoulders as he grabbed the bike's grips, and he hissed, a sharp exhalation between his teeth that settled into an uncomfortable grunt as his cock was trapped between the hard leather and his stomach.

Bass hooked his fingers into the waistband of Tag's jeans and tugged. Denim slid down over narrow hips and exposed his ass. The chill of the cold air made the lean curves of muscle twitch in reaction. Bass rubbed an appreciative hand over one cheek and then down to dip between Tag's legs. He worked his hand under Tag's balls, tight and hot against his palm, and rolled them in his fingers.

Tag's whine was a half-strangled, desperate sound as he pressed back into Bass's hand. He spread his thighs, the long muscles tensed under his skin, and managed a "Please."

"Please what?" Bass said. He squeezed his handful of tender flesh, and Tag flinched, clearly not sure whether he wanted to jerk away from the pressure or squirm back into it. "If there's something you want, Doc, all you have to do is ask for it."

The nape of Tag's neck was bare and vulnerable as he let his head fall forward, exposed between the collar of his shirt and the short-cropped hair at the base of his skull. "Really?"

Bass chuckled and let go of Tag's balls. "What? Consent is sexy, Doc," he said. "Besides, I like to hear you beg… especially for my cock."

"Fuck you," Tag said. "But first fuck me."

It was more of an order. Bass's cock twitched as a wire-tight string of hot pleasure strung through it and hooked to his spine at how unexpectedly hot it was. Not something Bass was all that interested in—he liked the way he could unravel Tag with a growled word or rough caress—but it worked.

Bass tried to think of an excuse for why he had a strip of lubed condoms in his back pocket for this absolutely unexpected and unplanned-for encounter. He didn't try that hard, and Tag seemed too distracted to call him out on it.

He caught the edge of the foil square between his eye teeth to peel it open, the sharp, fake, chemical-sweet smell of cherries sticky on his tongue. While he picked out the latex and rolled it down over his cock, Tag ground his erection against the leather of the bike's seat with jerky, eager thrusts of his hips.

The thought of how many hours Bass had spent in that saddle, until the shape of it softened to fit his ass like a glove, made Bass's balls pucker with interest. The thought of Tag as he fucked Bass like that, all hunger and impatience, made him fumble as he tried to get the slippery condom snug around the base of his cock.

Maybe next time.

There was excess lube left in the foil packet. Bass scraped it out with his finger until it glistened with sickly cherry lotion, and he worked it into Tag's ass.

"There's lube on the condom too, but if it's not enough," he said, "say something. I'll just fuck your crack."

Tag twisted around to squint at him over his shoulder. "You worry too much."

"I like your ass, Doc. I don't want to break it."

"You a bad boy or a romantic?"

Bass gripped Tag's backside in his hands and peeled his cheeks apart so he could nudge his erection against the already slick hole. It was just as tight as last time as it gave under the blunt pressure of his cock, but now he got to watch it as it stretched around the hard width of his shaft.

Short, slow thrusts of his hips worked him deeper inside Tag, the slick ring taut around his cock. Each stroke of his hips made Tag gasp and then push back into him. The bike moved under him, unsteady as his weight shifted, and the engine revved as Tag tightened his hands around the grips.

Fuck.

Bass could feel the harsh growl of the bike's engine in his balls. It reverberated through Tag's ass and caught in Bass's bones, liquified something hot and sticky in the crux of his thighs. He shifted his grip to Tag's hips to hold him in place.

Careful was hard to hold on to, and the next stroke of his cock buried him inside Tag. His balls pressed against Tag's ass, uncomfortably squashed and heavy with pleasure. He held himself there, the rumble of the bike an internal pressure that made his stomach clench until Tag squirmed impatiently under him.

"What are you waiting for?" he asked, voice ragged as he tilted his head back. "It's not broken yet."

Bass's laugh hitched raggedly in his throat as he rocked his hips against Tag's ass in a slow tease of rhythm. Each thrust stirred the hot, heavy syrup of want in his balls, slick and sticky as molasses. Bass freed up one hand to run it up under Tag's shirt and spread his fingers wide so he could feel the muscles clench and relax each time he thrust home.

There was another scar there. He could feel it under his thumb, angled slightly out from the pucker on Tag's ribs. When he spread his fingers out wide, pressed the heel of his hand against the small of Tag's back to stop his restless movement, his thumb just grazed the edge of it.

"I don't care who you fucked," he said. "They're not here now, and I am. That's all that matters."

In his head it had sounded magnanimous. Out loud he sounded like a dick.

Tag rocked back against him, and Bass's cock slid a fraction deeper. It felt more, an exaggerated ache of pleasure knotted up in his spine. He pushed forward again, roughly, and savored the frantic little "ah" that escaped Tag as his cock rubbed over leather that was slick with come and soft from wear. Under Bass's hand, Tag's back tightened with a ripple of tension that ran from his hips to his shoulders and then relaxed again as Tag exhaled raggedly.

"Why do you care?" he asked as he looked around. Sweat plastered his short dark hair to his forehead, and his expression was a mixture of confusion, hunger, and frustration.

Bass thrust into Tag with two deep, quick strokes that stoked the lust and pushed the other two emotions to the margins. He liked that better. The need that made Tag chew on his lips and squirm under him was something he could satisfy.

"I don't know, Doc," he admitted as he shifted both hands back to Tag's hips. "Small talk?"

It was probably the first time he'd made someone laugh when he was balls deep in them. He'd have expected it to prick his pride more, but Tag's breathless snigger as he bent his forehead down to the gas tank curled warmth in Bass's chest.

He fucked Tag down into the bike, hands clenched around his hips to hold him in place. Each hard stroke of his cock, Tag tight as a hand around him, made hot, sweet pleasure sink down into his balls. Sweat tickled against the back of his neck and itched in the crack of his ass as he tried to hang on just one more tight, deep thrust more.

Tag groaned as he was pushed down against the bike, his cock roughly stimulated, and choked out a whimper every time Bass got the right angle to jostle his prostate. His ass spasmed around Bass's cock, tight around the base of it as he came against the leather. Come smeared under him in a wet mess over the seat as Bass let himself come with a few rough, frantic thrusts.

Spent, come hot against his cock in the condom, Bass sprawled over Tag's back and pressed a kiss into the damp hollow of his neck. The usual stale lies scratched at the back of his throat, eager to get dressed up as a promise and out into the fresh air. This time he went with one that he thought he could keep.

"You don't need to worry about Shepherd or the MC," Bass murmured against Tag's throat. "They won't come near you again. I promise."

Tag inhaled deeply enough that Bass felt his ribs expand. Then he sighed. "You're in the club too, Bass? Does that mean you'll stay out of my life?"

Huh.

It hadn't occurred to Bass that Tag would still want that. Or that something in Bass's chest would knot up in blunt rejection of that idea. Apparently that sharp ache didn't give a damn about Bass's plausible deniability that this was anything other than a casual fuck.

"I can do that," Bass said as he lifted himself off Tag and stepped back from the bike. He discarded the condom, tucked his cock back into his jeans, and fastened them. "If it's what you want. Not like I can blame you, after everything."

Tag peeled himself off the bike and wiped the leather and his stomach awkwardly with the hem of his T-shirt. He didn't look at Bass.

"It's probably best. This is… you are… hard to say no to, but I've got a life. I want to put it back together, not smash it to pieces. I'm sorry."

"Don't be, Doc. Like I said, I can't blame you. I can stay away," Bass said. He cupped his hand around the back of Tag's neck, tucked his thumb under his jaw, and tilted his head back for a slow, hungry kiss. "We could start tomorrow. I've still got to get you home, after all."

Tag leaned into the kiss, mouth open and eager as he tangled his tongue around Bass's. He brushed his fingers over Bass's hip and up under his shirt.

"Tomorrow," he surrendered, the word murmured against Bass's mouth.

Bass smiled into the kiss and deepened it until Tag moaned. He finally pulled away and climbed onto the bike. He pulled on his helmet and tossed the spare back to Tag. A shiver of leftover pleasure prickled down his spine into his ass as, after a second, Tag leaned in and wrapped his arms around his waist, chest pressed against his back and breath against his neck.

Bass revved the bike. The growl of it was rough against his hips and tender balls as he peeled away from the curb. Tarmac flashed past his knee as he took the corner a bit too tight, and Tag squeezed his waist. Bass grinned to himself and enjoyed the moment.

It could be one of the last he had, but he didn't think so. He had until morning to talk Tag around to… something more than nothing and less than real, and he'd put money on it that he would. Otherwise….

He'd only *thought* it was a promise he could keep. It wouldn't be like Tag would be the first man disappointed when they realized Bass told lies after sex.

CHAPTER NINE

THE NEXT day, bad decisions tasted like salt, pennies, and drunken noodles from the Thai restaurant down the road. Tag groaned and rolled away from the insistent bar of light that had infiltrated through the curtains. The movement made Bass grumble sleepily and drag him back, a heavily inked arm wrapped around Tag's stomach and a knee tucked up between his thighs.

It turned out Bass snuggled in his sleep. He'd started the night starfished arrogantly on his—on the other—side of the bed, but in the night had moved over to sprawl on Tag instead. The first few times Tag had pushed him off, rolled him over, or swapped sides with him. It always ended up with Bass curled up around him again, his solid, warm body pressed against the line of Tag's back or draped over his chest. Twice in the night, Tag had stirred to some noise outside or upstairs and found Bass's hand cupped possessively around his cock.

In the end Tag gave up to a night spent tangled with Bass, tied together with the twisted, cheap white sheet. He slept better than he expected, but now it was morning.

That meant it was time to go.

He lifted Bass's arm from where it draped over his stomach, the fresh tattoo under his fingers, and passed it back.

"We made a deal," he said. "Time to go, Bass."

Bass groaned, stretched out on the bed—all muscle and inked, tanned skin—and scrubbed his hand over his face. He yawned and scratched at his short sweat-matted curls.

"Wha' time's it?"

"Five."

Bass peeled open one eye and squinted at Tag. "Fuck off," he said and rolled over with an impatient hitch to the sheet to drag it up over his hip. "Five my ass. That's not morning."

"My shift starts at seven," Tag said as he untangled his legs from the sheets. Last night had left his thighs and shoulders stiff and a dully pleasant ache in his ass. Despite a halfhearted wipe-down last night, he still had patches of come dried onto his stomach and in the crease of his thighs. "I need a shower and breakfast and—fuck—to work out how to get my car back if it hasn't been towed already."

"Fuck 'em," Bass mumbled into his pillow. "Stay in bed. Get a new job. I'll sort the car out."

Tag was tempted. That all sounded good. He loved his job, but…. Bass was naked and warm in the sweaty nest they'd made of his bed. The firm curve of his ass, tanned the same shade as the rest of him, was barely covered by the draped corner of the sheet. If Tag knew he'd get a macroreplantation of a severed limb today, it would be an easy choice, but if the best surgery was going to be a lanced boil? Why not just stay in bed? He could pretend the morning had never come and that he didn't have to be a responsible adult and *not* burn his life down.

Except the boil still needed to be lanced, and there was always a chance someone would cut their finger off. And even if he put it off until tomorrow, Bass was still a bad decision.

Fuck sake, Tag had fucked him on the back of a bike in a public street last night. There was no part of that sentence that was a good idea. Fuck, bike, public, and last night—all bad ideas on their own and probably criminal when stacked on top of each other.

Even if the memory—the bike's growl against his cock as it vibrated through the bones of his pelvis, and the cool air on his skin as Bass's heat pressed against his thighs and filled his ass—still made Tag's well-drained balls tighten with a feathery quiver of pleasure.

He pushed that thought down, grabbed the wrinkled white T-shirt from where it had landed on the dresser, and tossed it at Bass's head. It lay there for a moment, and then Bass dragged it off and propped himself up on one elbow to look at Tag.

"You seriously want me to get up?" he asked.

"I want you to get out," Tag said. "If you want to sleep in until morning starts for you, just lock the door on your way out. And then don't come back. You owe me that, remember?"

He stepped over Bass's discarded jeans, tangled in a knot with Tag's on the floor, and headed toward the bathroom. His shift really did start soon, and his colleagues would probably appreciate it if he didn't turn up with the stink of sex and last night still sweated out of his pores.

"You trust me to stay here on my own?"

Tag glanced over his shoulder at Bass, propped against the white metal frame of the bed with one knee cocked under the sheet.

"If you're going to rob me, you can just come back with your biker friends later," Tag said. "This way at least you won't have to kick the door in."

The rough rub of Bass's amused chuckle followed him into the shower. So, five minutes later, did Bass. Water dripped off the ends of his curls and ran down his shoulders as he pushed Tag back against the cold tiles.

"I still don't think it's morning," he said. "So we can talk about me leaving… later. You can get me breakfast."

Tag snorted. "What? Don't tell me that crime really doesn't pay."

It sounded like he meant it, but he always talked a good game. He just wasn't great at follow-through, which was why he slid his hands around to grip Bass's firm, wet ass, and his freshly-soaped cock stirred between his legs.

"Maybe I'm frugal," Bass said. "Saving for the future."

"Or cheap."

The wild, careless grin that flashed over Bass's face still caught somewhere in Tag's chest. "Could be that too, Doc," Bass admitted easily. "You know I'll pay you back, though, one way or another."

He shifted closer, body pressed against Tag's, and nudged his thighs apart with one knee. The pressure flicked pleasure along Tag's nerves and picked at the foundations of his good intentions. Tag licked his lips—the water was warm and dull against his tongue—and swallowed.

"Stop it," he said firmly. It took more effort than he could justify to make his voice sound undistracted. "This isn't going to work"

Bass raised his eyebrows and glanced down between their bodies. The corner of his mouth tilted in a wicked smirk. "Really?" he drawled as he rubbed his thigh against Tag's hard cock. "Because it looks like it's working okay."

Heat scorched through Tag from his balls all the way to his throat. He exhaled and blew drops of water off his lips. If he gave in to temptation now, it would just make it more difficult later. He knew that, but he already had. He tightened his grip on Bass's ass and pulled him closer, bodies pressed together from shoulders to thighs.

"It works fine," he growled as he twisted them around so Bass was pressed against the white tiles. "I'd be happy to show you if you want."

Bass rested his head back against the wall, out of the stream of water. His arms hung over Tag's shoulders, his hands dangled down behind him, and his lazy lust gave way to a thoughtful expression. "I like you, Doc," he said as he shifted so Tag's erection rubbed against his thigh. "You definitely like me. So why cut your cock off to spite your face?"

"Because you dragged me into an illegal surgery that could have cost me my license or gotten me killed? Or arrested?"

"Jesus, are you ever going to let that go?" Bass mocked him, a flicker of sharp frustration in his voice. Tag drew back, the month-old knot of anger suddenly tight again, but Bass caught the back of his neck. His wet fingers were rough as he pulled Tag back in. "It was a joke, Doc. I fucked up, and I won't do it again."

Tag sighed and rested his forehead against Bass's.

"How can I trust you?" he asked.

"You can't. You shouldn't," Bass said. "I lie to everyone, and I'm not gonna stop. It's like a shark. If I stop lying, a whole lot of shit is going to catch up with me. There's stuff I've done that you'll never know about and don't want to. Does it matter?"

What was more terrible, Tag wondered—the casual way Bass talked about a life built on, lived in, deception, or that, as Bass idly stroked the line of his throat with his thumb, he had already started to shift justifications around until it all sounded reasonable.

There was stuff he didn't, would never, want to talk about, and it turned out there was a hell of a lot his ex had kept from him—a whole nurse and his tattooed ass, in fact. Bass's secrets were more likely to be felonies than moral lapses or old traumas. Still, if Tag wedged this justification into the corner and that one over the trapdoor before….

"Eventually it will," Tag admitted.

Bass shrugged and dragged him down into a stubble-rough kiss.

"We aren't built for eventually," he said against Tag's mouth, his jaw. "That's obvious. Look at us. I have a criminal record, a lot of secrets, and an impulse control problem. You're still hung up on your ex, and you want some suburban daydream with a brat and the earning potential of that buttoned-up accountant from the fair."

"… lawyer," Tag muttered as he tilted his head to the side so Bass could scrape a hard kiss over his pulse. His hands drifted over the tight lines of Bass's back, from the lean waist to the thick straps of muscle across his shoulders.

Bass acknowledged the correction with a shrug but pushed on anyhow.

"Look at it this way. This, what we have, is like your shit-heap Mustang. You know it's going to crap out on you eventually, sooner rather than later, but while it lasts... it's hot to look at and fun to drive. So why not?"

"Am I the Mustang?"

Bass tilted his head back enough to give Tag a wry look. "Of the two of us? Not likely."

It wasn't as though he'd even made a bad decision. He'd just... put off the good one. But that wasn't fair to either of them.

"It won't—"

"Not morning yet," Bass reminded him as he broke the kiss. He ran his hand down Tag's chest, over the wet mat of hair, and across his stomach. He dipped his fingertips into Tag's wet navel and then lower. He closed his callused fingers roughly around a handful of hard cock and tender balls and squeezed gently. Sensation zapped through Tag's body, a little bit of pain and a lot of pleasure. Or the other way around. Whatever it was, it made Tag gasp and bite his lower lip. Bass looked smug. "Think about it. No strings—unless that's what you're into—just sex. Like this."

He loosened his hold on Tag's balls and went down on his knees in the halfway-to-overflowed shower tray. His breath was cold against the length of Tag's cock, and then his mouth was hot and tight around it. Tag hissed a curse, cupped his hand around Bass's head, and tangled his fingers through the wet curls. His balls ached, and the flick of Bass's tongue against the underside of his cock made Tag's nerve endings spark and splutter with want. He leaned back against the wall of the shower enclosure, the glass wall cold against his shoulders, and gave up.

Why not? He was going to write off this year anyhow and fill what was left of it with bad dates and one-night stands. This way he could streamline the process with one big really bad decision instead of a lot of minor ones.

Tag closed his eyes and folded his lip between his teeth as he felt the sharp, electric pleasure build in his balls. He didn't know if he was still hung up on his ex, but not once, all night, had he woken up in the groggy, sex-sweaty darkness and mistaken the body wrapped possessively around him for Kieran's.

Even half-asleep, he'd known it was Bass.

THERE WAS no time for breakfast. Tag slurped instant coffee, black, unsweetened—at some point, he had to actually get groceries—from a chipped black mug and shoved a forkful of cold noodles into his mouth. The combination was not great, but he choked it down.

"I gotta tell you," Bass drawled. He was on the couch, knee cocked as he pulled on his boots. "The scrubs kind of do it for me."

Tag half laughed and half choked on the noodles. He wiped his mouth on the back of his hand. "I thought the tux was what turned you on."

"That too," Bass said as he dropped his foot back to the floor. "I think I've got some sort of respectability kink. You want a ride to the hospital before you choke on that coffee?"

"Ah, no—"

"I can drop you off around the corner if you don't want to be seen with me."

It was a matter-of-fact offer. Tag bought himself a moment as he took another drink of bitter, scalding-hot coffee. Maybe no strings meant he didn't have to care if he hurt Bass's feelings, but he couldn't quite believe that. Besides, why not? Bass was handsome, funny, and enjoyed Tag's company. The details that made Tag hesitate to show him off—the betrayal, his connections, Tag's complete stupidity around him—weren't out there for public consumption.

"The bus would drop me off at the corner," Tag said dryly. He dumped his coffee in the sink and the empty take-out box in the trash. "If you want to give me a lift, drop me outside."

A slow, unexpectedly sweet smile spread over Bass's face. It wasn't the wicked, careless grin that Tag couldn't resist, but it took his breath away for a second. There was something soft about the expression, and from the way Bass tried to bite it back, lower lip caught between his teeth, it turned out Tag couldn't resist that either. Then it faded away, tucked back behind a smirk as Bass hopped up off the couch.

"What?" he asked when he caught Tag's stare. "You want me to bring the bike up the stairs?"

"No," Tag said, caught off balance. Again. He combed his fingers through his hair in an attempt to flatten it down, as though that would cover up that he was flustered. "Just… not sure how this works yet."

Bass shrugged. "Who cares, as long as it does. You ready to go? Otherwise even I won't be able to get you to work on time."

It felt like there should be more to it—papers to grab, doors to check, keys to find—but Tag supposed that was the advantage of an apartment you could see in its entirety from the door. The sheets were stuffed into the washing machine, and all he had to do was flick the switch on the coffee machine to Off.

"Yes, I'm good to go," Tag said. He patted his pockets and realized he had forgotten something. "I just need to get my—"

Bass grabbed the phone from the coffee table and tossed it to Tag as he pushed him out the door. "Here you go. And unblock me," he said. "You're taking my calls again."

"I am?" Tag asked as he unlocked the phone.

"Or I can track you around town like a fox on a chicken's trail," Bass chuckled as he slammed the door behind him. It locked automatically. "A text seems easier."

He had a point. Tag briefly scanned his messages in case he'd missed anything important, but the notifications were from Twitter, his sister in Eugene, and two texts that Beattie had sent before the date actually started, just a question mark followed by an exclamation point. Nothing he needed to deal with immediately.

"You never did say how you tracked me down at the fair," he pointed out absently as he navigated to Settings.

"No," Bass said mildly. He patted Tag's ass. "I didn't, did I."

It took a few false starts before Tag remembered where to find his blocked numbers. There were only three in there. Two were unstable patients who'd managed to get hold of his number somehow. He tapped Bass's number with his thumb as he leaned his shoulder against the door at the bottom of the stairs.

"Maybe you *do* just love artisan cheese," Tag mocked over his shoulder as he stepped outside. Half-blinded by the light, his attention split between his phone and Bass, he walked right into his upstairs neighbor and her baby. She yelped and stumbled backward in surprise, sniffling infant clutched to her chest. Tag caught her elbows to steady her and then let go when she flinched. He held up his hands. "Sorry. Sorry. I didn't see you."

She stared at him, eyes dark and tired as she jiggled the baby up and down in her arms on autopilot. There was a bruise on her jaw that gave Tag pause—dark purple against the warm brown of her skin. Without her makeup and tabard, her hair down, she looked a lot younger than he'd vaguely assumed she was whenever they passed in the dimly lit stairwell.

"Are you okay?" he asked.

She shuffled back from him, her feet bare on the rough concrete, and nodded. "Fine," she said in a quiet, anxious voice. Her eyes flicked to a point over Tag's shoulder as Bass came down the steps. She quickly looked back down at her baby. She stroked his flyaway hair down against his scalp with nervous fingers. "Nothing is wrong."

Bass jingled his keys. "We should go, Doc."

Tag hesitated. He hadn't heard the baby cry the last few mornings. It hadn't occurred to him to be anything but grateful, but now he could hear the thick, congested snuffle each time the baby breathed in. A baby who didn't cry was what every parent longed for. A baby who was too sick to cry was when doctors got worried.

"Is he sick?" He ducked his head to get a better look at the baby. "Coughing?"

His neighbor wrapped her arms tighter around the baby. "My baby is fine," she repeated. Her accent thickened and was heavier on the ends of her words as she got more nervous. "We don't need anything, mister."

The baby squirmed, wheezed, and waved his arms vaguely in the air. He looked miserable, his hair sweat-matted to his forehead and his skin tight and shiny with what could be fever. It was probably just a cold, maybe the flu. But there had been a couple of cases of whooping cough in local schools, and those were probably the parents whose houses Tag's neighbor went off to clean in the afternoons.

"If he has a fever—?"

"No," his neighbor insisted again. She tossed a nervous glance at Bass and edged away from Tag. "Nothing's wrong. We're fine."

She ducked around him and ran up the steps, baby pressed to her chest and pajama pants loose around her legs. The door slammed behind her, and Tag exhaled unhappily.

"She thinks you're going to call social services on her," Bass said. "Then they'll take her kid because she let it get sick."

"That's not going to happen," Tag said.

"Maybe not with you," Bass allowed. His bike was parked next to the building, up on the curb instead of in a space. He slung his leg over the saddle and backed it out. "But around here? It's happened before, probably to someone she knows. Don't take it personally, but she's not going to trust you, Doc. Your face doesn't fit."

"I just want to help."

"She doesn't want you to, though," Bass countered. He kick-started the bike and gave Tag a curious look as he revved the engine to warm it up. "How did you end up down here anyhow? Did your ex get your credit score in the breakup?"

Close enough, actually, but Tag could still have gotten a place in a nicer part of town. Half the surgeons at the hospital owned second "investment" properties he could have signed a lease on even before he hit the internet. Instead he'd dragged his unreliable car and two suitcases full of his clothes down here to an old apartment block with dubious water and an elevator that worked two days out of five.

"I could move straight in," Tag said as he climbed on the back of the bike. He wrapped his arms around Bass and leaned in against his back. "It's a month-to-month lease, so I wouldn't get stuck with any penalties when I found somewhere better. The building is clean enough, no rats or bedbug infestations. It was… convenient."

And the thought of anything better—anything that smacked of permanence—had scared the shit out of him. People who expected things to work out didn't sign year-long leases to an apartment in a building with access to a pool.

"There's worse neighborhoods," Bass said with a shrug. He passed a glossy black helmet back over his shoulder, the straps loose as he waited for Tag to take it. "But you start being nice to these people, Doc, and they'll drain you dry. A handout here, a favor there, and they'll pay you back when they get on their own feet again. Except they never do."

"It's a baby with the flu," Tag said. "My credit might be bad, but I can pull ten minutes and a packet of baby Benadryl if they need it."

"That's how it starts," Bass said, shreds of old bitterness in his voice. He revved the bike impatiently, and Tag fumbled the helmet straps tight so he could grab hold with both hands as they took off. "Trust me. I grew up around here. You might think you're Mr. Nice Guy, but everyone else will just think you're a soft touch."

He swerved out onto the road in front of an old Ford Escort, primer exposed in Rorschach patterns over the hood, and then between a camper van and a rental car with Nevada plates. They sped through the intersection as the lights went red, the indignant squawk of a car horn to the side of them.

Tag leaned into Bass's back and hung on to him as they took the next corner. He knew he should tell Bass to be more careful, to drive safely and slow down. At least once a week, some weekend biker was rolled into the ER after they came off their bikes, usually along the coastal route up to LA—broken legs, cracked faces, trauma to the spleen and liver, abraded skin, and lots of blood. On the other hand, Bass was all hard muscle and warm skin that still smelled like Tag's soap, and the flicker of possessive lust made it easy to ignore all those *shoulds*.

Besides, people came into the ER after they fell down stairs, cut off their fingers in car doors, or got dared to see if something would fit in their mouth. Life wasn't safe, and sometimes the occasional risk—bike rides, bad boys—was worth it.

Maybe.

"Do you think I'm a soft touch?" Tag asked cautiously, voice pitched to carry over the wind. The suspicion that this was—still, all along, somehow—a con on Bass's part dug in its claws behind his eyes.

Bass veered to the left and cut around a station wagon decorated with a dozen faded decals about their kid's school. He glanced over his shoulder and smirked at Tag.

"Naw," he said. "You're always hard enough when I touch you."

CHAPTER TEN

BASS SLOUCHED forward, arms braced on the handlebars of his bike, and watched Tag lope up the steps into the hospital. The rumble of the engine vibrated up his bones into his shoulders, and the memory of the night before tugged pleasantly at his balls.

He'd lied, of course.

Tag was definitely a soft touch. Look at who he'd spent the night under. Bass knew he was hot, but he wasn't *that* hot. He wasn't going to look his gift second chance in the mouth, but he still knew he didn't deserve it.

That was what soft touches did. They just-one-more-chanced their way into bankruptcy. Bass had watched his dad pour their lives down the drain after an ex-wife, two girlfriends, and one best friend whose new business idea would make them a mint. It never did, and his dad never learned.

"People want to be good," he'd always told Bass. "You just have to give them the chance."

It was a good thing that turned out to be bullshit, otherwise Bass would be out of work. Somebody like Tag, though, however much they played the cynic, always kind of wanted to believe that.

The fact that Bass was still pretty damn hot was just the sweetener.

"Excuse me." Someone stepped into view, a blur of gray and white in the corner of his eye, and interrupted his train of thought. "Do I know you?"

Bass supposed it was possible. Although most people who recognized him sounded a lot more pissed off about it. He pushed himself up off the bike, scratched his stubble-rough jaw, and turned his head to bring the blur into focus. The man had red hair styled back from a square, handsome face with green eyes and a wide, mobile mouth and wore a gray shirt and trousers under a white coat.

"Can't say you ring a bell," Bass said. He flexed his hands absently, working the buzz of the bike's engine out of his bones. "Last time I went to a doctor, it was for the clap, so—"

Two swatches of pink flushed over the man's cheeks, and he pressed his lips together in a thin, annoyed line. Bass assumed that was enough to discourage conversation and turned his attention back to his bike. He braced his foot against the pavement as he pushed it up off the kickstand.

It turned out Red wasn't so easy to put off. He stepped in front of Bass.

"That was Dr. Hayes I just saw go inside?"

"That?" Bass asked as he nodded toward the doors Tag had just disappeared through. His temper caught in his jaw with an ache that made him want to clench his teeth. "That was none of your fucking business."

The blond behind Red, with a party-boy pallor and a hard, pettish edge to his prettiness, leaned in.

"More or less what I said," he pointed out into Red's ear. "This is nothing to do with you. Not anymore."

Huh.

The ex? Bass wracked his brain for anything Tag had shared about his old boyfriend. There wasn't much. Either Tag hadn't talked about him much, or Bass hadn't listened. Maybe a bit of both. The only details Bass could swear to were that there was an ex, and Bass was hotter than him.

He gave Red—Dr. K. Reynolds, now that Bass cared enough to check the name embroidered on his jacket—a second look. Existed and no competition. This guy fit the bill.

"Not now, Freddie," Dr. Reynolds said, an exasperated sigh under the words. He shrugged off the younger man and stepped forward, one hand extended toward Bass's handlebars. "I just wasn't aware that Tag knew any bikers."

Behind him, Freddie rolled his eyes. "So he made a new friend. About time he stopped hanging around your place."

"Fuck off, Freddie," Bass said. He slid enough of a rasp into the words that Freddie backed up a wary step. Then he turned to Dr. Reynolds and smiled his best empty grin. "Don't touch my bike, and I won't touch your face. I just gave Doc a lift, because after I blew him in the shower, he was running late. Anything else you want to know?"

From the way Dr. Reynolds spluttered, there was, but Bass didn't wait to find out. He smirked at Reynolds, gunned his bike, and left him wreathed in exhaust fumes as Bass peeled away from the hospital.

Satisfying, but he knew he'd pay for it later when Tag got pissed off. It wasn't something they'd specifically discussed, but "no strings" could be assumed to mean that Tag wasn't Bass's territory to piss on in the first place.

Or, Bass corrected himself with a snort, at all. He might hang out with criminals and bikers, but he didn't have to pick up their screwed-up attitudes toward sex.

But if the ex had second thoughts about the breakup, Bass wanted him to know it wasn't that simple. Even though it should be. Bass needed to prove himself to Shepherd, get into his good graces as his go-to boy. The last thing he needed was to get into a dick-measuring contest with his hookup's ex... even though he'd win.

The problem was, good idea or not, he wasn't about to let Tag go that easily. Maybe they weren't built for the long haul, but Bass wanted more than what he'd gotten.

He laughed mirthlessly to himself as he took the off-ramp onto the freeway. That was the story of his life, wasn't it?

THE TRAILER smelled like a frat boy's armpit—scotch, sex, and sweat. A blond woman with a hint of mouse-colored roots sprawled on a chair with her legs spread wide enough to flash the stained panties under her leather miniskirt and the bruised injection site in the crease of her thigh. It could have been on purpose, although she'd have been barking up the wrong tree, but Bass doubted it. Her bloodshot eyes, the pupils shrunk to pinholes, tracked him as he moved around the space. But that was just mechanical. There was no one at the wheel.

He got a beer out of the fridge and used the bottle opener soldered to the wall to pop off the cap. Foam seeped out unenthusiastically and dribbled over his knuckles. He swapped hands and wiped his fingers against his jeans.

"What's she on?" he asked.

Shepherd looked up from the grimy pile of cash he'd counted out onto the scored coffee table.

"What's it to you?" he asked coldly.

Bass sucked a mouthful of foam out of the neck of his beer. "It looks like good stuff."

There was a pause as Shepherd stared at him for a second, the potential for violence ripe in the air. Then he grunted and went back to his crumpled notes.

"Stay away from that shit," he said as he wiped something sticky off a $100 note with his thumb. "Drop Dead will fuck you up too much to be any use to me, and you ain't got a pussy to pay your keep."

Nobody but the doped-out woman had their eyes on Bass, so he let himself grimace. Jesus. Drop Dead wasn't like Krokodil—he'd seen a couple of users of that in New York, Russian kids who didn't much care what happened to bodies they didn't own anymore—but it wasn't safe either.

"Not my place to tell you how to do business—"

"So don't."

"—but if it takes an elephant tranq to get her high, maybe your meth supplier is sending you the shit stuff."

Shepherd folded a stack of notes over twice and snapped an elastic band around the wedge. He tossed it into the bag at his feet and leaned back, his head cocked to the side as he watched the blond.

"After the fuckup at the junkyard, my... new friend gave me a free sample of his product as a goodwill gesture," he said. "Doubt it's going to unthrone meth, but you gotta offer some variety if you're going to bring in new customers. Club kids want something sexier than meth to get fucked-up on, at least to start with."

Bass shrugged and leaned back against the kitchen counter. The trailer had no air-conditioning, and sweat itched at the back of his neck and was matted into his hair and in the crack of his ass. He took a drink of cold beer and pretended it made him less sticky.

"Is the deal back on?" he asked. "Is that why you asked me to come by?"

Shepherd slung his arms along the back of the couch and pointed at the fridge with his chin. "Get me a beer," he said. "Counting all that cash is thirsty work."

It was half insult and half reminder that Bass was still on his probationary period at the bottom of the pecking order. He didn't get to ask too many questions. Bass drained his beer, tossed the bottle in the trash with the rest, and headed back to the fridge. He grabbed two bottles and sauntered over to slap a cold base against Shepherd's outstretched hand.

"You got any problem with how I run my business?" Shepherd asked as he rolled the damp glass over his forehead. "Complaints? Suggestions?"

Bass shrugged and took a drink. "Nothing worth rocking the boat over."

"Rock it. I wanna know what keeps my boys happy."

"It's been a bit slow for my liking," Bass admitted. "And it ain't easy to pick a bar fight when everyone knows you're a Brother. But if getting into a fight whenever you got bored paid off, I'd still be in New York."

Shepherd nodded. "And it's not like you've got nothing to do," he said. "I hear you hooked up with your doctor friend again."

"I had an itch. He scratched it," Bass said dismissively. "Not like he's my prom date."

Shepherd chuckled. He put the beer on the table, a stack of fifties as a coaster, and grabbed a pen to scrawl something on the back of a receipt. His knuckles were bruised and split. Fresh red scabs were clotted over the bones.

"Usually I'd send Ville," he said. The nib of the pen nearly cut through the thin sheet of paper as Shepherd circled part of what he'd written. "But apparently he's real unhappy with the way I run things, maybe even thinks he could step up. So you get to pick up some of his slack while him and me… hammer out a career path for him. Here."

He held out the scrawled-on receipt, the limp bit of paper pinched between his fingers. Bass took it and squinted at the blurred scrawl.

A name, circled, and then an address. Not the Heights. This address was the sort of neighborhood Bass would have expected Tag to live in.

"Who is he?" he asked.

"You don't need to know that," Shepherd said. He twisted off the cap of his beer against the heavy signet he wore. "Just that he needs someone to punch him in the face a few times, send a message that it's not a good idea to cross me, that people should keep their mouth shut. Now, see, Ville didn't get that. I expect you will."

He did. Bass squashed the guilt that tried to take root. He might have pushed some of Ville's buttons, but he hadn't made his old friend do anything. Besides, it wasn't like Ville didn't deserve what he had coming to him. Bass folded the paper over.

"It's not some weird sex thing, is it?" he asked as he tucked the square of paper in his pocket. "Because that'll stain your boots."

Shepherd pulled a disgusted face. "It's business," he said. "But it ain't that sort of business. Jesus Christ."

"Then I don't have a problem," Bass said. "You want it done today?"

Shepherd shook his head. "Take your time. He's not ready to be stupid yet. Next couple of days will do."

"Want me to give him a message?"

"Nah, he'll know why you're there," Shepherd said. He took a swig of beer and nodded at the arsenal of guns, knives, and assault rifles lined up against the wall. "Take what you need. But use some self-control. I want him piss scared, not dead or in the news."

Bass ran his eye over the selection. The sawed-off shotgun caught his eye, but even the truncated barrel would be hard to tuck out of sight on a bike. He grabbed one of the Magnums instead. The handgun was heavy in his hand.

"I'll see what I can do," he said. "And if I do a good job, maybe I get out from under the cars a bit more? Swear to fuck, Shepherd, Boone's aunt's brought that fucking car in so many times I think she's after my ass."

Shepherd smiled reluctantly and then shook his head. "You're a likable fucker, Bass. I don't trust likable fuckers. You make mistakes when you like people. But you make this guy shut his mouth, and I've got something else in mind for you."

Bass headed out the door. He paused on the threshold and glanced at the woman. Her eyes were fixed on a point in the corner of the room, and he couldn't remember if she was that greasy pale when he came in. He resisted the urge to check her pulse.

"You might need to get your man to rejig his gear," he said. "Dead junkies don't buy shit."

Shepherd looked at the girl too. When she didn't move, he flicked the bottle cap across the trailer at her. It bounced off her glazed blue eye, and Shepherd laughed when she blinked a second late.

"Not dead yet. Don't worry about her. She came here because she didn't want to be in her head anymore. Looks like it worked," he said. "Tell you what, Bass. She survives this? I'll give you a dose of the product. That Doc of yours is gonna be a lot looser with some of that in him."

He laughed again, thick and dirty in his throat. Bass didn't think it was funny, but he scraped up a grin from somewhere in time to play along.

"And I thought only wage slaves got target bonuses," he said.

"Stick with the Brothers, kid," Shepherd said. He drained the beer and went back to counting money with a swipe of a wet thumb to peel back each bill. "We'll see you right."

Bass glanced briefly at the girl again. Tears dripped out of her inflamed eye, and each breath she took was slow, wet, and shallow. Yeah, the Brothers would see him right. Or they'd see him dead. He doubted it mattered much to Shepherd either way.

GREEN STRIPES had corroded over the fancy copper-lettered sign for The Retreat. A kidnapped child, a scandal, and suddenly the local rich parents couldn't wait to stay away from the place. Rumor had it the old hippy who owned the place had tried to get back into the weed game, but it hadn't panned out for him. Times and tastes had changed since you could make a living out of a greenhouse and an unmodified strain. There was plenty of competition out there these days.

Bass stood behind the sign and pissed out Shepherd's beer on the calligraphed *T*. The trap-house trailer was pit enough. He didn't want to find out what the toilet was like. Even the hot stink of road-cooked dead possum somewhere in the undergrowth was probably better.

He finished, shook his cock, and tucked it back into his jeans. As he zipped back up, the paper in his pocket crinkled a reminder he still had a job to do, unfortunately for Nathan Cochrane, whoever the hell he was and whatever he had to mouth off about.

The vulture that had waited politely in the tree for Bass to finish dropped back down to its road jerky as he headed back to his bike. He swung a leg over the seat, the quick memory of Tag's body sprawled over it last night a brief, pleasant distraction, and started the engine.

He pulled back out onto the empty stretch of road and opened up the throttle. The bike surged forward, the rumble of the engine between his thighs harsher, and the needle on the speedometer ticked toward the red zone. The wind, cold at this speed despite the heat, caught at him as he hunched over the gas tank. A twitch of his hands veered the bike wide around a pothole, the buck of metal and rubber under him just about reined in.

Sometimes it felt like everything else—the fights, the parade of pretty boys and bad men, the danger—was just a poor substitute for this. Free, fast, and fuck 'em all. He wondered idly if Tag would like it, his body close against Bass's back and his hand—

The saw of the police siren as the cop car lurched out of the culvert behind him, blues on flash, cut his train of thought short. Probably for the best. He flexed his hands around the grips of the bike and weighed whether he should run for it. It wouldn't be easy, but if he cut through the feed store parking lot, took the old country road out into the maze of cookie-cutter new housing developments, he might be able to throw them off.

Instead he reluctantly laid off the gas and coasted to a stop at the side of the road. He stayed on the bike and waited for the deputy to stamp through the summer weeds to his side.

"Do you know how fast you were going, sir?" she asked by rote as she stopped next to him.

"Isn't that your *one* job?" Bass cracked. The Magnum felt like a brand against the small of his back, tucked into his jeans and hidden under his T-shirt. He tried not to think about it. "I mean, what else you got?"

She scowled at him.

"You were over the speed limit," she said.

"Yet a minute ago you didn't know how fast I was going," Bass said. "Make up your mind, sweetheart."

She clenched her jaw, and she pushed a stray spiral curl behind her ear.

"It's Deputy Tancredi, not sweetheart. Get off your bike, please," she said. "And show me some ID."

Bass rolled his neck, the crackle of his vertebra as they popped loud in his ear, and did as he was told. He paced back and forth on the edge of the road to loosen up as she ran his license and came back with... well, him. It wasn't a pretty read.

When she stomped back along the shoulder this time, she had her hand on her gun.

"I'm going to have to ask you to come with me, sir," she said. "You've got open warrants against you from Montana."

Bass held up his hands, palms out and fingers relaxed. "I've got a gun in the small of my back," he said. It was never a good idea to surprise a cop with a gun. "I have a license for it."

Tancredi grabbed him by the collar and marched him over to the patrol car. Her partner had gotten out too. He was stocky and had acne scars over his jaw.

"Assume the position," she snapped as she shoved him at the hood of the car. He did as he was told, the metal hot under his hands, and waited while she snapped on gloves. Once she was gloved up, she ran quick, practiced hands down his back and pulled the gun out from under his T-shirt. She pinched it between a blue-gloved thumb and finger as she handed it to the other deputy. "Do have any other weapons on you? Knives? Needles?"

"Pocket knife in my boot," Bass said. He bit a growl as she kicked his feet apart. "You know, this would be a lot more fun for me if your partner did it."

Tancredi put her hand between his shoulders and pushed him down onto the car. He grunted as she wrenched his arms back and cuffed him tightly. Then she pulled him back up and led him to the back of the car so she could push him in. At least she put her hand on top of his head so he didn't crack it against the doorframe.

The back seat was sticky, and from the faint ripe reek, someone had puked back there recently. So it was like every other cop car someone had bundled Bass into over the years. He slouched down, tilted his head back against the seat, and closed his eyes.

"Wake me up when we get there," he said. "If you stop for coffee on the way, I like it plain and black."

Tancredi muttered something under breath, but Bass was already halfway to a nap—he hadn't gotten that much sleep last night—and he didn't bother to wake up and work it out.

THE LAST time Bass had been in the Plenty cop shop, he was fourteen and, for once, actually innocent of the crime he'd been accused of. Not that he stuck to that for long, not once the detectives on the case beat some sense into him.

For a second he could almost hear the ringing in his ears that had hung around for a week after Detective... Peartree? Peterlee?... backhanded him with his class ring. His throat felt dry as well when he glanced toward the interview room they'd penned him in.

Jesus. He shook his head impatiently and swallowed hard. Talk about water under the bridge. It was half a lifetime ago, and by all accounts, the sheriff's department had cleaned out most of the crooks when they took over. Besides, they'd done him a favor. If he hadn't been routed to that money-farm juvie in Nebraska, he'd have stayed here and gotten to watch his dad rot away from failure and whiskey instead of just hearing about it.

Still. Bass turned his head and spat on the scuffed old tiles underfoot.

"Dirty bastard," Tancredi blurted indignantly. She yanked on his arm to pull him around the corner. "You want to spend the night in jail before we check the warrants?"

"Depends on the company." Bass swaggered along the hall, all heavy boots and confidence. That was who he was now, not some scared little petty thief.

Tancredi snorted at him and marched up to a door at the end of the hall. She rapped on it twice before she opened it and pushed Bass in ahead of her. He gritted his teeth at being manhandled, but held on to his temper as he stepped into the room.

It looked like the interview rooms here hadn't changed much since his day. Instead of the cracked, stark-white paint he remembered, the walls were painted an industrially bland slate gray. But the heavy steel table with the soldered-in handcuff ring was the same. It smelled the same too, like bleach over old sweat.

"Agent Merlo," Tancredi said. She closed the door behind her with the sharp click of an engaged lock. "I brought him in."

The Fed on the other side of the scarred steel table looked up from the paperwork he had spread out in front of him. Dark eyes flickered over Bass from head to toe as he stood up.

"I see that. Uncuff him, Tancredi."

Bass rolled his shoulders back to give her room as she unlocked the metal rings from around his wrists. They hadn't been tight or on for that long, but Bass's skin still itched once they were free. He brought them around in front to chafe them absently.

"I'm sorry that was necessary," Merlo said. He extended his hand. "It's good to see you again, Detective Sebastiani."

Nico Sebastiani, NYPD undercover detective on secondment to the San Diego County Sheriff's department, gripped Merlo's hand easily.

"Better safe than sorry." He glanced over his shoulder at Tancredi and grinned at her. "Deputy Tancredi was very convincing."

Chapter Eleven

MEL BYRON lay flat on her stomach on the stretcher and wept. It hurt too much to cry, so she just dripped water between shallow, shocked breaths.

"What's wrong with her?" her husband, Jeff, asked worriedly from the end of the bed. She'd banished him there after an ill-fated attempt to hold her hand to comfort her. He scratched his neck, which was sweaty under the gawdy polyester of his cheap Hawaiian shirt, and shifted his weight from one Birkenstock to the other. "She just slipped."

The woman hissed air out from between her teeth, pale lips pulled back in a grimace. She dug her fingers into the thin pillow, her knuckles white and bony under holiday-tanned skin. "He pulled. The fucking chair. From under me."

"I…. It was a joke," the man objected weakly. He looked nearly as gray as his wife. "We filmed it. For YouTube. It was just a prank. Nobody was supposed to get hurt."

Tag knew he'd made a face, but hopefully the man hadn't noticed. He took his hands off the woman's shoulders and moved down to her hips. When the ambulance brought her in, she described the pain as universal, a sheet of it from her shoulders to midthighs. From the way she'd fallen, though, Tag thought he could narrow down the point of injury.

"Maybe you should wait outside," Tag suggested to Jeff as he slid gloved fingers carefully under the waistband of Mel's jeans. Her skin felt hot, and she made a high, pinched whine through her nose as he touched her. "Just until I've finished my examination."

Jeff rubbed his hand through his bleached-blond hair and gaped at Tag.

"I don't know," he hedged. "Maybe I should stay with Mel in case she needs me."

The nurse on the other side of the bed snorted quietly. Unlike Tag, she wasn't lucky enough to have it go unnoticed.

"It was a *joke*," Jeff snapped at her. "She's my wife. I didn't mean to hurt her. It was just a laugh."

The nurse tucked her chin in and pursed her lips. "She's not laughing now."

Jeff glared at her and then swung his attention back to Tag in search for sympathy. "We do stuff like this *all the time*," he said. "She's never gotten hurt before. I wouldn't do that. I love her. She was just supposed to look like an idiot, not this."

"I'm sure," Tag said smoothly. "But right now I need to focus on—"

"I'm gonna divorce," Mel said in a breathy staccato that moved her body as little as possible. "You bastard. Get my lawyer… to show everyone that fucking channel. Get away from me."

Jeff grabbed her ankle. "You don't mean that, Mel," he said. "Come on. You think my jokes are funny too, after."

She tried to kick him and then made a strangled sound in her throat. He jumped backward, hands up in the air as Tag and the nurse pinned down his wife.

"I didn't touch her," he said. "I just want to help. She just *sat down* hard, how could that do this?"

Tag jabbed a finger at him. "Out. We'll tell you once we've finished our exam. Right now she's not in the mood to talk."

Jeff looked genuinely heartbroken as he gave up and retreated. As the hideous shirt left the room, Tag turned back to his patient. He repositioned his hands.

"Okay, Mel," he said. "Just bear with me, okay? Can you tell me when it hurts?"

"Now," she sobbed out into the pillow. Then Tag pressed down gently, and she sucked in her breath in a shocked, reverse scream that got stuck in her throat. Tag grimaced.

"We need to get her to X-ray," he said as he pulled his hands free and snapped the gloves off. He'd forgotten his antihistamines that morning again, and he gave the itchy spot on the web of his thumb a quick scratch as he stepped back. "Pain meds too. Morphine sulfate in a line."

Tag crouched next to the bed so he could see Mel's face. "We'll have to confirm with an X-ray, but I think you've broken your sacrum."

She looked almost relieved that at least it was something she could pin down. "Is that, like, my tailbone?"

"Same area," Tag said. "Slightly more serious, but manageable. Let's get you to X-ray and make sure first, okay?"

She swallowed hard. "Okay."

Tag rocked back on his heels and stood up. With any luck she wouldn't need surgery, but he would need to examine her again once the pain was under control to assess if there was any nerve damage that would need to be repaired.

"Get the line in before you take her to X-ray," he told the nurse as he stepped back from the bed. "It will make the transfer more bearable."

He left her to it as he stepped away from the bed and headed out into the waiting room to update her husband. The guy was already on his phone before Tag had walked away, a goofy expression on his face as he mugged for the camera.

"She's broken her *butt!*" he cackled.

Tag rolled his eyes and left him to it. He figured by the time Mel was back on her feet, Jeff was going to be sorry or single.

A teenager with a bug up her nose and hiking boots on—"Never. Going. Camping again!"—and two men who'd finally sobered up enough after the night before to realize they'd hurt themselves—broken fist in the first case, half a glass still jammed into his ass in the other—were next in line. It wasn't until Tag finished with them that he finally got a chance to check his phone.

It felt too good to see Bass's name hover in his notifications. He'd told himself he didn't regret the swipe that blocked Bass's number, that he'd been glad not to see any more videos ready to play in his inbox, but that was a lie. He swiped open the message.

One message, just text with no pictures.

I can still taste you.

Tag couldn't breathe for a second as lust hit him in the chest. He cleared his throat awkwardly and rubbed at the back of his neck. If he'd hoped that last night and this morning had gotten Bass out of his system, he was clearly wrong.

Just the thought of Bass's rough hands on him, a gruff voice against his ear, sent a quiver of awareness down Tag's spine. Any headway he'd made on not being a complete pushover had been rolled back again.

"Fuck sake," he muttered under his breath as he rubbed his eyes. "How hard is it to not screw my life up?"

Too hard for him, apparently.

"Doctor Hayes," Ennis called with the note of saccharine sweetness in her voice that meant she'd gotten out of something and didn't even have to feel guilty. "There's a patient in here who'd rather see a male doctor."

Tag sighed. That pretty much invariably meant that the guy had stuck something in his ass or in his penis. Which was fine—people had been doing that since the start of time—but it always involved a lot of lies and a lot of time convincing the patient you needed to stick the needle where you needed to stick the needle.

"On my way, Doctor Ennis," he said.

He typed out a quick response as he turned to head toward the curtained-off cubicle, Ennis's head stuck out halfway up like a bad magician's act.

Bass would just have to wait.

THE BABY carrier hit the barbeque and went up in flames.

Tag flinched in sympathy with Mel Byron's panicked screech. He knew it was a bad idea, but he flicked to the next video, where Mel thought she'd fed Jeff drain cleaner.

"Jesus," Tag muttered as he chewed on a slice of cold pizza. Part of him thought that, on some level, Mel had to know what was going on before her pained chuckle to the camera at the end when it was revealed her dad hadn't been arrested, her cat hadn't fallen out a window, but her husband was still a dick. After the first five, surely every time anything went wrong, she'd be suspicious of Jeff's camera somewhere.

But probably not to the degree where she expected to break a small but important part of her back.

Someone sat down opposite, white cuffs in the periphery of Tag's vision, and he looked up absently to nod his acknowledgment. He flicked his eyes over the pressed collar and the tie he'd gotten him… what, anniversary present? Birthday? … and braced himself for whatever he'd feel by the time he got to Kieran's face.

"Hey," Kieran said. His eyebrows creased together in a familiar "We've got something to talk about" frown.

Tag swallowed and reached for a napkin. He wiped his mouth and then his hands. "Hey." He balled up the greasy paper and rejected a dozen sarcastic comments like "Did Freddie finally fall off your ass?" before he settled on something neutral. "Long time no see."

Neutral-ish.

Kieran nodded. "It's been strange," he said mildly. "I used to see you every day for nearly five years, and now you dodge me in the hall."

Tag snorted. "Don't try and pull that Psychology 101 shit on me," he said. "You cheated on me."

"But you're the one who left," Kieran countered.

It was the sort of thing he said like he really believed it, even though he couldn't possibly think it was reasonable. Like it somehow canceled out his screwup if Tag did something Kieran didn't like. The spot at the back of Tag's head, where his spine slotted neatly into his skull, started to ache. He could, without much effort, plot out the next ten minutes of back-and-forth, and it didn't sound like fun. So he cut across it to the point.

"What do you want, Kieran?"

Kieran leaned forward and braced his arms on the table. "I'm worried about you, Tag," he said. The hint of his old accent, North Dakota born and bred, caught Tag the same way it always did, like it meant something that Kieran still let that slip around him. Maybe it did, but not enough. Kieran narrowed his eyes at whatever expression he saw on Tag's face. "And before you say anything, I get to worry about you if I want to. I don't need your permission."

It should have felt like… something. Hope? An opportunity? Tag just felt the ache of residual irritation in the back of his skull.

"I don't need it," Tag said. "I'm fine. We broke up. People do."

"Never thought we would," Keiran said. "Until we did. And maybe, yes, it was my fault."

Tag raised an eyebrow. "That hurt?" He got up and folded his paper plate in half to toss it in the trash.

"Little bit." A real smile tugged at the corner of Kieran's mouth and then faded. "But people do things you don't expect them to. Like get involved with… marginal elements."

"Like the margins of staying out of my business?" Tag asked.

"I saw you arrive this morning with the young man on the bike."

"Really?" Tag asked as he turned around. "You're trying to pull 'young man' on me? Because Bass is older than Freddie and doesn't work for me. So—"

The muscles in Kieran's jaw tightened in annoyance, and the familiar inescapable pink flush crawled up from under his collar.

"That's not the point," Kieran said stiffly. "I am genuinely concerned about you and what you could get yourself into when you're still… hurt.

The last thing I want is for this to turn into another referendum on my apparent failings."

Tag had to close his eyes for a second. He took a deep breath and made himself smile at Kieran.

"You're right. It's not my business who you f—are with," he said, the coarse alternative trapped behind his teeth. He swallowed it as he grabbed his phone off the table and shoved it in a pocket. "The thing is that it's not your business who I sleep with either. So there's no need to have this conversation."

"I've known you for over a decade, Taggart," Kieran snapped as he stood up. "Long before I ever saw your penis. I'm not just your ex. I'm your friend."

"No," Tag said as he stalked around the worn old lounge chairs and headed out of the room. "You're not. And you don't know anything about Bass, so drop it."

He was almost out when Kieran stated, "Ned told me."

"What?" Tag already knew, but maybe he was wrong.

Kieran huffed in annoyance. "Oh, what do you think?" he said. "He told me what this Bass did to you last month. The biker with the knife in his leg."

The door clicked shut again as Tag let go of it. "Screwdriver," he said as turned around.

"Do I look like I care?" Kieran snapped as he bumped his knuckles against his chest. He stopped, exhaled, and smoothed a hand back over his hair. Once his composure was back in place, he tried again. "Have you forgotten why we moved to Plenty in the first place? Because you did this, the exact same thing, in New York and nearly died."

The itch in his ribs was psychosomatic. He'd looked at X-rays and MRIs over the years, and the scarring was as good as you could hope for—no inflammation, no adhesions, no complications. But whenever someone noticed it or reminded him of it, he could feel it catch between his ribs like the knife was still in there.

"I didn't have sex with Mallick," he said. "He was just…."

He ran out of words. Always had. *Patient. Friend. Mentee.* None of that actually fit, before or after. *Mistake* did, although it kind of undersold the part where Tag had gotten stabbed.

Kieran covered his face with his hands in frustration and snarled against his palms. "You gave him chance after chance," he said. "I told you that the odds were against him, that kids from his background and his upbringing were nine times out of ten not going to turn their lives around."

"He was seventeen. No one is done at seventeen."

"Except I was right," Kieran reminded him as he pulled his hands down his face, the skin stretched tight and pale under his fingers. His voice cracked, and Tag knew it wasn't just frustration. "He nearly killed you, Tag. You tried to help him, and he stabbed you, robbed you, and left you to die in the road. How much blood did they need to replace? How many hours did you spend on the operating table?"

"A lot" was the answer to both. Old habits made Tag want to apologize, to offer an olive branch for that disruption of their lives. Under the circumstances, he resisted.

"It's not the same," he said.

It wasn't. If he tried to explain it, he'd look like a horny idiot, but it wasn't the sex. It wasn't *just* the sex. He liked Bass, and for some indefensible reason, he trusted him. There was no reason to, but he did.

But that wasn't the sort of thing he'd ever be able to explain to Kieran. He liked to strip people down to cause and effect, every passion just another neurosis from their childhood or their brain chemistry.

"You're a narcissist," Kieran said.

"I'm not."

Kieran snorted. "Every day you get up and decide that you trust yourself to cut patients open, to crack them open like crabs because you can put them back together. You're a surgeon. You might not be toxic, but you're on the scale. That means you want to be in control, and between our breakup—"

"Don't flatter yourself."

Kieran ignored him. "—and what happened last month with this biker, the echoes of what happened in New York. This is just you trying to take back control, to rewrite it so you didn't make a mistake with this man. With me."

"That's bullshit."

Kieran raised his eyebrows. "Really? So why didn't you go to the sheriff, Tag? Was it because you were afraid? Because you thought someone else would get hurt? Or did you just not want to admit that you—hotshot trauma surgeon Tag Hayes—had been made a fool of again?"

That caught Tag by surprise. It was a sharp, crushed pain in his chest that felt like gravel. He didn't know if it was because Kieran was right or because he was wrong and had only done a good impression of someone who knew Tag better than he knew himself.

"Why is this even your business?" Tag asked, his voice rough as it squeezed out of his throat.

Kieran gave him a pitying look. "I told you, I care about you. Just because I'm with Freddie now, that doesn't mean I don't still have feelings for you. That isn't going to change. I'll always care about you."

"Yeah." Tag opened the door. "Pretty sure the fact you think I give a damn how you feel makes you the narcissist."

Or not. What did he know? But it was a good line to leave on. The door slammed shut behind him, and Tag stalked through the ER toward the main doors. He needed some fresh air to clear his head before he got back to—

The doors clashed open around a stretcher as the paramedics shoved it ahead of them. A skinny blond lay on vomit-stained sheets, her eyes rolled back in her head and her skin gray and waxen.

"Overdose," one of the paramedics said between hard breaths as he pushed the stretcher. He gestured at the woman's groin, where bruises stained her thighs like ink. "Looks like she injected it into her groin. We've given her naloxone already, but it's had no effect. Her BP is—"

Tag registered the vitals, but his focus was on the woman's shallow breaths and the pinpoint pupil revealed when he rolled her eyelid back with his thumb.

"I need two more doses of naloxone," he yelled to any nurse who heard as he jogged alongside the stretcher. "And gloves. It looks like another synthetic overdose, and we can't afford to lose any of you guys before shift change."

The paramedic laughed, and, with the perfect timing of the ER, the woman spat out a mouthful of bile and coded.

CHAPTER TWELVE

"IT LOOKS like Shepherd's courtship of this new contact of his is about to finally be consummated," Bass said. "Luckily just as he started to trust me. At least enough to use me to do his dirty work. So I should be involved when the meet finally takes place, although I doubt I'll get much of a heads-up. Your people will need to be ready."

And that was that. Fifteen loudly ticked-by minutes on the cracked clock on the wall to summarize the last month of his life…. Most of it.

"They will be. I'll make sure of that. Did Shepherd give you any idea of why he needed to intimidate Cochrane?" SSA Merlo, the mover and shaker behind the last year of this organized crime investigation into the Corpse Brothers, asked. The note and the gun Bass had lifted from the Brothers' armory were laid out neatly on the desk in front of him, sealed into plastic bags for their expedited run through the crime scene tech's battery of tests. "Or why he needed him alive?"

Bass rocked back on the chair, balanced on the two rear legs, and tapped his hand on the table. The stark relief of being able to peel off the slick undercover mask had faded, and now he just wanted to get out of there and drop the mask of good cop Detective Nico Sebastiani as well.

"Nope."

Merlo looked at him. "Are you still able to do this, Sebastiani?" he asked. "If you need to be pulled out, we can do that."

When Bass first rode into town—his flight had dropped him off in Nevada so he could look dusty and road worn when he hit the town limits—he thought the supervisory special agent in charge of the local office was a buttoned-up prig, a pencil pusher with no idea how it worked in the trenches.

Just what he wanted in a handler. He had to break the rules, lie, fuck people over, break the law to fit in with the people he was there to take down. If he ever forgot where the line was—and he had, at least, lost sight of it a couple of times over the years—he wanted someone who knew what he was doing to pull him up. Once your handler started to cover for you instead, that was when shit got out of hand.

But sometimes in Bass's line of work, you had to cross that line to get the job done.

"Then what?" Bass asked. He rubbed his wrist absently, as though the healed ink had the same weight as the metal it represented. "You won't be able to get another agent on the inside with the Brothers. That's why you dragged me back here, remember?"

It took more than just a beat-up bike and a well-curated criminal record to get the Brothers to accept you. Oh, the Feds were able to run a couple of stings with drugs and guns and threw a handful of bikers in jail. Never enough to destabilize the gang, and never anyone they could coax into snitching to get out. Once the cell doors slammed, the Brothers clammed up and did their time.

They never even got close to the Brothers' inner circle. For all the Feds could prove, Shepherd was a law-abiding business owner who'd never so much as jaywalked and just had really bad taste in friends.

To get him they needed to get closer than a scabby dealer with a stack of heroin bricks to sell cheap. When the Brothers only swore in scumbags born and bred in Plenty, that was a problem.

Unless you found an undercover cop who was an aspiring local scumbag before juvie gave him a reason to turn his life around. Someone like that, if they were willing to take the risk, might just be able to make it work.

"I want to take down Shepherd and his organization," Merlo admitted. He sat back in the chair and laced his fingers together on the table. His voice was cool and unsentimental as he laid out his argument. "He's not the biggest fish in the area, but he's bad enough, and he runs interference and drugs for the cartels that greases the wheels for them. The information you've been able to get out is going to help me put him in jail where he belongs, but if you burn out, then everything we've done so far will go with you. I'd rather pull you out now with a good cover story. We can throw Bass the biker in jail, and Nico Sebastiani can go back to his life in New York."

That should have sounded better than it did. Bass raked his fingers through his hair and clenched them into a fist at the base of his scalp. Maybe it was just because the legend he'd been handed this time was too close to home—if broken ribs and a concussion hadn't gotten him pulled out of that Nebraska juvie and into foster care, if he hadn't decided that whatever crime paid, it wasn't worth going back somewhere worse.

"What is it?" Bass asked. "Do you think I'm going to turncoat all of a sudden?"

Merlo pursed his lips thoughtfully. "Divided loyalties are a problem for undercover cops," he admitted. "Good liars fool themselves before they fool anyone else, and you are very good at being a Brother, Detective."

Bass leaned in, and the front two legs of the chair hit the ground with a crack as he braced his elbows against the table.

"I was good at being a Long Island sleazebag who sold kids into slavery too," Bass said. "I gambled with Triads, I sold guns they'd never seen to white supremacists and convinced some made men that I had a market for stolen Bugattis. This is what I do, SSA Merlo, so trust me, if I need to be pulled, I'll let you know."

It was a lie. He figured Merlo knew that too, but he let it go this time.

"I'll hold you to that," Merlo said. He looked down at the table and tapped his finger against the receipt. Plastic crinkled under his finger as he did. "If you're still in, then we need to decide what to do about Ryan Cochrane. Obviously we aren't going to approve of you beating up a law-abiding citizen."

Officially. That went unsaid. It always did.

"If that's what he is," Bass pointed out. "I haven't heard his name before, but I might have seen him around...?"

Merlo nodded and stood up. He gathered up the gun and receipt off the desk. "I'll get Tancredi to look up, see if he has any priors or has come across our radar before. Once we know a bit more about him, it'll be easier to make a decision. If all else fails, I'll put him in protective custody. You can tell Shepherd that he either ran or you went too far and killed him."

Bass grimaced as he slouched back into his chair. He stretched out his legs under the table until his scuffed boots kicked Merlo's chair back. The metal feet scraped loudly against the tiles.

"I'd rather not mess up the first thing he asked me do," Bass said. "We want Shepherd to think I'm someone he can depend on, trust to get a job done, not another fuckup he can deploy as cannon fodder."

The key to being a good UC wasn't to get people to trust you, not in Bass's experience, anyhow. That was useful if you could pull it off, but half of the people he had arrested over the years didn't trust their own mothers—for good reason. Some criminals even a mother couldn't love. What they wanted was someone they could use, and for that, you needed results.

Merlo acknowledged the point with a nod. "That wouldn't be the ideal solution," he said. "But it might be the one we need to go with. See what Tancredi turns up on Cochrane."

"I take it she can keep her mouth shut?"

"She knows what's at stake," Merlo said. "Tancredi's a good officer. She's smart, and she's ambitious."

Bass laced his hands over his stomach, the buckle of his belt cold against his palm. "I don't want to know her arrest rates. I want to be sure she's not going to run her mouth and get me killed."

"I trust her," Merlo said. "And it's a bit late to worry about what she does and doesn't know."

Bass snorted and dropped his head back against the hard metal back of the chair. "Touché."

The door didn't close. Bass turned his head toward it and raised his eyebrows expectantly at Merlo.

"If you need a night off, we can keep you in overnight," Merlo said. A flicker of humor tucked the corner of his mouth as he added, "Not in the cells, but I could arrange a hotel. Or I have a couch, when the dog's not on it."

Bass considered it. Back in New York, he'd have taken the offer off at the wrist. Sometimes just being able to put your own skin back on for a night made a big difference. But in the city, a shave and a borrowed uniform were enough to dodge identification. When there were a couple million people around, at least five of them could pass for your brother. It was more of a risk in a town like Plenty, especially since he came from here.

He didn't have any family left—his dad died a couple of years ago, and Bass hadn't come back for the funeral—but there were still old teachers, the clerk from the gas station he robbed when he was twelve, or just an old neighbor. People went through life worried they'd made no impact, but the minute you didn't want to be recognized, there'd be some old biddy with a photographic memory.

"I appreciate the offer, but it's not worth the risk," he said. Besides, if he was going to spend the night anywhere, he'd rather it be on Tag and not a federal agent's probably minimalist leather couch. "Just cut me loose in a few hours and slap a court date on me. I'll tell the Brothers I'm being harassed by the pigs. Maybe it will get me a few brownie points."

Merlo accepted that with the relief of a man who'd made an offer he hadn't wanted to follow through with. He slipped out of the room and closed the door firmly behind him, but he didn't lock it. Bass appreciated that. He didn't care to be locked in a room he didn't have the key to.

The clock ticked off another loud minute. While he waited for some info to roll back down the chain of command, he checked his battered old phone. Just one message from Tag. The flicker of disappointment made Bass snort at himself. What had he expected? A sex tape from the operating theater?

Although that would be hot.

Tied up till later, he sent. *Your place tonight? 10. I'll bring food.*

The clock ticked off another loud handful of minutes, and then the phone buzzed three times in succession on the table. He turned it over, an unusual touch of doubt in the back of his throat as he wondered if Tag had finally come to his senses. Apparently not.

Drunken noodles... and you can Thai me up.

... fuck. Ignore that.

Just bring you. And noodles.

Bass snorted to himself and tossed the phone back onto the table. The back of the chair pressed hard against his shoulder blades as he stretched and wondered how the hell that sext misstep had managed to circle back around to sexy.

THE COFFEE was reassuringly bad. It was a touchstone of sorts for what skin he had on. Bass the Biker drank beer, with a chaser of whiskey if someone else lined it up. Detective Sebastiani drank his bitter, over-brewed coffee black and hot enough to scorch his tongue smooth.

"So who is he?" he asked.

"He's a urologist," Tancredi said.

That would... not have been Bass's first guess. He hitched his foot onto the metal seat and rested the coffee cup on his knee.

"I'm not saying that Shepherd's going to take the Brothers to Pride next year," Bass said. "But he's not homophobic enough to kill someone just so no one ever found out a medical professional touched him in his fun zone. Trust me. Most of these guys have been to the clinic to have their cock swabbed at some point."

Tancredi gave a caught-off-guard snicker and then glanced at Merlo and cleared her throat.

"Well, ah, maybe not," she said. "I don't think he's Shepherd's urologist."

Bass didn't need the glance at Merlo to know he'd slipped out of his cop skin. That wasn't a Sebastiani joke. He took another drink of coffee, somewhere between a reminder and a punishment, and waited for the awkward to fade.

"Go on," Merlo told Tancredi and lifted an eyebrow. "I assume there is an on to get to?"

She pressed her lips together and nodded firmly. "I don't know how or why this ties in, but last month, Cochrane's girlfriend was the drunk driver who took out Jason Morrow, the lawyer who'd just about talked his client, Logan Franks, one of the Brothers, into taking the deal we offered."

Franks had been a couple of months before Merlo requested Bass's secondment. Bass had read about it in the briefing when he got here. He rifled through his memory for the details.

"You arrested him for possession of illegal weapons. I remember you said you were trying to leverage access to his kid to get him to turn state's evidence," he said. "But Logan's always been close to Shepherd, so I'd assumed he was just yanking your chain."

Merlo held out his hand, and Tancredi passed him the incident report. "So had I," he admitted as he flicked through the pages. "Until his lawyer ended up in intensive care and Logan stopped talking to us. You're sure this Nathan Cochrane is connected to the driver? Her name's… Lowry."

"Same address," Tancredi said. "And records show that he was who she called before we booked her."

Merlo shook his head. "There was no connection to Shepherd. We looked. Besides, it's not like him to use a proxy, especially not such an unlikely one. He either does his own dirty work or he goes through the club."

"Not always," Bass said. The grim edge to his voice was another slip, but this time he was the only one who noticed it. He drained his coffee to the dregs and set the mug on the table. "If Shepherd knew that Logan was going to take that deal, then Logan's days are numbered. The minute he sent me or one of the Brothers to take this lawyer out, then Logan would know that too."

Merlo nodded. "And he'd have real motivation to take any deal we offer, even if it is only to move him out of state."

"I recommend Utah," Bass said dryly. He ignored Tancredi's curious look—Merlo didn't need to bother. He'd been filled in on Bass's history when they started—and shifted back on topic. "So Shepherd used this Cochrane as an in-between, someone Logan wouldn't know was attached to the club, to set up the accident—"

"Except he wasn't there, remember?" Tancredi interrupted. She pulled a photo out of the file and slid it to the middle of the table. "This was the driver, Rebecca Lowry. She's forty-five, she works three days a week in LA as an interior designer, and has a three-year-old son with Cochrane."

The woman in the photo was probably pretty on a good day, but it obviously hadn't been one of those. Her makeup stood out garishly in stripes of peach and teal against shock-pale skin, and mascara trailed muddy tracks down her cheeks to the corner of her naked mouth. Her blond hair was blown out in a perfect tousled fluff around all that devastation.

If she'd had a good day, Bass might not have recognized her.

"Right now she's a junkie in a trailer up past the Retreat," he said as he unfolded himself from the chair. "She was there when I went to see Shepherd today. He'd given her a dose of some new synthetic he had on hand."

"Are you sure?" Merlo asked.

Bass shrugged. "She hasn't had her roots done lately and she's ridden herself hard, but it's the same woman."

Tancredi shook her head. "That's not possible. We ran a background check, ran her against Shepherd's known aliases, and there was *no* connection to Shepherd or the Brothers. Lowry's a wannabe socialite who's on the board of her kid's preschool. She's not the sort of girl who runs with a biker gang."

"You'd be surprised," Bass said. "Some people like it rough."

"There's rough and there's Shepherd," Tancredi said. "He's industrial sandpaper, and I've seen that trailer when we raided it. It's gross, and your feet stick to the floor. You don't go from a mimosa brunch to that in a month."

Bass put a finger on the edge of the photo and turned it around. She wouldn't be the first perp to practice her crocodile tears on the booking sergeant, as though being sad you got caught was the same thing as remorse, but he didn't think so. It was hard to fake the pallor or the slack confusion that softened Lowry's mouth. She looked genuinely traumatized.

"Maybe not after you've run a man down and heard him screaming," he said. "After that you might think what Shepherd has to offer is what you deserve. And your boyfriend, or whatever Cochrane is to her, might start to have second thoughts about their involvement with the Brothers."

"In which case it would make sense for Shepherd to send someone like you to remind Cochrane that things could still get worse," Merlo said with a slow nod. "It fits the pieces we have. Just because it's a good story doesn't mean that it's true, though. All we have is a receipt with a name on it and a coincidence, albeit a compelling one. We need evidence if this is going to mean anything."

That put it squarely back in Bass's court, didn't it? It was why he was there—to get something they could use to take Shepherd's feet from under him hard enough that he didn't have time to damage control, threaten, and bribe his way out of it.

"If we're correct," he said, "then Cochrane's scared. But maybe he's not scared enough. Right now he's trying to come up with a way out of this mess, but he still thinks that he can get away free and clear. What if I go in and impress on him that he isn't going to? He's made his bed, and he's going to get fucked over in it."

Merlo grimaced at the crude metaphor, but Tancredi had already started to nod her agreement.

"Then when we come in and offer him protection," she said, "he'll be desperate enough to take the deal."

"He'd need to be," Merlo said grimly. Then he admitted, "It could work."

None of them looked happy with the plan. They were going to take advantage of a man's fear for his girlfriend's safety to get him to put his own life at risk. But it was the only idea on the table. Bass waited for a moment, just to see if anyone could come up with something better.

When they didn't, he scooped his phone off the table and slotted it into his hip pocket.

"I guess I get to go and beat up a urologist, then," he said with a bleak sort of humor. "At least if he ends up pissing blood, he can take care of it himself."

Chapter Thirteen

THE BIKER Express apparently only ran in the early hours. Tag had to catch the bus back from the hospital. When he got on, half the bus were faces he recognized from the hospital. By the time he got to his stop, it was just him and two of the orderlies. They had forgotten he spoke Spanish and thought he'd missed his stop.

He hunched his shoulders against the drizzle as he got off the bus. The street was dark, the only light splashed over the pavement by the cars on their way past, and Tag made a mental note to complain to the town council again. It didn't seem to do any good—the streetlights worked or didn't on some schedule he hadn't figured out yet—but he felt better for the effort.

Maybe one day they'd actually fix them, and Tag could tell himself that was his doing.

He nodded politely to the two orderlies as they parted ways at the corner. The two men ambled off as they argued over whether they should offer to walk him to the right bus stop or introduce him to the dealer who delivered.

Tag snorted and shoved his hands into his pockets. He supposed he should look for somewhere new. Not that he cared that he shared a neighborhood with the porters, but it obviously wasn't where anyone lived if they had options. Tag had options.

His credit was probably still shit—he'd always been bad with money—but Kieran was the one who wanted to buy. He was a Midwest boy, where you farmed your own land… or something like that. Plus he made the big money. Tag came from proud renter stock. He liked the security that came from the plumbing being someone else's problem.

It wouldn't hurt to see what he could get in his price range. It wasn't like he wanted to stage a return to the suburbs. It had never been a good fit for him, not really. Between his shifts and the commutes up to San Diego, he never got to know anyone that well. And he still didn't get the point of a garden when you didn't have kids, dogs, or a desire to spy on your neighbors through their fences.

The headlights from a passing car glittered on a broken bottle left discarded on the path, green smeared with red. Tag swept the bloody pieces into the gutter with the side of his shoe. He didn't look around to see if the bleeder was still nearby.

Somewhere that didn't have a homeowner's association or people who got glassed on the streets on the weekends, then. That would be a dream. He could even stay in the Heights. There were places here that met his criteria and would be closer to the hospital.

… and near Bass?

Tag grimaced at the skeptical thought as it settled like silt in his head. He could feel the slippery knot of self-doubt that Kieran had fed him earlier. It was still wedged behind his ribs despite his best attempts to ignore it out of existence.

It wasn't that he hadn't had his own doubts before, but they were easier to work around before Kieran pinned them down with words and history. He'd always had a knack for that. It made him a good psychiatrist and a pain in the ass when someone just wanted to enjoy blissful ignorance.

Although, to be fair, most psychiatrists were like that. People just didn't appreciate someone who pointed out their mental tripwires as much as they did the oncologist who confirmed that was just a weird mole.

Still, just because it wasn't something Tag wanted to think didn't mean Kieran was wrong. But this time Tag knew that going in. Unlike the thirteen-year-old gang members who died from gunshot wounds in surgery or the seventeen-year-old car thieves he patched up well enough that they could be taken to jail, with Mallick he'd seen a kid he thought he could help, and he ignored all the red flags that he couldn't.

Bass was just no-strings fun, and unlike a knife in a dark alley, Tag wouldn't be surprised when it ended badly. He might be a soft touch or a lovestruck idiot, but he wasn't a blind one.

If he signed a lease, it would be because he actually wanted somewhere to live, not just somewhere to stay until… something changed. And if it meant he got to sleep in with Bass or someone in the future, that would be a bonus. That's all.

When he got back to the building, his parking space, marked in cracked yellow paint with his apartment number and a greasy oil stain from the Mustang's undercarriage, was still empty. There was no sign of it anywhere else in the parking lot or slotted in between old vans and the cars with magazines pasted into the windows that families used to sleep in. Even in the dark, the long nose and cherry-red paint job made it hard to miss.

No sign of Bass either. It was—Tag checked his watch and grimaced—later than he'd promised. His shift had run over, and then he'd been drafted to cover the first half of another doctor's shift after Jameson got stuck in Seattle.

Maybe he'd been stood up.

Or Bass had decided to just man up and prove Kieran right. Tag pushed both hands through his hair and then locked them together behind his head. He really hoped that wasn't it, not after Tag had just done all this work to convince himself that the crash and burn would be painless.

He pressed his thumbs against the back of his neck and stared up at the bright, blind windows of other people's lives. Muffled music and TV shows turned up too loud created a discordant white-noise background track to the night.

Other people's lives.

Tag knew they weren't any better than his, but right then, they could easily be simpler. Not that anything would change while he stood out here… unless he got mugged. Tag dropped his arms from his head and dug into his pocket after his keys as he headed inside.

He trudged up the stairs, through the cloud of hash smoke on the third-floor landing, to his floor. The long day had started to hit, and the slice of pizza he grabbed for lunch suddenly looked even less sufficient. Tag doubted there was anywhere open to deliver, but he'd have a look while he charged his phone. It had died mid-*Words with Friends* on the bus.

He started to unlock the door and then paused when it swung open under his hand.

Fuck.

A chill ran down Tag's back. It wasn't fear exactly—he could have left the door open; he had before—but it was sharper than concern. The thought of Shepherd and his calculating eyes made the skin on the back of Tag's neck prickle.

He weighed his options. The stairs behind him loomed large in his thoughts as he considered flight. But his phone was dead, so he'd have to get the bus back to the hospital and then call the cops and come back here. If he was going to go to all that bother, he wanted to be sure there was someone here to run away from.

Tag exhaled slowly and gave the door a cautious nudge with one hand. It swung open with a slow creak, and Bass, legs propped on the coffee table and arm slung over the back of the couch, looked up from his phone.

"I was starting to think you'd stood me up," he said.

"Son of a bitch." Tag stepped into the apartment and slammed the door behind him. His upstairs neighbor stamped on the floor in response to the disturbance. "And you're in my apartment. It's kind of hard to stand you up."

Bass tilted his head to the side and smirked crookedly. He lifted his draped hand off the couch cushions and waved it at himself with a sweep of his fingers that took in everything from his halfheartedly tamed curls to his battered, dusty boots. "Also, well, all of this."

"Really?"

Bass grinned at him. "You gotta admit it's true."

"Asshole," Tag muttered. He shrugged out of his hoodie as he glanced around the apartment. "How did you—"

"It's a shit lock," Bass said. He swung his legs off the coffee table and got up to walk across the room. "I got you pad Thai. It's in the fridge. First, though…."

He grabbed Tag's wrist and yanked him across the distance between them until their bodies were pressed together from shoulder to hip and Bass's breath tickled against Tag's jaw as he waited. It was Tag who leaned into the kiss, his hand cupped around the back of Bass's neck and his body relaxed—as though he hadn't spent any five minutes he wasn't elbow deep in a patient worried that Bass was a liar and a criminal.

Which was stupid because they both knew Bass was both.

Bass growled appreciatively into Tag's mouth and ran a broad, warm hand up his back.

"Have I told you that you look really goddamn hot in scrubs?" Bass asked. The words grazed over Tag's lips as he leaned back slightly. His voice was a low rasp, and he tightened his hand around Tag's hip to pull him closer. "It's like fucking someone from *Grey's Anatomy*."

Tag licked his lips. The tip of his tongue flicked over the curve of Bass's mouth as well and dragged a groan out of him.

"I thought you might have stolen my car," Tag admitted.

Bass pulled back from him with a sigh. "Okay," he said. "I let the Thai thing go, but you suck at talking dirty, Doc."

Heat flushed up into Tag's ears. He tried to ignore it.

"I don't trust you," he pointed out. "Not even for a day. That's—"

"Common sense?" Bass suggested with a shrug. There was something brittle under his smirk, shadowed over the backs of his pale eyes. "You have no reason to trust me and plenty not to. Just because you want me to fuck you doesn't mean you have to pretend you're stupid and don't know who I am…. What I am."

Despite himself, Tag felt the ridiculous—Bass had just agreed with what Tag said—urge to defend Bass well up in his throat. He forced it back down. It was that urge to protect someone, even against themselves, that had gotten him into trouble before.

"I told myself that," he admitted. "That this wasn't stupid as long as I knew what I was getting into. Do I, Bass?"

Bass hesitated for a second, as though that question were hard to answer. Maybe he thought Tag wanted him to be honest. He curled his hand around Tag's hip and pulled him closer.

"This?" he finally said. His lips were soft and his stubble rough as he nuzzled the skin behind Tag's ear. "Me right now? It's about the most honesty I've got. I'm still a liar, and you still shouldn't trust me, but this is as close as anyone comes to knowing what they get with me. Good enough?"

Tag snorted. Of course it wasn't. It was a half-baked promise of nothing in particular, presented as though it were something real.

It *felt* real, but even an idiot wouldn't believe it was.

Maybe a lovestruck idiot.

"What am I going to do?" Tag asked with a wry smile. He cupped the side of Bass's face in his hand and stroked his thumb over the curve of his mouth. "Throw all of, well, this out?"

Bass turned his head into Tag's hand and bit him. The pressure of his teeth prickled a tight wash of pleasure up Tag's arm and into his armpit. His balls clenched in reaction, and he breathed out raggedly. The wet swipe of Bass's tongue soothed the injury.

"You sure about that?" he asked, breath ticklish against Tag's fingers. "This is your last chance to be rid of me without a fight. You might not want to be too hasty."

It was just a joke, but something still hitched eagerly in Tag's chest at the idea. He ignored the fresh heat in his ears.

"Pretty sure I could send you running just by suggesting you get a nine-to-five job," he said. "Or asked if you wanted to bring a toothbrush over."

"Why would I need a toothbrush? Your one is fine," Bass said. He turned Tag around and walked him backward toward the couch. "And trust me, you'd get bored if I weren't a bad boy."

The back of Tag's legs hit the cushions, and he dropped onto the couch. He sprawled back and looked up at Bass. "So what you've got going for you is all of that"—he gestured up and down with his finger—"and a bike?"

"It's usually enough." Bass leaned in and braced his arms on the back of the couch, either side of Tag's head. "What? It's doing it for you."

Tag hooked his fingers into the waistband of Bass's jeans and tugged. "Why don't you do me and—"

His stomach interrupted him with a gurgled complaint that sounded like Charlie Brown's teacher talking. Tag grimaced and pressed his free hand down on his stomach as though that would shut it up.

Bass stared at him for a moment, and then his composure cracked on a laugh. He shook his head as he folded himself down into Tag's lap.

"Seriously," he managed to get out through his laughter as he pressed a quick kiss on Tag's mouth. "You are shit at dirty talk. It ain't hard. Just tell me to fuck you some sorta way and then add that my cock's the hardest or biggest or something. Beg me to get you off."

Tag rubbed his hand over his eyes to block out Bass's grin. He was vaguely embarrassed about the ill-timed noise from his stomach, but it wasn't worth more than a flustered "sorry." It was Bass's grin, inexplicably delighted by the stupid noise, and the heavy weight of him sprawled over Tag's thighs that he couldn't deal with.

It felt real, even if it wasn't.

"Fuck off," Tag muttered, mostly to Bass, a little bit to himself.

Bass snorted against Tag's throat. "Getting closer, but you still haven't quite gotten the hang of it, Doc." He sat back, weight against Tag's thighs, and grabbed the bottom of his top to pull it up. "Maybe it's a bit advanced for you? Try being silent but grateful. Just moan a lot and throw my name into the mix every now and again."

Tag snorted and lifted his arms to squirm out of the shirt.

"If I'm that bad," Tag grumbled into the bleached folds of material as he dragged the shirt over his head, "what exactly are you doing here?"

Bass laughed. He ran his hands down Tag's sides in an impatient caress and bit a string of kisses along his shoulder.

"Well, I have no complaints about the sex, just the talking about it. Besides, I bet a smart guy like you helped tutor a few of the slower students in math and stuff when you were a kid," Bass said. "Same principle."

Tag snarled under his breath as he tossed his shirt onto the floor. He lifted his hips and rolled both of them over so it was Bass sprawled out under him on the couch. The heavy nudge of his cock pressed against Tag's stomach as Bass stretched, all solid muscle and bone.

"So that last chance to ask you to leave," Tag said. "Is it too late to take you up on that?"

The smirk on Bass's mouth deepened into a grin. He cupped his hand around the nape of Tag's neck and pulled him down.

"That?" he drawled as he nipped Tag's lower lip and tugged. "Oh, that was a lie, Doc. I'm not going anywhere tonight. Now, if you're still hungry...." He tightened his fingers as he scruffed Tag and pushed down. "I've got something you can put in your mouth."

"Seriously?" Tag asked. "That's your master class in dirty talk?"

Bass let go of him and folded his arms behind his head. He ran his tongue over his lower lip and tilted his head to the side. "Did it work?"

"What?"

The grin on Bass's face widened. "Now I've said it, do you wanna suck my cock?"

Tag narrowed his eyes. "No."

Bass folded his lower lip between his teeth and shrugged easily. "Pad Thai's in the fridge, then," he said and shifted under Tag. His cock pushed against Tag's hip, insistent now. "I'll have taken care of myself by the time you get back."

He waited, eyebrows raised expectantly. Tag glared at him.

"It'd serve you right if I did," he said.

The grin got away from Bass. Wide and charming as it crinkled the corners of his eyes, it was hard to resist. "You aren't going to, though. Are you, Doc?"

Tag really, *really* wished he could call his bluff. Unfortunately Bass was right. He really did want to, now that he thought about it.

"Shut up," he grumbled. He shifted back onto his knees and looked up the stretch of Bass's laid-out body. Old jeans clung to his legs and sagged around his hips, and the stark lines of his ink showed like faded shadows through his T-shirt.

"Make me," Bass said, a note of challenge in his voice as he spread his thighs. Worn denim pulled tight and threadbare over his groin. "I've got nothing else to do tonight. So show me what you got, Doc."

Heat wriggled under Tag's skin, a heady flush of hunger that started in his lips and fingertips and settled in his balls. His stomach was still empty, but his brain had apparently downgraded that fact in favor of his libido.

Tag unbuttoned Bass's jeans with impatient fingers and then pulled them to his thighs with one brisk yank. A low, ragged sound caught in the back of Bass's throat as the denim scraped along his cock. He was already halfway to hard, his cock heavy and interested as it lay across his stomach.

"Since you're the sex tutor here, any pointers?" Tag asked as he ran his hand up the inside of Bass's thighs. The muscles twitched and tightened under his caress until his balls rested in Tag's palm. He cupped the heavy weight of them and squeezed gently, the skin hot and fine as he kneaded them between his fingers. Bass sucked in a ragged breath and spread his legs wider. The waistband of his jeans was caught tight around his thighs, so Tag had access. "Dos and don'ts?"

Bass tilted his head back against his arms, the line of his throat drawn tight as he swallowed. "Do it, don't bite," he said raggedly. "Go with your instincts, Doc."

"You're such a dick," Tag grumbled as he shifted position until he had one knee on the floor and his hands curled around Bass's thighs.

"See?" Bass pulled one knee up and braced his bare foot against the couch cushion. "You're getting the hang of dirty talk. Now tell it that it's the biggest you've ever seen."

Tag mouthed a wet kiss against the crease of Bass's thigh. The skin was thin and smelled of sex and sweat. "I once saw a penis after a guy had tried to blow it up with a balloon pump, and then he got the valve stuck in it," he said. "So... not so much."

When Bass laughed, his cock bounced against his stomach. The precome was pale and slick against his skin. "Jesus fuck, Doc," he said. "You trying to flunk this class?"

"Maybe I just enjoy the after-school lessons."

Tag licked along the underside of Bass's cock, the clean, musky taste of it sharp against his tongue, and sucked at the slick head as he reached it. He flicked his tongue under the glans and over the head until it was slick, wet, and pink, and Tag could taste Bass all the way back into his throat.

"Son of a bitch," Bass groaned as he hitched his hips up off the couch. His cock pushed deeper into Tag's mouth, hot and hard against his tongue. Tag wrapped his hand around the base and stroked up as he sucked his way down.

He pressed his tongue flat against Bass's cock as he took as much of it into his mouth as he could. The pulse of it trembled through his jaw and down his throat with a familiar throb that made his ass clench and the afterimage of old pleasure flutter up his spine. He let the slick wet shaft slide from his mouth as he lifted his head.

Bass groaned in disappointment and then hissed as Tag worked his fist up the length of the shaft and turned his attentions to the base. He sucked at the dangle of Bass's balls, thin, silky skin creased and folded between his lips, and worked his way up to the thick base of Bass's cock. Tag folded his lips over his teeth. He couldn't wrap all of his mouth around the heft of it, but he licked, kissed, and sucked his way around it.

The muscles in Bass's stomach, tight and defined under his old shirt, tensed as Tag worked, and Bass reached down to curl his fingers around Tag's skull. Habit made Tag tense his shoulder, but Bass just tangled his fingers through his hair.

"You're a bad influence on me, Doc," Bass muttered, rough and ragged in his throat. "Or a good one. That'd be worse in my line of work."

Tag trailed wet, openmouthed, noisy kisses up Bass's cock and twisted his hand along the length in hard, impatient strokes. It made Bass hiss and squirm under him and flex his fingers against the nape of Tag's neck in time with each stroke.

Tag's cock ached with a dull throb in his hips and ass, but it came second to the ragged noises he dragged out of Bass and the vulnerable sprawl of his body.

He wrapped his mouth around Bass's cock again and sucked it into his mouth. Then he curled his tongue around it as he worked his head down, pushed it against the roof of his mouth, and traced the long ridge of veins. His fingers were slick with spit as he squeezed and stroked

Bass's cock, and after a second, he slid them down. He gave Bass's balls, pulled tight and ready up against his body, a quick squeeze, and then followed the tight thread of nerve-rich tissue to his ass. Tag rubbed slick wet fingers around the tight pucker and then pushed one inside.

"Fuck." Bass gritted the curse word out between his teeth. He dug his fingers into the back of Tag's neck. "Doc. Tag. You're going to fucking kill me."

His body was one long, tense line of muscle, pulled tight as wire from one end of Tag's couch to the other. His free hand was dug into the couch cushions, knuckles white under the skin. Tag lifted his head, dragged his lips slowly along the hard sides of Bass's cock, and sucked on the head as he pushed up with his finger on the smooth curve of Bass's prostate. All that hard muscle was undone as Bass came, wet and penny metallic as he spilled over Tag's tongue.

Bass slumped on the couch, spent and boneless. His head was tilted back, and his throat worked as he gulped hard, as though he were the one with a mouthful of come. Tag swallowed and then pushed Bass's shirt up his stomach. He licked his way over the fine skin drawn tight between Bass's hipbones, dipped his tongue into his navel, and then traced sticky kisses over the thick, curved lines of ink marked on his stomach and ribs.

He got halfway up Bass's ribs. Then Bass growled under his breath and scruffed him by the back of the neck to drag him the rest of his way up. Tag kissed him, the taste of sex slippery between their lips, and then groaned as Bass shoved a hand down his scrubs. He wrapped his long, callused fingers around his already aching cock.

"Unless," Bass teased in his ear, "you want to get your goddamn pad Thai."

He didn't make Tag come up with an answer. Tag appreciated that. He wasn't sure he could have strung the words together. He swore against Bass's shoulder as hard strokes of his cock dragged him unceremoniously toward orgasm. It dragged at his thighs and stomach, hot and tight under his skin as he dug his nails into Bass's shoulder. He came with a groan as he jerked his hips and spilled into Bass's hand. It slid, sticky and slippery, down his cock.

"And for the record," Bass said. "I wouldn't steal your car if you paid me. I might be a criminal, but I'm not an idiot. Besides, if you had a working car, you wouldn't need a lift in the morning."

Tag laughed and then untangled himself from Bass so he could get up off the couch. His padded over in the kitchen, washed his hands, and ferreted out the carton of noodles from the fridge. Then he popped the lid, grabbed a fork, and went back into the main room. Bass moved his feet out of the way and then dropped them back into Tag's lap once he sat down.

"You know, if we weren't just casual, I'd tell you to get another job," Bass said as he watched Tag poke through his dinner. "Shepherd might be a monster, but at least I get a lunch and he lets me clock off at a reasonable hour."

"Just a bad day," Tag said as he leaned back. For the first time, the sparse little apartment didn't feel so much like a hotel room. Typical. The minute he decided to move, the place started to feel more homey. "There's this new synthetic opioid doing the rounds. The local junkies don't get how strong it is, so it takes them straight out. Some woman got brought in today, and it turns out her partner works in the hospital. So that was fun."

"Yeah," Bass said quietly. "How is she?"

"Alive. This time," Tag said. He scowled at his noodles as he swirled them around his fork. "I didn't know her husband, that was something, but their kid was in the day care there too. I don't know if that's more convenient or tragic."

"Me either," Bass said quietly. After a second he swung his feet off Tag's lap and got up. He dragged his T-shirt down over his stomach and stretched lazily, all canted shoulders and unbuttoned jeans hung low around his lean hips. "I need a shower. If you finish your dinner in time, come join me."

Tag twisted to watch Bass walk away. Then he glanced down into his pad Thai. It *was* already cold, so it wouldn't be any different in ten minutes.

Chapter Fourteen

One day.

That was how long Bass had managed to steal from his real fake life—one Sunday to play at being someone whose life wasn't hedged about with lies, legends, and violence. The sad thing? Bass wasn't sure if that described Bass or Detective Sebastiani, the cop or the crook.

Neither of them was someone who'd wake up on his stomach in Tag's bed.

Mostly on Tag. He sprawled over his bony back with a shoulder blade for a pillow and his hand folded under Tag's stomach so he could hang on to his cock. They'd gone to dinner, talked about movies, and looked at houses together.

Okay, so it was loft apartments for a single doctor with a shit Mustang. Bass had just... not thought too much about the fact that he'd never see the apartment. Or that if it were real, he'd have probably chewed off his arm to get away. They'd only hooked up a couple of times. For anything real, that was too early to move in together.

If things went according to plan, this legend would be burned with a handful of others that Bass had retired over the years. It wasn't like Bass could hang around after he'd fucked over the Corpse Brothers. Even in jail, Shepherd had enough clout to organize payback. Not, Bass added to himself hastily, that he wanted to stay in Plenty anyhow. He'd spent half his life on the run from this place, from this *him*.

So what the hell, right? In fifteen minutes Tag's alarm would go off, and Bass would lie to him. For the next time, not the last time. Until then he could lie to himself for a while. He'd earned it.

The ceiling creaked overhead. The rhythmic, predictable beat of a tired parent who needed to pace the floors to get their baby to sleep. It was already a familiar sound to Bass.

Tag turned his head to the side, hair kinked and face sleep-creased from the pillow, and opened his eye.

"Not your problem," Bass grumbled into his back.

"I'm a doctor," Tag objected sleepily. "Sick people literally *are* my job."

"In the hospital," Bass said. "Go back to sleep."

"Too late."

Tag untangled himself from the sheets and wriggled out from under Bass. He sat up on the edge of the bed and scratched his head as he listened to what was going on upstairs. Bass sat up too, but only so he could sling an arm over Tag's shoulder and press a kiss against his neck.

"It's your job when you get to the hospital," he said. "Right now it's a weird hobby. The woman knows her own kid. If there's something wrong with it—"

"She's young," Tag pointed out even as he leaned back against Bass's shoulder. "She could be here illegally and not know she can get the baby treatment, or be scared what could happen if she does."

"Then she probably has someone else to ask for help," Bass pointed out. He slid a hand over Tag's hip and stroked his thigh. He was all long, wiry muscle and spare flesh. Bass chewed a bruise into his shoulder. "What are you going to do, walk up there and demand she hand over her kid? She'll think you're crazy. *I* think you're crazy. So come back and be crazy in the sack, where it does me some good."

Tag twisted around and grazed a quick, awkward kiss over Bass's mouth. It was a brief taste of sleep-sour tongue, not that Bass figured his breath was better, and then a soft, chaste buss against his unshaven cheek.

"No strings, remember," he said. "So you don't get a vote on what I do."

"Yeah?" Bass worked his hand back up to cup and squeeze Tag's balls. That got him a ragged moan from Tag and a twitch of interest from the limp cock dangled over his knuckles. "I count a couple of votes in my favor."

Tag grumbled, but he didn't resist as Bass pulled him back into bed.

Fifteen minutes to an hour, Bass decided as he tangled himself around Tag's lanky, eager body, and then he'd get back to work. He'd waited too many years for a chance to get even on Shepherd. He wasn't about to let it slip through his fingers now for the sake of... what? Long legs, a nice ass, and the worst dirty talk in history?

But for a second, that trade-off almost made sense. Almost. Bass used Tag's mouth to drown out his regret that he couldn't quite convince himself of that lie.

"TELL YOUR ex to go fuck himself," Bass told Tag as he dropped him off outside the hospital. He waited until Tag had dismounted the bike and pulled off the helmet. Then he pulled him back in for a slow, thorough kiss. "Because you've got a better offer."

Tag slid an arm around Bass's waist. His fingers were cold as they dipped under his jeans to brush against the curve of his ass.

"You slept over. Don't get cocky," he said into Bass's ear.

Bass let him pull away. "Three nights in a row," he reminded him with a wink. "Hey, if I make it to five, do I get a free prostate exam?"

A grin flashed over Tag's face. "That's complimentary. Trust me, it feels fine."

He turned and loped over to the doors with a wave tossed over his shoulder. Bass watched him go and then tugged his phone out of his pocket. He hadn't ignored the messages he'd gotten while he played hooky—two from his handler under the front of a tattoo shop with its own Facebook page and an inexplicable cadre of devoted fans who'd definitely never been tattooed there, four from Shepherd, and one from Ville—but his replies had leaned into a holding pattern. Now he needed to get things moving again. He slid his thumb over the screen as he typed, half his attention on the road.

Two messages to two men on different sides of the law, but the same content—*I'll get it done today.* The first time he went undercover, Bass thought the hardest part would be tripping the switch between identities. It wasn't. There was never, even when you weren't playing a "road not taken" version of yourself, as much clear blue water between who you pretended to be and who you were. There was always bleed through. That's what made it convincing, and, cop or crook, his bosses always wanted pretty much the same things from him. It was only at the end game that their plans diverged.

No wonder he sometimes lost sight of what he was supposed to want.

Bass shoved his phone back in his hip pocket and pulled away from the curb. Luckily he knew where he could go to jog his memory. It wouldn't even put him behind the loose schedule he had laid out for the day. His old neighborhood wasn't that far from here, only a quarter of an hour.

That prediction turned out to be a few years out of date. Traffic had gotten a lot worse since the last time Bass had driven down this way in a social worker's blue Accord. Not since his dad's truck had broken down again. He was glad that trip hadn't taken half an hour. The social worker's awkward attempts at encouragement to clean up his act had been hard enough to bear.

Nothing much had changed since then. The street had gotten older, the yards had gotten more sparse, and the broken-down cars parked in the road outside had gotten more battered and sun faded. Bass parked behind a canary-yellow Firebird and kicked down the stand on the bike. He leaned on the handlebars and stared over the road.

It was his house now, he supposed. He paid taxes on it, ignored the letters from developers who wanted to buy up the property. Every now and again, the council would try to force him to provide upkeep for it, but he was a cop, and in this neighborhood, it was only a token effort anyhow. He could have paid through the nose to plaster up siding and rip out the rotted-through windows, and the neighbors' houses would still have dry rot in the roof and dead trees in the garden. Still, everyone and the government agreed it was his, the only thing his dad had to leave him when he died.

Bass hung his helmet off the bike and crossed the road. The chain-link fence was rusted and ragged-looking, loose panels kicked back to list into the neglected yard. A ginger cat, crop-eared and scrawny, sprawled on the sun-warmed concrete path. It shot up and disappeared into the weeds with an indignant yowl as Bass wrestled the gate open.

When he was a little kid, the walls were white with yellow trim on the roof and windows, but it had been some shade of its current dirty gray since Bass was a teenager. There was a stack of paint cans in the shed, ready to finally fix the place up. But either Dad had too much work to make the time, or when the work dried up, he didn't see the point.

He walked up to the front door and gave it an exploratory shove. It should have been locked—there was a heavy padlock fastened over the frame—but the screws pulled out of the wood as it swung open.

There were drifts of old leaflets in the hall, kicked to the sides where they'd dried out like leaves, and bottles lined in neat rows on the stairs. It didn't stink since the summer sun had baked out the ripe notes, but there was an undernote of cheap tequila and piss on the air.

Bass leaned against the ripped-up doorframe and rubbed the back of his neck. He didn't need to go any farther. The stairs were where everything shit in this house happened to him, every bit of bad news and every fight.

He snorted. If he went on what he remembered, he'd spent his life between eleven and fifteen either halfway up the stairs or locked in his bedroom. Presumably he'd watched TV in the main room and ate in the kitchen with his dad, but he couldn't swear to it. Maybe if he'd stayed, things would have been different. Or they might not have been. He'd been on a straight shot to a bad end back then.

But it didn't matter because things weren't different.

Dad's hand was clammy on the back of Nico's neck as he dragged him downstairs. His breath was hot and smelled of whiskey—not enough to get him drunk, just enough to give him a dose of Dutch courage.

"Just admit you did it," he hissed in Nico's ear.

"I didn't," Nico protested as he tried to wrench away. Dad fumbled his grip on his neck, and they stumbled on the steps in a clumsy, foot-mashed struggle before he grabbed a handful of Nico's hair and dragged him back. "Get off me! I didn't do anything, Dad!"

It wasn't the first time he'd said it, but this time it was true. The old woman in the hospital had nothing to do with him. He hadn't broken into her house, he hadn't scared her, and he hadn't pushed her down so she hit her head. What would she have that he'd want?

"Shut up," Dad said as he shook him. "It doesn't matter what you did. They don't care. All they need's a body in the cells."

He manhandled Nic down the last of the stairs.

There. Bass's eyes tracked up the wall until he found a torn strip of wallpaper at the right height. He'd ripped his nails down to the quick on that. Bass rubbed his thumb over the nail on his index finger, the ridge on it that had never quite grown back right.

"I found this in his room," Dad told the burly salt-and-pepper cop at the door. He pulled a thin purse out of his back pocket and shoved it out in front him. His hand shook. "Hidden under his bed."

"A law-abiding citizen," the cop drawled. "Look at that. It's going to be more than a slap on the wrist this time, Sebastiani."

Nico knew that. He broke away from his dad, dodged between the cops in the doorway, and made a run for it. He didn't get far. The salt-and-pepper cop caught up with him and grabbed him by the arm, twisted it all the way up to his shoulder blades, and slammed him into the side of a car. He cracked his head against the metal hard enough that the drone of his Miranda rights was almost drowned out.

"Don't make it difficult, kid," the cop said quietly as he snapped on the cuffs and pulled Nico off the car. "Play along. We'll cut you a good deal. Good enough."

He marched Nico, barefoot and shivering even in the summer heat, back down the street to the cop car. As he was shoved roughly into the back, Nico saw Ville at the end of the street, sickly pale and with a black eye. Shepherd stood behind him, one hand clenched on Ville's shoulder. He glared at the cops as they looked his way.

His Dad had done the best he could, Bass supposed. The cops had already been paid off, and it wasn't as though they could afford some hotshot lawyer to oppose the charges. At least this way they got something out of the deal—money and safety from reprisals.

Bass rubbed the back of his neck as though the memory of that clammy grip had left sweat residue on him. Just because he understood why his dad had taken the money didn't mean he forgave him.

Or anyone else.

The old anger was back, hot and sour as bile in the back of his throat. It was bitter, but it was familiar too. Most of the time he drugged it with adrenaline and hard work, stuffed it down where it couldn't get him in trouble, but it was always there when he poked at it.

This was what he'd come back to town for, why he'd agreed to Merlo's plan that might end up burning his real name. He wanted payback, not a doctor with pretty eyes who gave out too many second chances. And he couldn't have both.

Bass spat onto the mildewed carpet. He left the door ajar—what did he care if some squatter moved in—and headed out of the yard and back across the road. A dog in one of the yards leaned on the end of its chain, collar dug deeply into its neck, and barked monotonously at him. Bass ignored it as he tugged his helmet back on and buckled it under his chin. He let the eager itch scratch under his skin and obscure any doubts he had.

The endgame of this operation was coming up, and he needed to stay sharp to keep both sides happy.

He left the street behind on a growl of over-revved engine and a cloud of white smoke. As he drove away, he took one glance back in the rearview mirror.

The last time he saw that exact view was in the cop car as they drove away. The bank was two days away from foreclosure on the house when Bass got turned in to the cops, but after he was charged, his dad paid off the note, free and clear, a fair trade of a house for a son. And he even got to die with a clear conscience after he unburdened himself about what he did—and why and for whom—on his deathbed.

It was the house that Shepherd bought, and Bass left it in his rearview mirror. He took his grudge with him.

THE WHITE stucco house in the end lot of the suburb was a lot nicer than the one Bass grew up in. It was clean and well-maintained, with golf-course smooth green lawns and floor-to-ceiling windows that gave passersby a glimpse at pristine walls, waxed wooden floors, and perfectly curated cushions on the couch.

It made Bass wonder if Dr. Cochrane had gotten better terms on his deal with Shepherd or if it was just down to inflation.

He crossed the road and cut across the smooth lawn to the front door. Cochrane's car wasn't in the drive, but that wasn't a problem. Bass hadn't expected it to be. His girlfriend was in the hospital, and he'd been by her bedside since she was taken in.

Guilt nudged at Bass about the source of that information—he'd claimed he just called Tag with a question about the Mustang, asked about his friend—but he ignored it. He'd gotten good at that over the years. When he finally bowed out of undercover work, that would be hard to unlearn.

Right now, Bass needed to lay the foundations for his threat to Cochrane. It took a bit more work than just giving a corner dealer a brisk workover so they remembered not to short the hand that supplied them. Someone like Cochrane had invested a lot of time and student debt on the idea that he could ward against that sort of thing. His conviction might have been shaken recently, but probably not enough.

Bass scraped garden mud off his boots at the front door and hammered his fist against the lacquered black surface. On the other side of it, someone dropped something heavy on the floor with a clank and a yelp. A child started to wail. Bass hooked his thumbs in his pockets and waited. When no one answered the door, he kicked the bottom of it in a vicious tattoo that rattled it dangerously in its frame.

"I can fucking hear you," he said conversationally when he stopped. "Open the door."

After a moment the door creaked open, security chain looped securely across as though it would do any good, and a vaguely familiar girl in a neat gray uniform peered out at him. He couldn't place her immediately, but the girl didn't have any such problem as the color drained from her face and she tried to slam the door on him. He jammed his boot in the gap just in time and wedged it open.

"I don't need help," she stammered out, her accent thick with fear. "I told him that. We don't need help."

The background wail of a miserable child jogged Bass's memory. It was Tag's neighbor, the one with the sick baby. *Great.* The girl glanced nervously over her shoulder, and Bass let himself grimace. The last thing he needed was this to come home to roost. Tag might have given him a second chance, but Bass didn't think even Tag was softhearted enough to offer up a third.

Unfortunately it looked like Bass might have to find that out.

"Where's Cochrane?" he said as he leaned on the door.

The girl flicked her attention back to him and shook her head. "Gone," she stammered. "His wife is… is sick. Not well. Not *here.*"

Bass tilted his head to the side. "You wouldn't lie for him, would you?" he asked.

Something flinty cut through the girl's eyes. "No," she said sharply. "Leave now. I am not to let anyone in."

She shoved the door. Behind her, a little boy in a fire-engine T-shirt and jeans, dark curls stuck up in matted commas, appeared at the top of the stairs. Tears and snot slicked his round cheeks and the arm he used to wipe them away.

"Where's Mama?" he whined. "I want Mama. I don't wan—"

Bass caught the kid's eyes and gave him a nod. "Hey."

The little boy shut up, shocked out of his whine. He stuck his snotty thumb in his mouth and shuffled to the side to hide behind the banister. A big dark eye peeked around the carved wooden pillar.

"Good-looking kid," Bass said as he turned back to the girl. "You the nanny?"

She gave a small, nervous shake of her head and pushed the door again. It squeezed Bass's foot, although he couldn't really feel it through the heavy leather.

"I just.… I clean for them," she said. "Today I help with… ah.… While Mrs. Cochrane is in the hospital, I help to watch Johnny. Please. I will get in trouble. I will not tell. I won't talk to the doctor."

Bass hesitated. He could feel the bad idea like a balloon in the back of his head, but that didn't help him resist it.

"Tag, the doctor?" he said. "He's not a part of any of this. Okay? He really just wanted to help."

The girl stared at him as though it were a trap and slammed the door the second he pulled his foot out of the jamb. Bass grimaced and shoved his hand through his hair. Sometimes he felt bad about lying to people who trusted him, even if they were crooks. But he could justify that. It never felt good to scare some innocent bystander.

But now Cochrane would know that his house wasn't a safe haven, that there was nowhere safe in Plenty. Like everything else Bass did, that served two masters. On the surface Cochrane would be scared enough to shut his mouth about whatever he knew about Shepherd, but hopefully it would scare him enough that he'd take Merlo's offer of protection in return for information.

Chapter Fifteen

"Hypothetically," Tag said as he set a Starbucks latte down on the desk in front of Ned.

"Ah, no," Ned said sharply as he looked up from his computer. He waved his hands in the air. "That's always a trap. People *say* 'hypothetically' when they mean, 'I fell in the shit, and I want to pull you in too.' Never answer a question that starts with *hypothetically*. There should be a class on that in med school."

Tag pulled out the chair on the other side of the desk and folded himself into it. It wasn't much of an office. Most of it was given over to filing cabinets, and the only window was an envelope of glass high on the wall behind Ned that let in nicotine-yellowed light. A box of tissues was set prominently on the table, and there was a dent in the wall that building management hadn't spackled over yet.

Pediatric oncologists gave out a lot of bad news. Tag would have assumed the trade-off was that they didn't get asked for as much bad advice.

"I would have thought I'd get that more in the ER," he said. "I figured peds would be more... upfront."

Ned laughed at him. "You're joking, right?" he said. "No. When kids are involved, everyone lies more. The parents gave the kid a 'hypothetical' McMuffin before surgery, or a nurse 'hypothetically' let it slip to a parent that there was no hope. It's a rich tapestry up here, Taggart."

"So hypothetically," Tag said as he ignored Ned's groan, "if a baby were wheezy, quiet, and not thriving, what would your diagnosis be?"

Ned sucked down a hot mouthful of coffee. "Cancer," he said with a shrug. "But that's confirmation bias. By the time a case makes it up here, eight times out of ten, the doctor that referred them was right to do so."

"What if you were the first doctor to lay eyes on him?" Tag asked.

Ned squinted at him. "Why ask me?" he said. "That's more your wheelhouse, isn't it? If this kid was brought into the ER, what would your first thought be?"

"That I could order tests," Tag said. "There's a girl in my apartment with a newborn, or close as. It cried a lot when I first moved in, but now the baby has respiratory difficulty, bad color, and is too listless to cry."

The chair creaked as Ned sat back in it. His tie slid to the side, under his arm. "Never good. Tell her to go to her pediatrician. Or bring the baby to the ER."

Tag leaned forward and rested his elbows on the edge of the desk. "I tried that. Even if she understood, and I don't know how much English she speaks, I don't think she will. Most likely diagnosis is bronchitis, right?"

"Uh-uh," Ned said. "Hypothetically, Tag, you're heading for thin ice here. If you treat that baby outside the hospital, what if something happens? You won't have access to an OR, equipment, medication. You won't be covered by the hospital's insurance either, and trust me, I don't care how little English this girl speaks, there will be a malpractice lawyer with a phrasebook on her doorstep before you can say 'hypothetically.'"

"I know."

Ned shook his head. "I thought you would have learned your lesson after what happened with that"—He glanced at the door and dropped his voice to a mutter—"guy and the bikers. That could have been real trouble, and censure from the hospital would have been the least of it. They could have killed you, you know, and dumped you in a shallow grave. Jesus, Tag, I know that you're not from Plenty, so you don't understand, but it is *not* a good idea to get involved with those people."

The thought of Bass sprawled on the bed, sheet tangled around his thighs and his clothes slung over a chair, made Tag shift uncomfortably. It wasn't the sort of involvement that Ned meant, not anymore, but it was still an unwelcome reminder that it probably was a bad idea. No matter what it felt like.

"I think I managed to pick that up from context," Tag said.

Ned snorted and chugged his coffee. He wiped his mouth on the back of his hand as he finished. "You should ask Nate about context."

"Who?"

Ned grimaced as he dropped the cup over the edge of the desk into the trash. The milky dregs of liquid spilled over the torn envelopes and sandwich wrappers.

"Nathan Cochrane," he said. "Dr. Cochrane. Forget it. I shouldn't have said anything."

After the last few months, Tag knew he should be sick of gossip. He was when it was about him. But this was someone whose wife he'd treated a few days ago. He couldn't help but be intrigued at the idea there was some connection.

"You probably shouldn't have told Kieran about me either," Tag pointed out. "Yet he said you did."

Guilt made Ned's ears go red. He scratched his head. "I…. Sorry…. It wasn't like that, though. I told Jenny, and she told Kieran because she thought he should know that something had happened to you. I mean, maybe she thought it would, you know, remind him of when he…. How he used to feel."

Back when he cared about Tag, that was what Ned was trying not to say. Tag appreciated the effort, but it actually didn't hurt anymore. It didn't feel great, but it was more odd than awful. That "Oh, right" feeling when you reached for something and then remembered that it had broken last week.

"How was Cochrane involved with the Corpse Brothers?" Tag pushed. "He doesn't seem like a biker."

"He wasn't. It's nothing like that." Ned hesitated. It took a second as he struggled between his good intentions and his desire to gossip. He finally leaned forward as though someone were going to burst through the door and hear them. "Look, don't repeat this. Nate used to have a fondness for the, ahh…."

Ned put his finger against his nose and snorted noisily.

"I know it's the pediatric floor," Tag said, as he narrowed his eyes in mock seriousness. "But I think you can say *coke*."

"Well, you know what I mean," Ned said impatiently. "It happens, but with Nate it wasn't recreational. It turned into a habit, then a problem, and then a very large chunk of change that he owed to the Brothers."

Tag thought of Shepherd's shark-empty eyes in the dingy bar. He didn't seem like the kind of man who'd forgive a debt.

"What happened?"

Ned scratched his ear. "I don't know the full story," he said. "I was new here then, just a resident down from LA, and the only reason I heard anything is that my roommate dated his sister-in-law for a while. So I just picked up the edges of the story as it happened. He apparently got in far too deep, made some really bad choices that ended his marriage, and the whole thing wrapped up with Nate being questioned over scrips he'd sold to the Brothers to try and stay on top of his debt."

"He was charged?" Tag said in surprise. "And he still works here?"

Ned shrugged. "It was a while ago," he said. "Now they'd have made an example of him, but back then, they just wanted it to go away. Since there was no concrete evidence that he'd done anything—although I will admit I don't think they looked very hard—the administration cut a deal with him instead. He was suspended for a year, and he had to go to rehab, get himself clean, and pay the hospital back for what was 'missing.' In the end it all went away, but he was shit scared of those people, Tag. I heard that they took him out on a boat and tied weights to his legs like they were going to throw him over and let him drown. That's what he told the review board, anyhow. After that he did whatever they wanted."

"What about the debt?" Tag asked. Drug dealers weren't like the utility company. They didn't come up with a payment plan for you when you fell behind. He'd seen enough drug addicts and prostitutes sent to the ER because they owed a dealer a couple hundred dollars. A habit as substantial as the one Ned described would rack up a tab they wouldn't just write off. "What happened to that?"

"Paid it off at the same time he paid off the hospital?" Ned speculated. "I know he sold everything he owned back then—the house, the boat, his car. I think his wife got a lump sum in the divorce too, instead of alimony. I guess it was enough, and he wasn't much use to them while he was suspended. Even now he can't write his own prescriptions."

"I didn't know that."

Ned nodded. "Yeah. It wiped him out personally and professionally. And you know what? He still thinks he got off lucky. And so did you, Tag, if—"

His buzzer went off before he could get properly into his lecture. He pulled it off his belt to check it and cursed as he scrambled to his feet.

"One of my AML patients is going into liver failure." He whipped his white jacket off the back of the chair and dragged it on as he ducked around the desk. "Get your neighbor to bring her baby in to be looked at. If she won't, call CPS."

"I don't want to do that," Tag protested as he got up. "She's just scared—"

"If the baby is sick, so is he," Ned said firmly on his way out the door. "And he can't do anything about it. CPS won't act without cause. Now get off my floor and go back to work, Dr. Hayes. See you later."

Ned jogged away down the corridor.

The anxious mother was already out in the hallway as she looked for him, her hands twisted together and face gaunt with pre-prepared grief. Tag looked away. It was hard enough to lose a patient you'd known for all of twenty minutes, never mind one you'd known since they were three or four.

Ned was a terrible gossip, but a good doctor and not the worst friend in the world either, although Tag already knew he probably wouldn't take his advice.

AS SHIFTS in the ER went, the day was uneventful. Tag even managed to leave the hospital within a reasonable time from the end of his shift and walk home in daylight once he got off the bus. The neighborhood wasn't improved by being able to see it better, but a row of food trucks was set up in one of the abandoned lots. So he grabbed lunch on his way by.

He leaned against the kitchen counter in his apartment and ate his *carne asada* fries from Styrofoam—grease, melted cheese, and spicy, skinny fries. Hot food. Who'd have thought that made it taste better?

Tag glanced up at the ceiling as he chewed. He was halfway through the fries, and the shower was still running up there. It had been on when he came in.

Not that it was his business, he reminded himself. Maybe she liked good, long showers. Tag knew how hard it was to wash a bad day off your back, and he didn't have to clean toilets.

He took a drink of soda and poked at the fries. The cheese had hardened into curd, but the fries were still good once he picked them out. Overhead the footsteps paced back and forth on the floor, and the drone of an exhausted lullaby caught at his ear.

The shower was still running, so either she just liked to waste water or she was trying to steam out her apartment.

Shit. Tag reached for his phone. Maybe Ned was right. And it wouldn't be the first time he'd called CPS. Besides, if he was wrong, he wouldn't be the one who paid for it. He had a dozen new places in his price range earmarked to view.

He pulled up the number and was about to hit the call button when he changed his mind. It had been days since he'd heard much from the baby, but someone had started to cry upstairs. Tag shoved his phone in his back pocket and left the fries to congeal on the counter while he raided the fridge.

Five minutes later he stood on the landing outside the upstairs apartment. There was a threadbare Welcome mat in front of the door, the *W* and *ME* worn down to the nub. It was more than Tag had done to make his place homey.

He rapped his knuckles against the wood and waited. And waited.

"If you don't answer the door, I'm going to have to call CPS," Tag said. He shifted the paper sack full of peace-offer leftovers onto his hip and hoped she understood him. "All I want is to put my mind at ease that the baby is okay. If he is, no need for CPS. Okay?"

There was no response. Tag hoped she didn't call his bluff, because he might not call CPS tonight. But if the baby didn't get better soon, he wouldn't have a choice.

"I've got leftovers and a bottle of soda," he said, the last hand he had to play and the most ridiculous. "It's yours. I just want to check on the baby."

The door opened a crack, just enough to let a nose and one eye peer out dubiously.

"I'm not a whore," she said. "I've got a job."

"I'm not straight," Tag reassured her. She looked blank and still suspicious, so he tried again. At the same time, he handed her the leftovers. "I sleep with men, and I don't want anything from you. Just to check the baby out."

She licked her lips. It was obvious she was so tired she could hardly make her eyes focus, but she still shook her head after a second. "I told you, no help."

Tag shifted his weight onto one foot and stuck out his hand. "I'm Taggart Hayes. I live downstairs. You're…?"

He waited expectantly. After an uncomfortable moment a thin, scar-knuckled hand came out and shook his carefully.

"Maria" was all she gave him, which he already knew. It wasn't an uncommon name in Plenty. Tag had hoped for a surname, but he didn't push. "But the baby is fine. He has the, ah… the… umm… chills?"

A chill. A cold. It could be, but Tag had come this far, and he wasn't going to be put off until he knew the baby was okay.

"It's me or CPS," he reminded her.

That was one word she didn't need put into context. She pulled back and closed the door in his face. Tag swore under his breath in disappointment, but before he could reach for his phone, the door opened again. This time the security chain wasn't strung across it.

"Come in," she said with an impatient gesture from one square, practical hand. "You say you have to, so come in."

Tag squeezed through the door into a room that could, more or less, have been his own. The TV was smaller, and there was a bucket of baby toys next to the couch, but those were the only differences at a glance.

The bathroom door was propped open and the shower was turned on full blast. Wet clouds of steam filled the small room and made the air in the rest of apartment sticky and humid. Tag could taste the hint of old soap and shampoo on the back of his tongue. The baby lay on a blanket in front of the open door, in a faded onesie, and coughed miserably.

"I would have got you some fresh food," Tag apologized as he handed over the crumpled bag. There was a stain at the bottom where something had leaked. "But I didn't have any in the apartment."

Maria peered into the paper mouth of the bag and shrugged. She rubbed her hand over her face. "I have food most times," she said. "For me. For him. But he is so sick, I haven't time. Or I forget."

"It's hard enough being a parent," Tag said. "Never mind to a sick baby. Can I—"

He gestured at the baby. Maria shrugged from behind the sack of food.

"I let you in," she said tiredly. "I will already be in trouble. Why not more trouble?"

She lifted the food onto the counter and started to unpack. Styrofoam containers and paper boxes were lined up neatly on the counter. The burger she half unwrapped and took a huge bite from, her spare hand raised to brush crumbs and sauce from the corners of her mouth.

"He makes that noise all the time," she said as she chewed. "Coughs sometimes, but not as much as last week. Maybe he'll be better soon?"

She sounded hopeful but unconvinced. Neither was Tag.

He knelt down on the floor next to the body, warm steam in his face, and put his hand to the small chest. The baby wheezed and waved his arms and legs listlessly. Tag could feel the rattle of small lungs against his fingers.

"What's his name?" he asked.

Maria didn't answer. He glanced up at her. She took another bite of cold burger and shrugged as she chewed. "I call him Ribka," she said after she swallowed.

Tag studied her for a second. Her English was better than he'd thought. Apparently she just hadn't wanted to speak to him before, and his Ukrainian was still scant. But the few words he knew, he picked up in the ER as people fretted over injured friends and relatives.

Ribka meant *little* something. *Fish*, he thought.

Nobody had used it as a given name, but then some people named their child Abcde. Something wasn't a name until it was.

"How old is he?" he asked.

"Six months," she said promptly. "Six months and a week."

Without a scale or measure, Tag couldn't commit to it, but the baby looked small for that. He unfastened the poppers on the onesie and checked the baby's chest with careful taps. The congestion was obvious.

"Have his bowel movements been normal?" he asked. When Maria didn't answer, he glanced up and reframed the question. "Has he pooped?"

"Shit, you mean?" she asked and then pulled a face. "All the time and bad. Worse than other baby."

"You have another child?" Tag asked. He felt Ribka's forehead. His skin was damp and hot, but it was hard to tell if that was internal or from the steam.

"Not now," Maria said. "Not for as long as him."

She sounded matter-of-fact, almost dismissive. Tag folded Ribka's onesie back over his chest and wondered if he should push. People didn't have one-size-fits-all responses to things, even things like the loss of a child, but….

"What happened to the other baby?" Tag asked cautiously as he picked Ribka up off the blanket. The baby coughed at the shift in position and rubbed his not-quite-chubby-enough fists over his eyes. Tag supported his head with one hand and made faces to see how the baby reacted. His dark eyes were filmed, but he traced Tag's face.

Out of the corner of his eye, he saw Maria shrug. She finished the burger and crumpled the greasy paper into a ball between her hands.

"They went someplace better," she said. "What's wrong with him? You said if you looked at him, you could fix him."

There was always a mental assessment you did when a child came into the ER. The younger the child, the earlier it started. Maria's affect was askew, and the mention of the absent child was a concern, but she was still worried about the baby and had obviously cared for him. He had on clean clothes, there were no visible bruises or marks, and if he was underweight, that could be put down to a failure to thrive from illness. Something was off here, but right now it wasn't something that had to be his business.

"He needs to go to the hospital," Tag said as he rested the baby against his shoulder. "This isn't just a cold, Maria. Your baby could be really ill."

She glanced at the child and looked conflicted, but she shook her head again. Dark hair stuck to her sweat-damp neck and curled under her ears.

"He can't go," she said. Her voice tightened, breathy and high in her throat as she stepped forward and reached for Ribka. "It's a cough. That's all. You'll tell them that, yes? It's a cough, and I'm taking good care of him. I'm doing a good job. Someone was meant to get him already, weeks ago, but I'm still doing my best."

Tag backed up. The steam made him sweat and itch as tried to get through to her. "It's not a cough. He could be really ill, Maria. He could die. You don't want that, for him to…." He pulled up how she'd put it a minute ago about the other baby. "Go somewhere better?"

She pulled her hand down her face in exasperation. "If he's ill… bad ill… he won't go somewhere better," she blurted. Stress cracked the edges of her accent as she struggled to work out how to explain something that needed words she hadn't come across in English. "They don't want a baby that's… sick like that. Bad sick. Healthy babies are what people want. If they find out Ribka is bad sick, they'll… send him back. If they find out I talked to you? They will kill me. No hospital!"

This time when she lunged for the baby, Tag let her pry Ribka out of his arms. She backed away from him, the baby tucked against her shoulder and her cheek pressed against his head as she murmured reassuringly to him. Dark eyes flicked suspiciously at Tag as she put the kitchen counter between them.

"You should go," she said agitatedly. "Get out! If you tell, he'll be mad at you too. Go away, please!"

Tag wished he could. He set broken bones, put people's guts back into place, stitched on the occasional finger. This was either a delusion or a crime. Unfortunately there was a very sick baby in the middle of it, and Tag had, in a fever of idealism after med school, taken the Hippocratic oath.

He held up his hands, palms out and fingers relaxed, and waited for Maria to look at him again. She finally did, resentfully, and Tag licked his lips.

"Does he taste salty?" he asked.

Maria blinked at him, fear short-circuited by confusion. "What?" she spluttered. "That's a stupid thing to ask. Just go."

"If you answer me, I will," Tag lied. "Does the baby taste salty?"

She looked exasperated but pointedly kissed the baby's head. Then she hesitated as she licked her lips slowly. She ran her thumb over her lower lip and slowly, grudgingly, nodded.

Tag took a deep breath. "I think Ribka has cystic fibrosis." He tried to find the right tone to deliver the diagnosis without alarm, but it just sounded vaguely condescending to his ears. It wasn't that he never had to deliver bad news in the ER, but it was usually confirmation of what they already knew. "It's a genetic condition to do with the lungs, a sickness he's had from when he was born and nothing to do with you. But he needs to go to the hospital."

Tears welled up in Maria's eyes. She dashed them away with the back of her hand. "They won't want him if he's sick like that. Forever sick."

"Maybe not," Tag admitted. "But he is. If we take him to the hospital, we can help him… and you."

She barked out a harsh laugh and sniffed. "You'll put me in jail. Send me home."

"That could happen," Tag admitted. "I hope not, but if he doesn't get help? He will die. I don't think you want that."

Maria grimaced and looked down at the baby. Her lips pleated together in a thin line, bled pale around the edges, and she exhaled shakily before she finally nodded.

"Okay." She wiped her nose on her sleeve, sniffed hard, and bounced the baby gently. "What now?"

Tag gave his face a quick scrub with both hands to get the blood flowing again. He patted his pockets for a second—hips, back pockets, hips again just in case—and realized he'd left his phone downstairs. His car was still being "not stolen" with Bass.

"We need to call an ambulance," he said. "Do you have a phone?"

Maria didn't look up from the baby as she shook her head. "It only lets you call them. No one else."

It sounded like paranoia, but it also didn't sound impossible. Some of his friends with kids basically used the phone as electronic tether. They could track it, shut it off, take a photo with it, all from the comfort of their own screen, wherever they were. Maybe Maria's parents had given it to her.

"All right, then," he said. "I left my phone downstairs, so I'll go and make the call. Why don't you pack up your stuff and anything that Ribka will need?"

Maria looked around her flat with blank eyes, as though the idea was too much for her, but then she shuffled toward the bedroom. Tag went into the bathroom and turned off the shower. The sudden silence made him realize how loud the batter of water had been. He took the stairs down two at a time and ducked into the apartment just long enough to find his phone—on the charger, where else—so he could make the call on the way back upstairs.

In hindsight, he supposed, it wasn't really a surprise when he burst back into Maria's apartment to find her gone and Ribka strapped into a baby carrier in the middle of the room.

Shit.

CHAPTER SIXTEEN

NATHAN COCHRANE, dick doctor to the scumbags in town, spat a surprised mouthful of frothy, bright-red blood onto the concrete floor of the parking lot. He hunched over, shoulders curled in and the back of his hand pressed over his mouth and nose as he stumbled backward. His keys swung from one hand, but modern life had pared them down to a fob and a small locker key, so they weren't going to be much use.

"What the fuck," Nathan spewed between his fingers. Flecks of blood caught on the toes of Bass's boots as he prowled along in pace with Nathan's unsteady retreat. Nathan fumbled his wallet out of his pocket and half dropped it, half tossed it Bass. The folded leather dropped onto the ground about halfway between the two of them. "Here. Take it. Just leave me alone. I don't want any trouble. Trust me, I have enough of my own."

There was a greasy black stain on the richly textured leather when Bass picked up the wallet and a wad of notes inside that made it flip open. He peeled out the notes, because why not, and stuck them into his back pocket. The wallet itself he pitched away between the rows of parked cars.

"Thanks," Bass drawled. "But I'm just here to pass on a message."

Nathan finally unhunched long enough to squint at Bass over his newly crooked nose. He peeled his hand away from his face and wiped it on his shirt.

"From who?" he asked, voice thick with mucus and blood. From the flicker of fear on his face, he already knew the answer. He'd just decided to hang on to hope until he was done. "Look, I told them—"

Bass grabbed him by the tie before Nathan could stagger into a BMW, and reeled him back in. The muted pink-on-navy silk creased as he twisted it around his fingers.

"You know what," he said genially as Nathan panted blood over his T-shirt, "I think we've pinpointed your problem, Nate. You don't tell Shepherd anything."

He bounced Nathan off the BMW. The jolt made it flash its lights and the alarm go off, and the nasal drone of it bounced back and forth from the high, bare concrete ceilings. It was like being at the world's most irritating rave—a combination of off-beat light show and designed-to-pierce music.

"You listen."

"Jesus," Nathan blurted. His eyes flickered nervously around the room. "Someone's going to fucking hear that. They'll come down to see what's happened."

That was the point. It also didn't matter. Depending on what POV you looked at the situation through.

"And what the fuck are you going to say if they do?" Bass asked as he leaned into Nate's face. He could hear the gurgle of blood in the man's broken nose and the nervy hiss of his breathing. Bass pulled his voice up into his nose, a nasal, singsong whine in his words as he went on. "You going to ask them for help? Whine about the big bad biker upsetting you?"

Nathan swallowed hard and shook his head. He looked like the photo Tancredi had given him in the station, with a narrow, pleasant face and blue eyes behind heavy, smudged glasses. What the photo couldn't convey was how aggressively bland Nathan was. It wasn't his appearance—he was reasonably good-looking, tall, and he wore well-cut suits that made the most of whatever was underneath—but the way he carried himself. He was an *ummm* made flesh.

"No," he said in a small, tight voice. "I won't."

Bass pulled air through his teeth in a skeptical noise. "See, thing is, Shepherd ain't so sure of that, Nate. He thinks that you're feeling chatty, maybe wanna get some stuff off your chest."

Nathan licked his lips. The taste of blood seemed to catch him by surprise, and nausea flickered over his face. Then he lifted his chin and tried to take a deep breath. It didn't quite squeeze all the way past his chest, but he made the effort.

"Did you go to my house?"

"What? Am I not welcome?" Bass taunted. "Are you ashamed of me, Nate? And I thought we were friends."

The sudden shove from Nathan, the heels of his hands angled up to hit under the breastbone, caught Bass off guard, and he rocked back onto his heels.

"You stay away from my family," Nathan hissed through his teeth. His eyes shone wet through his glasses as he shoved at Bass again. "Isn't what Shepherd did to my partner enough? My son has nothing to do with this, you son of a b—"

The words got stuck in his throat as Bass twisted the tie tightly enough to dig into Nathan's neck. It wasn't that he didn't appreciate the sentiment, but it wouldn't exactly be on-brand to let it go. He kicked Nathan's feet out from under him and used the tie to catch him as Nathan went down onto his well-suited knees.

"Maybe you should have thought of that before," Bass said. "You, your wife, that spoiled whiner of a son you got? All of you belong to the Brothers now, and we'll do whatever the fuck we want to you. Just like Shepherd did to that pretty blond wife of yours. Tell me, Nate, was it worth it?"

Nathan shuddered and then folded in on himself in a welter of tears, blood, and snot. He slumped over Bass's arm, as he shook with broken, horrible sobs. His collapse was so complete and unexpected that Bass recoiled from it. He wanted to push Nate to the point he realized this wouldn't—couldn't—end well for him, prime him to accept Merlo's offer when the SSA made his approach.

He hadn't expected success to be quite so immediate.

"Hey!" someone yelled across the rows of cars. The high beam of a flashlight cut through the dimly lit parking bay and flicked over the two of them. "What's going on over there?"

Bass hauled the still-shuddering Nathan to his feet and slung a heavy, fake-companionable arm over his shoulder.

"My friend here just had a bit of an accident," he said. "Fell into that car and gave himself a bit of a knock. He's all right now, though, ain't you?"

Bass slapped Nathan roughly on one shoulder and squeezed. He dug down through shirt and muscle to pinch the nerves against the bones. The bolt of pain made Nathan's legs buckle under him for a second. Bass held him up until Nathan recovered and pulled a grimace and a tight excuse up out of somewhere.

"I'm fine," he said in a thready, unconvincing voice. He reached up and wiped his fingers under his nose. "I tripped. It's nothing."

The car alarm persistently droned its insistence that something *was* wrong. Bass squeezed Nathan's shoulder again until he felt the collarbone shift under his grip.

"Keep your mouth shut," he told him. "Until Shepherd tells you to talk."

He let go. The sudden cessation of pain made Cochrane stagger. Bass steadied him and then gave him a shove back toward the hospital.

"And clean yourself up," he said. "You look pathetic. Even a junkie doesn't want to see that at her bedside."

Nathan wiped his face again, on his sleeve this time. "Go to hell," he tossed back over his shoulder as he walked away.

The guard shifted his flashlight to Nathan's face as he got closer. "Damn," he blurted in alarm as he made out the mess of Nathan's face. "Do you need to go to the ER or something?"

A sharp jab of panic caught under Bass's ribs at the thought. He could hardly pretend he didn't know why. The last thing he wanted was to drag Tag back into this and push his luck on being able to explain it away.

It wasn't like he could justify the state of the good urologist with an explanation. Even if he could admit he worked for the Feds, Tag would probably want more of a reason than "He was probably involved in a hit-and-run... peripherally." That was dangerous thing about real life for a UC. Even if they were okay with you pretending to be someone else for 80 percent of your day, it mattered what they thought of you for that other 20 percent. It leaked into the job, into your head, until it was time to do something shitty to push the operation forward and you hesitated.

If you were lucky, that got you bounced back to uniform, a lifetime of disciplinaries in your future as you struggled to get used to rules and regs again. If you weren't.... Bass had no idea what happened to some of the guys he had worked with. Well, he could guess as to the what, but he'd probably never know where their bodies ended up.

Stick to name-optional hookups and run the hell away if someone talked about house hunts—those had always been Bass's rules of engagement. He should have known that would bite him in the ass one day. He'd always broken the rules. It's why he ended up a UC and not in IA.

At the other end of the parking lot, Nathan put up his hand to block the guard's light. "No," he said harshly. He exhaled and cleared his throat before he tried again. "No. No, I'm fine. Thank you. My, um…. He broke my fall."

Bass inhaled in relief. Any explanations to Tag wouldn't be tonight, at least. He let his breath out on a short, controlled sigh and smirked.

"Don't mention it. I'm just being a good friend," he said with dark humor. Nathan glanced over his shoulder, and Bass raised a hand in casual salute. The strobe of the BMW's headlights picked out the bloody spots in bright relief. "See you soon, Nathan. Give your boy my best."

Anger and fear blanched Nathan's face. Hopefully in the right proportions for Merlo to use as a lever.

Bass flipped his fingers and sauntered back to his bike.

"Sir," the guard said. The tone of his voice wobbled uncomfortably between demand and request. "Sir, could you wait for a minute? We'll need to make a health and safety report."

"Sorry," Bass yelled over his shoulder as he gunned the bike. "Can't hear you over the alarm."

He turned hard out of the spot and coasted down the ramp as the guard yelled at his back.

"DID YOU have to break his nose?" Merlo asked.

Bass leaned against the frame of the one-way glass, arms crossed, and watched as Nathan folded his arms on the table and rested his head on them. Black bruises had spread out from his nose and settled under his eyes in livid smears.

"He actually did trip into a car."

Merlo gave him a skeptical look from under a raised eyebrow. "Really?"

"He saw me leaning against his car, tried to run for it, and bang." Bass punched his fist into his palm. "Right into the wing mirror on a pickup. Did it work?"

He didn't get an answer right away. Merlo tilted his head and studied Nathan for a moment.

"I'm hopeful we'll be able to get something out of him," Merlo said finally. "Or that he'll at least incriminate himself so I can put pressure on the wife."

That was the sort of cold calculation you had to do on an operation like this. When evidence never quite made it to court and witnesses either clammed up or disappeared, you had to build a case the best you could, even if it rolled over some people who weren't all that bad. You couldn't care what civilians would think about it because they didn't see the full story.

Except when you couldn't help but wonder what a soft-touch doctor with nice eyes would think about it.

"Some days I miss being a uniform," Bass said. It was a lie, but like the best lies, there was a bit of truth to it. He didn't miss the starched collars or hours spent in a car so soaked in piss and puke the smell got into your hair and followed you home. But sometimes he missed the person he'd been. "Back then I still thought I could make people's lives better in the job."

Merlo took off his jacket and hung it over the back of a chair. He unbuttoned the cuffs of his shirt and folded them back.

"If we get Shepherd off the street," he said. "A lot of people's lives will be better, Sebastiani."

"If," Bass repeated pointedly. He nodded through the glass at the sack of a man sunk in on himself in the uncomfortable metal chair. "Until then this is what I do to people."

"On my orders," Merlo pointed out.

"Yeah, well, I guess we're both assholes."

Merlo hooked a finger into his tie and pulled it loose from his collar. A dry smile sketched over his mouth. "I know people who'd agree with you," he said. "But none of them are here to do the job their way instead. Until they are, us assholes just have to do the best we can with what circumstances drop in our lap."

"After this," Bass said. "I think I might go and join them for a while."

"After this you're due some downtime," Merlo agreed. "It's been a hard job."

"No, it's not," Bass said. "That's the problem."

It was perilously close to the sort of admission that could get your legend retired and you pulled off the streets. Once this was over, maybe that was what Bass needed, at least for a while until he got his head straightened back out.

Merlo picked up the prop folder of evidence from the table, officiously stamped and stuffed with cold, graphic images of the Brothers' sins. He tucked it under his arm and glanced briefly at the door to make sure it stayed closed.

"Will it be a problem?"

"Not for you."

That was apparently good enough. It wasn't as though they had anyone else he could put in. Merlo glanced at his faded reflection in the glass, made a face, and straightened his tie back up.

"Are you going to observe?"

"For a bit," Bass said. He fished his phone out of his pocket and glanced at it. A few messages from Shepherd. One from Tag. Instinct twitched his thumb toward Tag's name, but he resisted. He might have gotten more entangled than he expected from answering *Sure* to a *Wanna fuck* from a stranger, but he didn't need to be pathetic about it. "Then I'll need to go show my face at The Sheep's Clothing, protest I did my job when they can't find Cochrane to bring him to heel."

Merlo nodded. "You've done a good job here, Sebastiani, and I know that Frome wants to get more locals in the ranks here in Plenty. If you wanted to stay, I'd put a good word in."

It was simultaneously the last fucking thing Bass wanted and a tempting offer. He settled for a shrug.

"Might not be too good for my health," he said. "Unlikely as it sounds, Shepherd does have friends."

"I'll put a word in wherever you settle," Merlo said. "Just didn't think you were the type to be scared out of somewhere."

Bass quirked up the corner of his mouth. "I don't think I'm the type to take that bait either. Besides, pretty sure my boss in New York expects me back."

Merlo acknowledged the failed gambit with a smile and headed into the interview room. As the door clicked closed, Nathan pushed himself up off the table. He wiped his hands over his face and blustered preemptively as Merlo pulled out a chair to sit down.

"Before I say anything, I want some guarantees in writing," Nathan said. He jabbed his finger against the table to underline the demands he spat out. "I want protection. My family is to be relocated to a location of our choice, and I get immunity from prosecution for anything I did under duress."

Merlo sat down and laid the folder out neatly in front of him.

"Just for you?" he asked as he opened the folder and started to lay photos out in front of him. "So Ms. Lowry is still going to take the rap for her attempt on Jason Morrow's life? I hope her commitment to paying her debt to society goes over well with the judge when it comes to sentencing."

The high, defiant flush washed out of Nathan's cheeks. He opened his mouth to say something, but when no noise came out, he closed it again. Merlo waited patiently as he pushed a photo across the table. Nathan looked at it and then looked away. His throat worked as he swallowed hard.

"Rebecca didn't want to…. We had no choice," he said. "I take full responsibility for that. Rebecca just wanted to protect me."

"Mr. Morrow had threatened you?" Merlo asked. "Ms. Lowry had to mow him down in the street in defense of your life?"

Nathan touched his nose. "Shepherd threatened me. He threatened us both," he said. "Rebecca didn't want to be involved in any of it. She's in the hospital right now because she couldn't cope with what happened to that man."

"What you and your wife did to him, you mean?" Merlo corrected smoothly.

"Yeah," Nathan said after a second. "I guess I do. It wasn't anything to do with Rebecca, though. She didn't want to do it, any of it, but I owed Shepherd. He said this is how I could pay him back. It wasn't a *choice*, I couldn't say no. But we couldn't afford for me to go to prison either. The hospital would fire me. I could lose my license."

"Again."

Two red stripes of color stood out on Nathan's cheeks at that.

"If you know that, then you know I… I had some problems a few years ago, with drugs and… everything. It wiped me out financially. I have no savings, no investments, and Rebecca works three days a week fluffing cushions. She couldn't live on that. Without my wages from the hospital, we'd lose the house. The car. Everything. That's the only reason that Rebecca ran that man down. To pay off my debt, to protect our family. Our son."

"What does Shepherd have to do with your son?"

Nathan rubbed his hand through his hair. "Rebecca can't…. She couldn't get pregnant, and we couldn't adopt, not with my past. Not easily. Then she heard from one of her clients that Shepherd could…. He could provide more than drugs. That's why I got back in touch with him. It wasn't cheap, but it was cheaper than IVF. And it was a guaranteed result. He'd get us a baby. He *got* us a baby. All it took was money, some favors.

Nothing we couldn't live with until this. Rebecca couldn't live with this. She thought she could at first, but when she saw what she'd done to that man and…. I want Rebecca to have protection too," he said. "Immunity for her when she gets better. Otherwise I won't tell you anything."

"You already have, Nathan," Merlo pointed out, not unkindly. "More than you could afford to if you planned to walk out of here with the rest of Shepherd's secrets. But you knew that wasn't going to happen when you came in. That's why Shepherd sent one of his boys to do that to your face, didn't he? He knew you wanted to come clean, get the guilt off your chest."

Nathan barked out a harsh laugh and rested his forehead on his fist. "You make me sound brave," he said. "I'm not. Never have been. I'm just more scared of what Shepherd is going to ask me to do next. Because I'll do it, do it to pay him off, get him off my back. I've done it before."

Merlo nodded. "Except somehow you always end up deeper in his pockets?"

The hint of sympathy in Merlo's voice, something closer to fellow feeling than pity, pulled Nathan's head back up. He stared with desperate eagerness over the table.

"Yeah," he said. "Every time."

There it was. The hook had caught. Bass glanced down at his phone as it rattled against his fingers. It was Shepherd again.

Where R U?

The next few days—or it could be weeks, sometimes it could even drag out to months—were the riskiest. Once the net started to close in, Shepherd would be on high alert for signs of disloyalty, even if he didn't suspect a UC, as his allies saw blood in the water. Yet at the same time, Bass would need to stay close in case Shepherd reacted unexpectedly, and violently, to the applied pressure.

He texted back, *Getting laid*, as he pushed himself off the wall.

At this point Nathan and whatever incriminating evidence he had was Merlo's business. If anything came out that Bass needed to know, there were ways to get in touch with him.

"FIFTY THAT Ville shit the bed," Mick muttered in an aside to Bass as he passed him a beer. He pointed at Ville with his chin. "That's the face of someone whose boss isn't pleased with him."

That was one way to describe it. Another would be that it was barely a face. Ville's eyes were puffed up, bruised like blood blisters, and his face was so swollen it looked like raw meat ready to slide off his skull. Bass looked away.

One way or another, Ville had brought this on himself. He'd left Bass to take the rap for something Shepherd had done—bought his way into the bad boy's good books—and he'd probably done a lot worse over the years between then and now to keep his name in there. That didn't mean Bass couldn't feel bad. He set Ville up for this particular beating, and he hadn't even done it for revenge. It was just useful to have that dissent to keep eyes off him.

"I'll take that bet," Bass said as he took a swig of beer. "It looks like Shepherd's already beaten the sorry into Ville. You gotta show your work for a good object lesson."

They clinked bottles to seal the bet. Bass took another drink and made himself slouch back against the bar. Nerves crawled under his skin, itchy with adrenaline as he tried to judge the mood.

Most people seemed to be in the same boat, on edge. Sonny, balanced on a crutch under one arm, looked grim as he talked to Fat Boone in the corner. Bass looked them over quickly, registered the guns shoved into the waistbands of their jeans, and turned his attention back to his beer.

"Maybe we're gonna move against the Albanians," Bass guessed aloud. He bit the side of his tongue in irritation the second the words were out. People with nothing to worry about didn't feel the pressure to fill the silence. Mick was content with his beer and whatever he'd picked out from between his teeth as they waited. But now that he'd opened his mouth, he needed to finish the thought. "Get some payback for Sonny and for my fucking love life."

Mick scratched under his chin. "I heard you still had a soft spot for that doctor."

"Nothing soft about it," Bass cracked. The echo of his flirtation with Tag made him feel uncomfortable and sort of dirty for a second as Mick sniggered. "And trust me, he made me pay for it. Literally. You know what new shocks for a Mustang cost?"

Mick leaned his elbows back against the bar. "You know what your problem is, Bass? Gay guys have high standards. The key to a happy house is low expectations. My old lady is happy I buy her a pizza. She doesn't expect much from me, and I don't expect much from her."

Bass gave Mick a sidelong look. It wasn't something Bass's dad had ever said, but other than the part about gay guys, it could have been the guiding principle of his life. Don't expect too much, and you might be happy with what you get.

"I didn't know you knew so much about the gay dating scene," he said.

"I watch TV," Mick said with a shrug. "I got YouTube."

"Yeah, well—"

Before he had to think of an answer, Shepherd kicked the door to his office open from the inside. It slammed into the wall hard enough to crack the skin of paint and plaster and sagged crookedly from loose hinges. Shepherd stalked out, blood splattered over his white T-shirt and a girl's long, dark hair tangled around his fist as he dragged her behind him.

"The fuck—" Mick muttered as he straightened up.

"We got a fucking problem," Shepherd rasped. He threw the girl down on the floor. The big bad bikers shuffled backward as though her bad luck might be contagious. "This stupid bitch had one job, and she fucked it up. And after Ville told me she could be trusted."

Nobody bothered to pretend they hadn't turned to look at Ville. He lurched painfully out of his chair and swung a kick at the girl. She rolled out of his way before his toe could connect to her ribs.

"Stupid bitch," Ville slurred through swollen lips. "What'd you do now? All you had to do was a watch a fucking baby. How hard is that?"

Shepherd casually backhanded Ville into his chair. "I could ask you the same question, Ville," he spat. "I send you on vacation, all expenses paid for you and your favorite whore here—"

"Not a whore," the girl muttered.

"Shut up." Shepherd used his boot to shove her back down on the floor. "All you had to do was find someone to sell you a healthy baby and bring it back. Instead what the fuck happened? You bring back some defective inbred Mexican brat, and now we've got a problem."

He lifted his foot. The girl shuddered and pushed herself up on skinny, wiry arms. She shoved her hair back from her face with the back of her hand. "The baby was going to die. I didn't tell anything, just gave Ribka to doctor and left. No one was told anything, no one has your name, and no dead baby."

It was the girl from Tag's building, the one with the sick baby.

Fuck.

Bass took a long, cold drink of beer and wondered what the odds were that Tag wasn't involved.

CHAPTER SEVENTEEN

"I THOUGHT your diagnostic superpowers were restricted to the ER, Dr. Hayes," Deputy Tancredi said. She wiped at the shoulder of her uniform with a wet paper towel an apologetic nurse had run to the bathroom to get. "What made you pay special attention to this child?"

Did she sound suspicious? Tag couldn't tell. He slouched down in the molded plastic chair in the hospital waiting room and stretched his legs out in front of him. His sneakers almost touched Tancredi's polished police-issue boots.

"I don't know," he said. "They lived above me, and I heard them a lot? I was in a good mood one day and noticed she was worried? I thought I was going to hand over a packet of antibiotics and have that warm feeling of being a good guy."

Tancredi sniffed the damp spot on her shoulder. "You save lives every day. Wasn't that enough?"

He shrugged. "I guess? Deputy, I don't know why I decided to stick my nose in. But I assure you I thought Ribka had bronchitis, *maybe* whooping cough from the unvaccinated suburbs. Not that he was...."

The sentence trailed off as Tag shrugged helplessly. It hadn't taken long to confirm Tag's diagnosis once they got the baby to the ER pediatrician, but the other questions around Ribka were still up in the air. All they had was Maria's name, the fact that she disappeared rather than come to the hospital, and Tag's account of what happened.

It was possible, although hopefully unlikely, that they thought he'd killed her and stolen the baby.

"Ribka," Tancredi said as she sat down next to him. She pulled a notebook out of her pocket and unclipped a pen from it. "Is that his name?"

Tag shrugged again. "It's what Maria called him," he said. "It means little fish. I've never heard it used as a given name before, but it's a common Ukranian nickname and I guess people have called their babies weirder things."

"You know a lot of Ukrainian?"

"That and 'where does it hurt,'" he said. "I've never had enough Ukrainian patients to make learning more a priority. Look, I don't know what's going on here. The only reason I got involved was because the kid was—"

"Do you know the name Ville Ritola?"

"No."

"Nico Sebastiani never mentioned him to you?"

"Who—" Tag stopped midquestion as his brain tripped over the surname. He'd known Bass was only a nickname. That's what they agreed on. It was just not something he expected to come up in the middle of a police interview. "Bass? No, he never did. It doesn't ring a bell, anyhow. Why?"

Tancredi scribbled something and turned a page. "The girl in the apartment, Maria, she never mentioned Ville Ritola?"

"No. Why?"

"The apartment is in his name," Tancredi said. "Maybe he's the child's father?"

"I never saw her with anyone," Tag said. "But I work shifts, sometimes nights. It doesn't make it easy to socialize with the neighbors."

A quick smile creased Tancredi's freckled face. "Tell me about it," she said. "I think my neighbors think my partner lives there alone."

"Maria never mentioned anyone else," Tag said. "We didn't talk much. I used to live in New York. It didn't seem that odd."

"Until today."

"Well, yeah. When she implied this wasn't actually her baby and then ran away, even in New York, that'd be considered a bit odd." Tag scrambled up out of the chair and paced across the room. There was a shelf of small toys tucked in behind the door—a teddy bear and a couple of ragged-cornered board-game boxes. *Operation* and *Kerplunk*. He wondered if anyone had ever actually cracked them open for a game while they waited for word on their baby. "What's going on, Deputy? Maria…. Look, I don't know what she did, or if she did anything, but she couldn't have been older than nineteen. Whatever is going on, she's probably in danger right now."

"Probably," Tancredi agreed. "And we are looking for her, but as far as we can tell, you're the only person in that building who ever spoke to her. So if you want to help Maria, you need to talk to me."

Tag clenched his hands at his sides and breathed through the urge to throw something. He knew the deputy was just doing her job, but it felt like a call to a computer helpline. Yes, he had turned his computer on and off. No, he hadn't forgotten the time Maria talked about her mother who worked in the new Starbucks.

"I don't know what else to tell you," Tag said. "Maria didn't tell me anything. I think I did most of the talking, to try and convince her to let me bring the baby here."

"The baby was sick," Tancredi said. "Why wouldn't she want to bring him here?"

"She said he couldn't be sick, that they wouldn't want him if he was sick," Tag said for the sixth time. He understood the theory—make people say it often enough, and they'd eventually slip up and tell the truth—but he was still tired. Nervous. "And she said that if someone found out she'd asked for help, they'd kill her. So I suppose it was mostly that."

"That didn't alarm you? You were happy to still leave her with the baby while you went to get your phone?" Tancredi watched him as he paced back and forth, her dark eyes interested. "Weren't you worried that she might hurt the baby rather than let him go to the hospital?"

"No," Tag said. "She'd taken care of him, she tried to hide that he was sick so he wouldn't be sent away, and she'd sing to him when he couldn't sleep. I don't know if Maria is involved in something criminal or having a break from reality, but she obviously cared for this baby."

Tancredi nodded and wrote that down. Her pen scratched across the narrow span of paper from one side to the other in a wall of neatly rounded-off letters. Tag watched her for a second and then shoved his hands into his pockets.

"What does Bass have to do with this?" he asked. "Nico Sebastiani?"

It was a good name. Tag was caught between the old scrape of fear that he'd been played for a fool—*Again*, an inner voice that sounded a lot like Kieran noted—and idle curiosity about whether the name fit Bass or not. He tried to focus on the more important question.

"That's nothing for you to worry about, sir," Tancredi said. She licked her thumb and turned the page. "Did Maria mention any other names? Marc Gulliver? Nathan Cochrane."

Tag gave her a started look. "What…. No."

"But there's something?" Tancredi said. "You know the names."

"I'm a gentleman," Tag said. "I try to remember the names of everyone whose internal organs I've stuck my fingers in recently."

Tancredi stared at him for a moment and then gave a grudging nod. "Fair point," she said. "Although if you weren't a surgeon, that would be a very disturbing thing to say. But you never heard those names or anything like them from Maria."

He could honestly answer no to that, and it seemed like Tancredi had finally run out of ways to ask the same question over and over. She tucked her notebook back into her pocket and scrambled up, vaguely graceless, from the chair.

"If you think of anything, call me," she said as she handed him another one of her cards. "If you see Maria again, get in touch. She isn't going to be in trouble."

Tag took the card. He flicked the stiff edge of it with his thumb. "You don't know that," he said.

"No," she admitted. "But I hope it's true."

Tag tucked the card in his pocket and turned his back on her as he stared at an old poster on the wall. In a series of useful vignettes, a cartoon heart encouraged people with depression to talk to someone.

"Are the Corpse Brothers MC involved in this investigation?" he blurted before he could think better of it. "Is that why you asked about Bass?"

There was a chance he'd missed her, that she wouldn't hear him on her way out the door. He wasn't sure if that would have made his life easier or not. Unfortunately he didn't think his conscience would take "Well, I tried" as good enough. It didn't matter anyhow because he heard the creak of the door as it swung back against her hand.

"That isn't something I can comment on at this stage of the investigation," Tancredi said. "Why do you ask?"

Tag gave the little heart a dirty look, as though this were its inspirational fault, and turned around. He hesitated uncomfortably as he weighed his loyalties. This was information he'd been told in confidence by one friend and that he knew someone he cared about probably wouldn't appreciate him sharing.

"Why would Maria know Doctor Cochrane?"

"I don't know if she does," Tancredi said. "His name just came up in connection with our inquiries. Do you know something about him?"

"I don't. I just heard some gossip. Somebody could have just made it up and passed it around."

"Or?" Tancredi closed the door. "This can be in total confidence, Dr. Hayes. If there's something you know that can help that baby, you have to tell us."

"The rumor is that Nathan sold Shepherd prescriptions for pain pills to pay for his own addiction. The hospital hushed it up back then, but Nathan lost everything—his house, his wife, nearly his career. He had to sell everything to pay back the hospital and get Shepherd off his back."

He'd meant it to be news. Tancredi just looked slightly disappointed, as though he'd built her up to expect more.

"Thank you, Dr. Hayes," she said. "I appreciate the…. Wait, back then? When was this?"

"Before my time," Tag said. "Ten, twelve years?"

Tancredi bit her lower lip as excitement sparked in her eyes. That was more the reaction he'd expected, although he wasn't sure why the timeline mattered.

"That could be… useful," she said. "Thank you, Dr. Hayes."

This time it sounded as though she meant it.

TAG FELT a wash of relief as the social worker finally arrived after nearly a week to take Ribka to his foster home. It didn't really make any difference to him, he supposed. The police had taken the carrier and the small bag of clothes that Maria had put together for the baby, so he had nothing to hand over. And just because he was the one to check the baby into the hospital, that didn't give him any actual legal standing.

It felt as though he'd passed the baton of responsibility. Ribka was now Annette Davies's problem, and Tag could go home with a clean conscience. Clear of this, at least, since he still wasn't sure how he felt about his involvement with Bass… or how he felt about himself over it.

Tag leaned against the bus stop pole and shoved his hands into the pockets of his hoodie. He couldn't even plead ignorance. Sure, for that first week, he'd been in the dark, but after that? He knew perfectly well what Bass did, what he was, and he overlooked it because he liked him. It was easy to enjoy the bad boy and the bike until he saw the actual cost of his thrills.

Now? Tag still wanted the possessive sprawl of Bass's body over his in bed, the hunger for him, and the open, confident affection. But it wasn't easy anymore. Once you realized something, it wasn't so easy to pretend it away again. He could probably manage it for a while, but he couldn't overlook terrified women the same way he could being fucked over himself.

He absently fingered the phone in his pocket. He didn't actually need to worry about that, he supposed, since he hadn't heard from Bass in days. The last text had been brusque and four days ago.

Be careful. Trust me.

As though he could do both of those things at once.

"Tag?"

Kieran. Tag thumped his head gently against the pole in frustration. Even if he was more or less over being dumped, he wasn't quite at the point where he wanted to be friends with his ex, especially not today, when he could hear the "I told you so" in his near future.

"I've told you before," Kieran said. "Ignoring something doesn't make it disappear."

"You don't know that," Tag said. "It just hasn't worked so far, but maybe I haven't tried hard enough."

Kieran didn't reply. The weight of his refusal to play into Tag's mood was almost tangible. After a second, Tag gave up and looked around.

"Kieran," he said with mock surprise. "Where did you come from? No Freddie?"

"He's at his nephew's birthday party," Kieran said. "I'm headed back over there. I was called in for an emergency consult."

Tag snorted to himself, but not quietly enough, because Kieran gave him a disapproving look.

"I just always imagine him being the Other Man," Tag said. "Either sprawled seductively over a table or propped sexily against a wall, rubbing whiskey and truffles into his nipples."

"He'd lose his job."

"I just never imagined him playing musical chairs at a kid's birthday party." Tag glanced down at his feet and scuffed his sneaker over a weed in the pavement. "I guess people aren't always who you want them to be."

"I wasn't for you," Kieran admitted. "I try to be for Freddie, even though it's not always easy. Are you okay with that?"

For fuck's sake. Apparently Tag couldn't have one politely distant conversation with his ex without said ex making it a thing.

"No," Tag said caustically. "I'm not. The idea makes me want to sit on the ground and scream until I pass out. What are you going to do about it?"

He waited expectantly for a second. When Kieran didn't come up with anything, Tag snorted impatiently. "Don't flatter yourself, Kieran. I'm fine. If you and Freddie make each other happy, get on with it."

Kieran's shoulders relaxed. "I suppose I should wish you and your biker the same," he said, but then he didn't. "I didn't come over to talk about Freddie. Ned told me about why the police were here last week. A girl abandoned her baby with you?"

"Ned can't keep his mouth shut."

Kieran chuckled and put his hands in the pockets of his jacket. "You've noticed. Still, it sounded awful. Is the child okay?"

There was a lot to cover there, and Tag wasn't sure how much he could actually share. Legally.

"Better now he's getting the care he needs," he said. "No news on his... um... my neighbor yet."

"And you?"

"Great."

"I've known you for years," Kieran said. "And I'm a psychiatrist. That is clearly not true. Look, why don't I give you a lift? We can talk. Whatever happened between us—how we got here—doesn't mean we have to hate each other."

"I'm fine, really," Tag said. He smiled at Kieran. and it was mostly genuine. "The bus ride will give me time to think, and don't you have a birthday party to get to?"

Kieran spread his arms, hands still in his pockets so his jacket flared like wings. "It's a one-year-old's party with clowns and an open bar. I love Freddie, but I can love him and be late to this. Jimmy's appreciation of Chuckles the Dancing Clown won't be dimmed just because I'm not there for the cake." He pulled one hand out of his pocket and put it on Tag's arm. His fingers were warm through the thin blue cotton sleeve as he squeezed. "Come on, I know you hate the bus."

There was a possibility in that offer, in the way Kieran's hand lingered. It wasn't concrete, nothing they'd have to actually acknowledge, but they *had* known each other a long time. If they wanted, it could just happen. It wouldn't even have to mean anything. Tag would get even with Freddie for every sly smile he'd looked back at after the truth came out, and he'd see if an old flame could burn Bass out of his heart.

Or head. One or the other.

Tag didn't know what Kieran wanted to take from the moment, but then, that was Kieran's problem.

"I've gotten used to it," he said and stepped back. The thread of "we could" pulled tight between them, stretched, and then snapped. It dissolved as though it had never been there at all, not even awkwardness left. Tag waved a hand at the schedule under scratched plastic. "Ten stops. It gives me time to think."

Kieran hesitated for a second. Then he discarded whatever he was going to say and stepped back.

"I guess I could still make it for the cake—"

It all happened at once. A white van veered across the road and mounted the pavement. It screeched close enough to Tag that he jumped out of the way, and the van's mirror snapped off against the bus stop. Glass splintered and scattered over his feet. The panel door slammed open, and a big man swung out and grabbed Tag by the hood.

"Doc," the fat, dark-haired biker Tag vaguely remembered from the bar—Fat Boone—said. He twisted the fabric around his fist and yanked. "Shepherd wants to have a fucking word with you."

Tag staggered as he lost his balance. Panic flared, and he swung his elbow back in a sharp, gut-aimed blow. It connected—he felt it sink into the hot flesh—but there was solid muscle under the layer of flab. Boone just grunted at the blow and hauled Tag off his feet. Hung by his hoodie, Tag tried to squirm out of it. Before he could shed it, Boone shook him like a dog with a rat and jabbed a payback fist into his kidney.

Pain flushed through Tag like boiled water. He choked on it, and his legs went out from under him like someone had bodychecked him.

"Let go of him," Kieran shouted in alarm. He fumbled his phone out of his pocket. "What the hell are you doing? I'm going to call the police!"

"Shut him up," Boone snarled over his shoulder as he dragged Tag into the van.

A biker with close-cropped hair and a deceptively genial face, one thigh still thick with bandages from the operation, swung a shotgun up onto his hip.

"Kieran, get out of here," Tag yelled. He grabbed at the biker's leg to try to pull him off balance. "Get inside."

The biker grunted in annoyance and kicked Tag away from him. He braced himself, legs spread for balance, and fired. Blood sprayed from Kieran's shoulder and splattered the wall behind him. His satchel, the strap torn apart, slid from his shoulder and hit the ground.

Then so did he.

"Kieran," Tag yelled. He lunged forward and grabbed the side of the door. The protocol of a shotgun injury ran through his brain on a loop, dispassionate and useless from here. "Let me go. I can help him. Just let—"

A meaty hand clipped him around the ear, hard enough to rattle his brain. "Get your hand out of the door," Boone ordered as he grabbed the handle to swing it back. "Or lose your fingers. Not gonna stitch anyone back together again after that."

Tag let go.

The van door slammed shut, and it jolted down off the pavement. Tag half slid, half scrambled over to the far side and pressed his back against the metal. Panic rattled against the inside of his skull, but there was nothing to do with the flood of adrenaline. His hands shook, and he clamped them between his knees.

"What do you want?" he asked.

Boone glanced at him. He wiped a hand over his sweaty face and then wiped it on his jeans. "A peaceful life, Doc," he said. "But looks like you fucked that up."

CHAPTER EIGHTEEN

THE CHEAP air freshener glued in the corner of The Sheep's Clothing toilets oozed the heavy, overpowering smell of gardenias. It wasn't enough to cover up the smell of shit, and it mixed oddly with the salty, meaty smell of old blood.

It had been a bad week for Shepherd—two consignments of drugs intercepted, three of his trap houses closed down, too many of his street dealers picked up, frisked down, and locked up—and he'd shared the misery. A middleman for a client in LA questioned Shepherd if he could actually come through on the deal. Shepherd had broken the sink with the guy's face, blood scabbed on the white porcelain and a bloody tooth jammed in the plug, and put his unconscious body on a bus up the coast.

Bass paced the small space nervously as he waited for Merlo to call him back.

"Shit. Shit. Shit," he muttered to himself under his breath. Where the fuck was Merlo? The only reason to have a handler was so you could get in touch when something went wrong, either side of the line.

Ten wide, dirty tiles from the door to the far wall, under the small window that was cracked open onto the alley. The smell of garbage and cat piss from the dumpster was an improvement on the stink in here.

Bass made the trip twice. Then he stopped in front of the wall and, with a surge of frustration, cracked his fist off it. His hand came off worse than the wall. One of the pale blue tiles chipped from his ring, and his knuckles split open.

"Shit," he muttered again, resignedly this time.

The sink was out of order, so he wrapped the hem of his T-shirt around his hand. It would stop bleeding eventually.

His phone finally buzzed in his hand, and he snatched it up to his ear.

"Something is going down," he said sharply. "Shepherd sent Boone and Sonny an hour ago, tooled up and on a mission. He didn't tell anyone else why or what next. I think he suspects that someone in the club has informed on him."

There was a pause on the other end of the phone as Merlo absorbed that. Bass fidgeted as he waited and shot nervous glances at the door. There was only so long you could spend in the bathroom before people started to ask questions.

"Fuck," Merlo said after due consideration. "There's just been an incident at the hospital. Someone was shot."

Bass closed his eyes and braced his bloody fist against the wall for support. His stomach sank like a stone into his boots. A quiet, terrible voice strung a series of *fuck, fuck, fuck*s together in the back of his head.

"Tag—"

"No. It was a doctor, but it wasn't Hayes," Merlo said. In the background of the call, Bass could hear raised voices and sirens in the background. His stomach lurched queasily in an attempt at relief, but it was halfhearted. The last twenty-four hours Bass had felt that itch that meant the shit was about to hit the fan somewhere. "He was shot in a drive-by near the hospital this afternoon. They called me in case it was related to some of the cases he's consulted with the agency on this year."

The unsettled feeling in Bass's gut latched on to that. "Psychiatrist?"

"I'd say that was an impressive guess, but it's a fairly safe bet," Merlo said. "Why?"

"Redhead?"

"The odds were against you getting that one right," Merlo admitted. "You know him."

"He's Tag's ex," Bass said. He scrubbed his knuckles over his forehead in frustration as he turned away from the wall. What he wanted to do was call Tag, make sure he was okay, and go find him if he didn't answer. But he was pretty sure his number had been blocked again, and if he walked out of The Sheep's Clothing right now, he wouldn't get far. Merlo hadn't touched the core MC yet, but he'd gutted their business interests and pulled in enough people they knew would squeal. It was the closest anyone had gotten to actually defanging the Brothers in a long time. "Check in on him. Make sure he's either at work or at home."

Merlo made a distracted noise on the other end. "A deputy is on the way to his house. I'll check in with the hospital administrator to see when he's expected on shift. If we track him down, I'll put a protection detail on him. He's not just your boyfriend. He's a witness in the case."

"Let me know if you don't find him," Bass said.

"Why? There's nothing you can do," Merlo pointed out bluntly. "Stay where you are, keep out of trouble, and I promise that I will keep Dr. Hayes safe. Do your job, Detective Sebastiani, and trust me to do mine."

He hung up, and Bass clenched his fist around the phone.

"No," he said aloud to the small bloodstained room. "I don't think I will."

BIKERS WERE different from other criminals. That was the idea they bought into, anyhow. They weren't like the Mafia or the Russians, who were just in it for money and power. They liked to pretend they were Robin Hood on a Harley, modern-day Vikings. Once a year one of them would punch some wife beater in the face and pretend that made it okay to turn out fifteen-year-olds with track marks on their thighs.

It was a brittle lie, and it was almost always where the cracks started to show first when law enforcement put pressure on an MC.

Bass went behind the bar and grabbed a bottle of tequila. He took a swig straight from the bottle and swilled it around his mouth for a second before he let it slide down his throat. The cheap liquor burned from the back of his tongue to the pit of his stomach.

"Fuck," he growled as he wiped his mouth on his sleeve. "It tastes like cactus piss."

Mick glanced up from the game of solitaire on his table and scowled. "Why the fuck drink it, then?" he snapped. "You can't even hold your whiskey. You think you can guzzle tequila?"

Bass stared back at him, bared his teeth in a fuck-you smile, and took another swig. He ignored the urge to grimace at the taste for a second time. Tequila wasn't his drink to start with, and this was barely tequila. It tasted more like rubbing alcohol someone had soaked a vanilla pod in.

"Getting a head start on you, Mick," he said as he slammed the bottle back down on the bar. "After this shit hits the fan, the border's going to be the only option. I might as well get used to the taste now."

Mick dealt out three cards and scowled as the suicide king came out to play. He swept them back up off the table and shuffled the unlucky royal back into the deck.

"You think this is the first time the Feds have tried to close us down?" he said. "Merlo's got a hard-on for us because he thinks taking us out will make his reputation, but his old boss was no better. He tried to get rid of us too, but we're still here, and he's in the boneyard. Shepherd's like fucking Teflon, Bass. Nothing sticks."

Bass pressed the palm of his hand down over the mouth of the tequila bottle. His knuckles were swollen with blue bruises under the skin around the scabs, but no one had noticed yet. Or if they had, they didn't care.

"Yeah?" he said. "Well, I've seen the Feds take other gangs down like this, and it's fucking surgical. First of all they cut our supply lines so the money dries up, then they start on anyone that does business with us. It doesn't even matter if they have anything that sticks. They just need to make it a royal pain in the fucking ass to deal with us."

He abandoned the tequila—he'd made his point with it, and another swig would land him on his ass—and grabbed a beer from the bar fridge instead.

"Then what?" someone asked.

Not Mick. He had more sense. Bass used the edge of the bar to pop the cap off the beer. He licked the froth of it as it bubbled down the glass.

"No money. No business," he ticked off on his fingers. Then he stopped, took a drink, and stuck his thumb out on the third point. "No friends. Then they just pick us off, one by one, as we're stuck shaking down hookers on street corners like pimps to get the money to buy a pack of smokes. I don't know about you guys, but it's real nice to have J.J. Diggs in a suit that costs more than the DA's education turn up in court to call them all bastards. I am not looking forward to whatever scrub that washed up in the Public Defender's office getting my name wrong when he accidentally pleads manslaughter up to murder."

He drowned any other complaints with a long draft of beer. This time he didn't actually drink any of it, just blocked the bottle with his tongue and swallowed his own spit, but it gave the right impact. Out of the corner of his eye, he could see frowns groove deeper into sun-leathered faces, and the small puddles of conversation dried up as people thought about their own best interests.

Usually he'd let it drop there, let the ideas settle, and take private bets on who'd go to Merlo first for a good deal. Tonight he was going to have go off book a bit.

"Jesus Christ, tequila makes you a miserable fuck." Mick broke the silence as he gathered up the solitaire spread. He shuffled the cards, the scrape of them loud against callused palms, and slouched back in his chair. "Do you even speak Spanish, you ignorant bastard?"

Bass snorted. "I grew up here," he snorted. "I'll get by."

Over by the pool table, Ville spluttered a curse as he sank the white ball. He shrugged off the offer of a rematch from his opponent with ill grace and a handful of bills tossed onto the table. The other guy shrugged and picked the money off the blood-stained baize as Ville walked away.

It wasn't a bad exit—he'd always been a bad loser—but he played his hand too soon. His phone was already up to his ear as he ducked out the door into the back office. Bass turned his head to watch as Ville shoved the door shut behind him.

He should have known it would be Ville. It wasn't like the guy even had to sell out his best friend to get into Shepherd's good books this time.

Bass leaned his elbows on the bar, the beer bottle clasped in his hands as he waited for everyone's attention to fully shift from him. It didn't take long. Just because what he said was true didn't mean that anyone wanted to hear it. As a muted buzz of conversation started up again, Bass pushed himself off the bar and sauntered over to the back office. He nudged it open and leaned in, shoulder braced against the frame.

"Peace offering?" He held up the beer expectantly. "I didn't mean to get you in the shit."

Ville gave him a sour look through faded bruises. "No?" he said skeptically, even as he extended his hand for the bottle.

"We can call it even, then," Bass offered as he stepped into the room and kicked the door shut behind him.

"Even?" Ville asked. He started to frown, but the expression died as it touched the edges of his bruises. Instead he settled for a snort. "For what? Telling Shepherd about that doctor you fucked?"

The beer bottle slapped against his palm, and he looked surprised as he registered how light it was. His eyes flicked from Bass to the half-empty bottle, and Bass took advantage of the moment of inattention to punch Ville in the face.

His nose, still swollen from Shepherd's beating, flattened under Bass's knuckles. Blood spluttered out, hot and thick, and Ville sucked in his breath to scream. Bass grabbed his face to shut him up, with the heel of his hand braced under Ville's stubbled chin and his fingers dug into the bruised cheeks. The scream bubbled against his palm, choked out through clenched teeth. Bass used the leverage to shove Ville against the filing cabinet.

"Actually I meant for framing me to the cops back in the day, but that's water under the bridge. Now shut up."

Ville swung his arm blindly in a clumsy roundhouse. It was beyond telegraphed, but if Bass let go of Ville's mouth block, they'd have company. Bony knuckles and weighted glass caught against his forehead. The bottle broke in a spray of green glass, and pain grayed through Bass's skull.

He felt warm liquid drip down the side of his face and something scratch at his eyelid when he blinked. It made his eye itch. Ville snarled against his fingers and rammed his knee up toward Bass's groin. Bass blocked with his thigh and clenched his teeth against the dull jolt of pain as Ville's kneecap dug into the muscle.

"I will break your fucking jaw," he said as he tightened his grip. Bruised skin blanched under the pressure, and he felt Ville's jaw creak as he pushed up. "Where's Shepherd?"

Ville glared at him, eyes black and desperate in the soft bed of bruised skin. His breath huffed against Bass's fingers as he panted with anger and pain. Fear too. His answer was garbled through mashed lips, but it wasn't that hard to decipher.

"Fuck off."

"Wrong answer."

He loosened his grip enough that Ville could form words. "Fuck off," Ville spat at him. "I had beatings before, and you aren't going to kill me. Who'll tell you where to find Shepherd then?"

Bass reached around and pulled a gun. Not the one Shepherd had given him. That had been used in two gas station holdups and just had to wait for its day in court, but close enough. He pressed it hard into Ville's groin against his half-done zipper.

"I will blow your fucking cock off."

Doubt flashed through Ville's eyes, and then he visibly firmed his resolve. "You wouldn't."

"They sent me to fucking Nebraska," Bass said. He pushed harder against the gun, and Ville squirmed as it dug into soft flesh. "Because of you."

"And your dad. Nobody shed any tears when you left," Ville hissed.

Bass pushed up under his chin and forced his head back. "Yeah, but he died. So I can't have it out with him. That leaves you or Shepherd. Whose cock is more important to you?"

It was the sort of question that helped to focus the mind. Ville closed his eyes, slits against the bruised skin, and Bass thought he might actually pick Shepherd. The smell of fresh piss filled the air.

"I don't know where he is," he blurted. He squirmed when Bass moved the gun up so it pushed against the base of his cock. "I swear to fuck, I don't know. Not for sure. He had me move the trailer, though."

"Where?"

"Halloran. The old Halloran farm, around the back of the old barn. Jesus Christ, don't shoot me in the dick, man. I'm telling the truth."

Bass moved the gun away from his crotch. "You're a piece of shit, Ville. You know that?"

Sweat stood out in fat, greasy drops on Ville's face. "Shepherd would have gone down just because some old lady fell over her own slippers. You were a minor. You got juvie. Shepherd would have seen you right when you got out. It's not our fault you got sent away."

"I think it was," Bass said, and he hit Ville over the head with the butt of the gun.

Ville stared at him for a moment in slack surprise. Then his eyes rolled back in his head. His body went limp, and Bass let him slump bonelessly to the ground. There was blood on his gun. He wiped it against his jeans and crouched to pull Ville's phone out of his pocket. It was locked. Bass grabbed Ville's hand and pressed his thumb, crooked and black-nailed, against the sensor.

He quickly got into the settings and changed it so it wouldn't relock. It might come in useful later.

The door creaked. Bass scrambled to his feet gracelessly and aimed his gun at Mick's face. It wasn't the first time someone had done that, and the big man was unfazed. He looked at the gun and then down to Ville, battered and in a puddle of his own urine.

"Shit," he drawled and then looked back up. "What the hell have you done, Bass?"

"Shepherd took Doc," Bass said. He stepped over Ville's legs and edged toward the door. "I'm not going to let that go."

Mick heaved a sigh that puffed out his cheeks. "If the Feds get something on Shepherd, Bass, we'll get sent up with him. You think the warm feeling of saving your boyfriend is going to do you any good when you're behind bars for five to ten?"

Lie, truth, or something in the middle? Bass wouldn't be able to stay under anymore, but Merlo might still be able to use the legend.

"I'm hoping he's waiting for me when I get out," Bass said dryly. "He's a surgeon. If I go straight, he can keep me in the manner I'd like to be accustomed. Move away from the door, Mick."

They stared at each other for a second, and then Mick decided to do as he was told, held up his hands, and moved obediently out of the way.

"You sure you want to burn this bridge, Bass?"

Bass pointed his chin at Ville. "I think I already took this bridge out," he said. "Stay here and stay quiet until I leave. Then nobody else gets hurt."

"And if I don't?"

"Somebody does. Maybe you."

Mick leaned back against the desk and crossed his arms. It wasn't an agreement, but it wasn't a disagreement either. Mick's expression was stoic and hard to read. Bass supposed he'd find out what Mick was going to do in a minute.

He flicked the safety on the gun on and stuck it into his jeans. The weight of it pressed against the small of his back. Bass waited, but Mick just smiled sourly and hitched his hip up onto the desk.

"Five minutes," Mick said quietly.

Bass turned to go but hesitated at the door. He liked Mick. He had probably—definitely—deserved to go to jail as much as any of the other Brothers. Still, Bass was going to give him a chance that none of the others would get, just because Mick didn't give a fuck who Bass liked to fuck.

"If you went and got that girl from wherever Shepherd stashed her, took her to Merlo—he'd give you a deal," he said. "I'd burn that bridge, if I were you."

"I'm not a snitch."

"Someone will take the deal," Bass said. "Sonny won't want to limp into jail as a lame duck, Carter needs to see his kids grow up, and Ville's just weak. I'd rather you got the second chance."

Mick raised his eyebrows, and deep wrinkles scored over his forehead. "How come you don't want it for yourself?" he asked. "You got some other arrangement, Bass?"

"I've got Doc. I don't want to push my luck. It's up to you, Mick, but if you wait too long, Shepherd will sell you all out."

He pushed the door open just wide enough to slide out and stalked through the bar.

"Where you going?" Ville's old pool partner called across the bar. "And what the fuck happened to your face?"

He'd forgotten. Bass reached up and rubbed at the gluey stripe of blood on the side of his face.

"Shepherd shot some guy at the hospital earlier," he said. "He wants me to go and shut him up. And my face is my own fucking business."

The pool player backed off with a shrug and an upraised hand. No one else bothered Bass on his way out of the bar. He loped over to his bike and swung his leg over it.

Second chances, he mused as the engine coughed and spluttered for a second before it caught. He'd already had more than most—the foster family that took him out of juvie, even when most people didn't want to take an angry teen into their life, the police department who looked at that juvie record and decided not to prosecute, Tag and his soft heart. He didn't deserve another, but maybe he could get just one more.

He gunned the engine and roared away from The Sheep's Clothing.

CHAPTER NINETEEN

THE BARN smelled of old hay, the lingering BO of generations of cows, and a sharp, mineral smell that Tag assumed was gun oil.

He knelt on the splintered wooden floor of the barn, bits of old straw sharp and hard under his knees, and watched as heavyset men unpacked a stash of guns from the storm cellar under the age-warped boards. Competent, black-gloved hands racked magazines and checked sights and then repacked them in crates below layers of paper and trays of fancy iridescent forks.

The short, gray-haired man who'd arrived in the back seat of a matte-black Hummer turned an ugly black semiautomatic over in his hand. Tag tried to run the numbers in his head, the ratio that figured out casualties versus injured through the rate of fire and bullets used. The answer always sounded exaggerated, even when it wasn't.

"You said you had bump stocks," the man said as he pulled back the slide. "I don't see any."

"I said I could get bump stocks," Shepherd disagreed. "I still can. There's just been a… hitch… in delivery. Never use UPS. They're fucking unreliable."

Shepherd grinned wide, with shining white teeth. It almost disguised the edge of black temper that pulled his upper lip tight and lingered around his cold eyes. If the buyer noticed, he didn't care.

"So, it seems, are you." He shoved the semiautomatic butt first into Shepherd's chest. "I told you I wanted serious firepower. Not one that the local MILFs put their stamp of approval on."

"I told you. I can get the stocks," Shepherd said through his smile as he took back the gun. He flipped on the safety and tucked the gun into the front of his jeans. "Besides, what are you going to do? Get your men to unload again? That seems like a waste of time."

They buyer glanced over his shoulder. "They're bought and paid for, Shepherd," he said. "Their time is mine to waste. If I tell them to unpack the vans, they will. If I tell them to kill your family, they'd do that too."

The smile on Shepherd's face faltered as he clenched his teeth, muscles in knots under his stubbled jaw. Behind him, the fat man who'd grabbed Tag outside the hospital growled and stepped forward, one hand under his jacket on his gun. Shepherd held up a hand to stop him.

"Don't push it, Morales," Shepherd said. "It's a long drive back to the border."

Morales glanced around at the bikers who slouched, arms crossed, in the shadows of the barn as they watched his men work. Their bikes were lined up outside, matte black and unremarkable.

"Luckily," Morales said. "I can afford the gas."

Shepherd glared. "You want the guns or not?"

Morales picked at his lower lip as he considered the question. "I'll pay you half of what we agreed," he said. "Since you did come up short on product."

"You were already getting a good deal," Shepherd said. "Pay up, and you'll get the bump stock. You have my word on it."

"Half," Morales said flatly. "If you get the bump stocks, we can talk about the rest of the money."

"Deal," Shepherd gritted out through clenched teeth. "But I'll remember this, Morales. Don't come asking the Brothers for favors next time you need something."

Morales chuckled as he reached into his jacket for his phone. He tapped the screen as he talked.

"Don't try and gaslight me, Shepherd. I pay for your favors the same way I pay for an hour of a prostitute's time. I don't mistake either for friendship or love."

Shepherd spat on the floor. It dampened a coin-sized spot of dust into mud. "That ain't the song you sang last time your boys came up, Morales. Then we were all fucking brothers, weren't we?"

"And you gouged me on the price for those grenades," Morales said. "Now you need me more than I need you, and I've returned the favor. That's how capitalism works."

A stocky man in a dark suit came in carrying a suitcase from outside, his eyes squinted against the dim light in the barn. He walked past Tag, close enough that Tag could smell the sweat of the drive off his suit, but didn't even glance at him. Morales took the suitcase and held it out to Shepherd.

"Half," he said.

Shepherd took it. "Go fuck yourself."

"Good doing business with you," Morales said. "Oh, and when SSA Merlo arrests you, tell him I haven't forgotten what I owe him either."

He didn't bother to wait on Shepherd's reaction. He just turned and left. The Hummer growled to life outside, and then the noise of its engine retreated into the distance. His men packed the last of the guns into the crates, hoisted them up between them, and headed for the doors. One of the bikers stepped in front of them before they reached it, head down and bullish. The men with the crates slung between them paused midstep and reached into their coats.

Tag didn't know if he should hope they'd start a gunfight or not. The chances he'd dodge all the bullets weren't good, but it might still be his best shot at getting out of there. He closed his eyes and hunched his shoulders as that thought sank in.

"Let them go," Shepherd snapped. "We've got enough fucking problems without Morales tattling on us to the cartels."

Tag opened his eyes and listened as the men left the barn, slammed the van doors, and then drove away. He stared at his knees and the three battered boards in front of him until Shepherd's heavy, scarred leather boots stamped into his field of vision.

"You know why I wanted you to see that?" Shepherd asked.

When Tag didn't answer immediately, someone cuffed him around the back of the head. He clenched his hands against his thighs.

"No," he squeezed out through tight lips.

"Because the reason I have to grovel to the likes of fucking Martin Morales is that you"—Shepherd rapped his knuckles hard against the top of Tag's head—"can't mind your own fucking business. I should have gotten rid of you after you fixed up Sonny's leg, but I thought we had an understanding. You. Kept. Your. Mouth. Shut."

He ground his knuckles into Tag's skull with each word. It ached down into Tag's brain like an external migraine.

"The baby was sick," Tag said. "I didn't know that Maria worked for you or that it wasn't her baby."

"Did anyone ask you to get involved? Did Maria knock on your door at night and offer up her scrawny ass in return for antibiotics?" Shepherd asked. He pinched the top of Tag's ears between thick fingers and squeezed until Tag couldn't stop the yelp of pain that escaped him. It hardly counted as pain, a pinched ear when he'd had a piece of rebar punched through his gut once, but it made him squirm in place as tears sprang to his eyes. "Did Bass tell you to get involved? Slip a quiet word in your ear after he fucked you? Does he think he could take my fucking place?"

"It was a sick baby," Tag said raggedly as he tried to concentrate around the throb of his ear. "Most people wouldn't need an ulterior motive to want to help."

"Ulterior motive," Shepherd mocked as he let go of Tag's ear. "Thinks he's a smart fucker, doesn't he, Boone?"

Boone grunted in agreement. He hooked his thick thumb into the belt loop of his jeans, and the worn denim sagged under his gut. "Never trust a man that wants to cut you open," he said. "That's what my dad always said."

"Shut up," Shepherd said. He slapped the side of Tag's head. "What did Bass tell you about me, Dr. Hayes? Did he say anything about the MC?"

Tag lifted his arm to block the slap and got kicked in the chest instead. The sharp, hot pain made his lungs and heart seize at the same minute. He rolled onto his side and curled up around the pain as he tried to suck in a breath. His heart jumpstarted itself after a missed beat, but his lungs took a moment longer before he managed to force air back into them.

"Did that two-faced fucking bastard put you up to this?" Shepherd roared in his ear. "The fucking Feds had no idea about the adoption racket. Drugs and guns, they had their noses up our asses. No fucker ever mentioned babies until you stuck your nose into my business."

He kicked him again. The heavy toe of his boot caught under Tag's ribs and skidded him over the floor. Something made a brittle *pop* sound, and it was hard to breathe again.

"Suddenly you want to keep quiet?" Shepherd asked. Instinct made Tag start to clench a fist, but Shepherd crushed his fingers against the floor with a heavy boot. "What the fuck did Bass tell you about us?"

Tag swallowed hard as Shepherd leaned his weight on him. Blood throbbed painfully in the tips of his fingers, and his joints popped and grated.

"To stay away from you," Tag said. "That being around him didn't mean I had anything to do with you. Bass never even met Maria."

Not exactly true. Tag remembered Maria's nervous glance at Bass as they spoke outside the building for the first time, and Bass's bored discouragement of Tag's interest. Reverse psychology, to make sure that Tag didn't stick his nose in? One more bit of manipulation.

Tag didn't know, but it wouldn't help him to hurt Bass, so he bit his tongue and breathed raggedly through his nose.

"Did Bass even know about the adoptions?" Boone asked. He flinched back when Shepherd turned to glare at him, hands raised. "Just saying. Sonny didn't. Mick neither. Not their sort of racket, so who'd have told Bass?"

"Maybe Ville ran his mouth," Shepherd said as he ground his foot down. The growl of an approaching motorbike cut through the air. "He likes to preen."

Boone huffed a sigh and raked his fingers through his hair. "Then why not look at *Ville*? It ain't like our problems started when Bass came back. Besides, why? You go down, me or Sonny will step up till you get back. Maybe Mick or one of the long-timers. Bass's been back a couple of months. He only got inked in a month ago. You go down, and no fucking thing changes for him."

After a second, Shepherd lifted his foot and stepped back.

"Maybe," he said, although he didn't sound convinced. "I don't trust him, though. He's in The Sheep's Clothing now, into the tequila and telling everyone to fuck off to Mexico while they still can. Never mind the fact that he was the one I sent to talk to Cochrane. Next thing you know, Cochrane is on Merlo's leash."

Boone shrugged. "It happens. You put a scare into someone, sometimes you scare 'em too much. Why send Bass if you didn't trust him? Why make him a Brother at all?"

A nasty smile flickered over Shepherd's mouth. "I wanted to see what he'd do," he said. "And because you keep your enemies close."

Tag cradled his hand against his chest as he sat up. It felt thick and hot, like a glove overfilled with blood, but he didn't think anything was broken or snapped. That was good. It would heal.

"Why's he your enemy?" he asked because he was still in… fatuated. Or stupid in love, and it would be nice to die with the idea that he hadn't been a total idiot.

Shepherd scowled at the question. "Because you don't shut the fuck up," he snapped as he grabbed Tag's ear again. "If he's not a traitor, then what does he want?"

"Payback," Bass said as he stepped into the barn. His shadow sprawled long and dark over the floor as the sun settled behind him. "After all, you did frame me for what happened to that old woman. You and Ville. Did you really think that my dad would take that to the grave?"

Silence settled over the barn, and nobody looked at Shepherd.

Not even Bass, who dropped his gaze to Tag. His pale eyes were full of a complicated mix of determination, regret, and worry. There was a bloody, roughly cleaned cut on his forehead, a gouge of scabbed red that cut through his brow and nicked the corner of his eye.

"You okay?" he asked.

Tag glanced down at his hand, already swollen and with hints of pale blue under the skin as the damage settled. His chest crackled when he breathed, and his ear throbbed with a distinct, hot pain that made him assume it was the size of a fist.

"No," he said. "Not really. You?"

"Don't worry," Bass said. His smile creased his face and cracked the cut in his eyebrow. A trickle of blood ran down his cheek. "This will be over soon."

Shepherd kneed Tag out of the way and stepped forward. "Yes," he said. "It will. Kill him."

The bikers went for their guns. Bass already had his in hand. It barked twice as he threw himself to the side and scrambled behind the rusted hulk of old farm machinery. One biker staggered as blood sprayed from his thigh and his legs folded under him. The second bullet missed and punched into a support. The two men nearest it yelped as splinters caught their hair and stippled their faces with blood.

That still left six other bikers. Bullets flew across the room, chipped gouges in the worn floor, bounced off the thresher, and ripped through the walls.

Pencil-thin beams of light painted dots on the floor as though it were a game of laser tag. The noise echoed up to the peaked ceiling, loud enough to roust a few pigeons that creaked their way into flight, and bounced back down again.

Tag scrambled out of the way on his one good hand and knees. He got splinters under his nails, sharp little jabs that pinched down to the bed, and in his knees. Adrenaline made his heart thunder painfully against his bruised chest wall. He crawled behind the few boards that were left of a makeshift stall. It felt safe even though it wasn't.

"Tell me something?" Bass yelled. He took another shot, and one of the bikers squealed in pain, surprised, as though they hadn't known they were in a firefight. "How do you plan to clean this up, Shepherd? This isn't a poor old woman and a kid everyone knew was on a fast track to fuck up. You were selling babies to the highest bidder."

Tag squirmed around and peeked through a crack between the boards.

He could see Shepherd. He had taken shelter behind a metal tub. He crouched, heavy shoulders hunched under a grubby T-shirt, with the briefcase at his feet.

"Supply and demand. Women got kids, their husbands can't seal the deal, and I get them," he yelled. "What's so bad about that?"

"You think that's what they'll believe?" Bass mocked. "We all know what sort of pervert buys little kids, Shepherd. What sort of pervert sells them. How long do you think it'll last when that gets out?"

One of the bikers cursed and fired a stuttered line of bullets across the length of the thresher. It sparked and rattled as they struck it and either lodged or bounced.

"Shut the fuck up," Shepherd yelled over the noise. "Nobody's going to believe that."

"They will when Merlo spreads the word," Bass said. "After you murdered two doctors to keep them from testifying?"

One of the bikers looked around. He shook his head and tossed down the gun. "This ain't worth it," he said. "It isn't what I signed up for."

He ran for the door, but Shepherd shot him in the back before he reached it. The man lurched, arms thrown out in surprise, and fell face-first into the dirt.

"Son of a bitch," someone gasped—a soft sound that would have been lost if not for the sudden, startled silence.

"You want out of the Corpse Brothers," Boone yelled despite a slight shake in his voice. "You go out feet first. Brothers for life."

"Yeah, like Cain and Abel," Bass yelled. "Guess who's Cain here, boys. Or was I the only one he didn't tell about this baby-selling racket?"

"You're a fucking snitch," Boone yelled, face red over his salt-and-pepper beard. "So shut your snitching mouth. You're outnumbered, outgunned, and you're going to regret ever coming back here. Believe me."

"You're a lackey," Bass jeered back. "And—"

The low, heavy chop of helicopter blades interrupted him. Everyone glanced up at the ceiling. Boone jabbed a thick finger across the barn at one of the bikers, a skinny boy with more Adam's apple than muscle.

"Check it out."

The boy gulped and edged toward the door. He gave a wide, spooked berth to the corpse on the floor and peered around the door. Then he dropped his gun and raised his arms.

"This is Special Supervisory Agent Javier Merlo," a smooth, controlled voice said from outside, amplified so they all heard him without any need to shout. "You are surrounded. Come out now with your hands in the air."

Bass laughed. "And I got backup on the way."

The guy at the door glanced back at Boone and shrugged. "I just wanted to get laid, man," he said and dodged out the door. When he didn't catch a bullet in the back, others followed until it was just Shepherd, Boone, and the dead.

"You're done, Shepherd," Bass yelled. "Go out with dignity."

Shepherd spat on the floor and glanced over at Boone. His mouth twitched into a grim smile as they made eye contact. "We're Corpse Brothers," he said. "We go out feet first."

Boone nodded grimly and hefted his semiautomatic. "Feet first. Together. Like always."

He roared and charged the door, finger tight on the trigger. Bullets hammered into his body and made him judder in place. He dropped over the dead man in the doorway, and the gun fell out of his hand.

Alone.

Tag registered that at about the same time he felt a hand on the back of his collar. He was wrenched to his feet, and the hot muzzle of a gun was pressed to his forehead. Shepherd dragged him out of the scant shelter of the stall.

"You move," Shepherd told him with a rough shake, "I blow your brains out your other ear."

"Let him go," Bass said. He stepped out from behind the tractor and held up his hands to show he'd dropped the gun. "This isn't going to make it better."

Shepherd laughed, his breath hot and sour against Tag's ear. "Yeah, see, that look on your face? Scared to fuck, just like your dad when I told him to sell you out? That makes it worthwhile."

"He's not part of this."

"Will it hurt you if I kill him?" Shepherd asked.

Bass glanced at Tag and then away. "No."

An inappropriate laugh caught in Tag's throat. Of all the times for Bass to suddenly turn out to be a bad liar. Shepherd laughed at him.

"He's part of this."

A tall man in a crisp shirt and a bulletproof vest stepped over the dead bodies that blocked the door. He aimed his gun at Shepherd.

"David Shepherd," he said. "I'm Special Agent Javi Merlo. Put the gun down."

"I don't think so." Shepherd stepped in front of him. Out of the corner of his eye, Tag could see the briefcase shoved under Shepherd's arm. "I think what I'll do is walk out of here, and you'll let me. Or else you'll have the good doctor's death on your conscience and his brains on your shoes. Your choice."

Merlo glanced at Bass and then lowered his gun. He held up his hand, palm out, while he slid the gun back into his holster.

"Don't do anything rash, David," he said. "This won't end well if you hurt anyone else."

Shepherd shifted the gun to the back of Tag's head and walked him forward.

"I don't have any plans that end me today," Shepherd said. "Get out of the way."

Bass walked sideways to block Shepherd. "Take me. Let him go. You want a hostage? I'm the one you want."

"Don't," Merlo said.

"Thing is," Shepherd said. "No one cares if you live or die."

"I'm an undercover cop," Bass said. He dropped his gun and kicked it away. "Detective Nico Sebastiani, NYPD. They care."

Merlo grimaced. "Goddamn it, Sebastiani."

Under other circumstances, Tag knew he'd care about that. He wasn't sure if he'd be angry, relieved, or just confused, but he'd care. But at the moment, his brain refused to spare it any attention.

"Shut up, Bass," he said through clenched teeth. "Don't be an idiot."

Shepherd tightened his hand on his neck, and his breathing went harsh. "You son of a bitch," he rasped out. "I knew this was all your fault. You fucked everything up."

The grin that spread across Bass's face was a bad idea. "That was the plan. Although I'd have rather you were dead than Boone."

"You first," Shepherd spat as he pulled the gun away from Tag's head.

Then everything happened at once.

"Tag! Run!" Bass yelled as he lunged forward, hands out to grab Shepherd's wrist.

But he was too far away, and Shepherd's finger had already tightened on the trigger. There were a lot of things—more than he even realized—that Tag didn't know about Bass. But he knew he didn't want him dead.

Tag grabbed Shepherd's wrist, thick muscle and bone, and shoved up at the same time he threw his head back. The back of his skull crunched satisfyingly against Shepherd's face, and Shepherd staggered back.

"I said, run," Bass snarled as he got his hands around Shepherd's wrist and wrestled it up. "Is the only place you fucking listen in bed?"

Shepherd roared in frustration and slung Tag bodily away from him, hard enough to bounce him off the bullet-riddled wall of the barn. This time it was definitely more than one rib that bent too far and snapped. As Tag slid down the wall to the ground, Shepherd swung the heavy steel briefcase in a short, brutal arc. The reinforced corner caught Bass on the side of the head, and he staggered backward, unsteady as he shook his head and tried to focus.

"Cop killers do okay in jail," Shepherd said as he jerked the gun back down. He tightened his finger on the trigger as a low, rough voice barked, "*Fass!*" from outside.

The big black dog shot in through the door like an arrow and launched itself into the air. It latched on to Shepherd's forearm, sank its sharp white teeth in to the gums, and whipped its muscular body from side to side.

Shepherd howled and staggered as sixty-five pounds of K-9 tried to take him down. He swung his arm out and around in an attempt to dislodge the black dog as it snarled through meat and bone. When that didn't work, he remembered the gun and tried to jam it into the thick ruff of the dog's neck.

Before he could pull the trigger, a different gun barked and blew most of Shepherd's shoulder joint out through his back. Shepherd finally went down. The dog hung on to him, head slick as an otter with blood, and growled steadily until its handler came in with the order to loose. Then its sharp black ears pricked up, and the plumed tail wagged in happy arcs.

"She okay?" Merlo asked.

The handler slapped the dog's shoulder with rough affection. "She's good."

Tag pushed himself off the wall and limped over to Bass. Bass ignored the attempts to wave him away as Tag caught Bass's face in his hands and probed at his skull with cautious fingertips. Bass flinched away from the pressure with a grimace, and blood stained his sandy curls, but his eyes focused and nothing moved under Tag's fingers.

"You're going to be okay," Tag told him.

"What about you?" Bass asked. He reached up and brushed his fingers along Tag's jaw. "Us?"

That was… not a question Tag had an answer to right then. He pulled away from Bass and loped over to Shepherd. Blood puddled under the man's shoulder, and he had the gray, glassy look of someone going rapidly into shock. The wound on the front of his shoulder wasn't pretty, but it also wasn't the main problem.

Tag pulled his shirt over his head and rolled Shepherd onto his side so he could press the makeshift bandage against the bloody hole.

"You need to get an ambulance up here right now," he said over his shoulder. Blood had already soaked through the green cotton and oozed between his fingers as he kept pressure on it. "And get me a first aid kit, if anyone has one."

"There should be one in the van," the K-9 handler volunteered. Merlo turned and nodded to someone outside.

"Trust me," Bass said as he dropped into a crouch on the other side of Shepherd. "The world's not going to be any worse off if he dies."

"I don't make that decision," Tag said. "This is my job. I'm not going to cry if he dies, but it won't be my fault either. Where's the first aid kit? I need gauze and bandages."

CHAPTER TWENTY

"ARE YOU sure?" the contractor asked. He scratched the back of his head as he leaned back on his heels and took in the stained walls and sagged roof of the old house. "This place has been here for a long time."

Bass put his hands in his back pockets and stared at the house he'd grown up in. He tried to feel sentimental, but any good memories he had under that roof had been overwritten by that one awful night on the stairs.

"I'm sure," he said. "It's been a weight around my neck for years. Just do your worst and bill me when you're done."

The contractor, Danny Lloyd, a stocky Welshman with a ponytail that had shrunk back from his forehead enough that it was noticeable, sucked his teeth.

"Not going to be a small job," he warned. "Done right."

"Whatever you need," Bass said. "I just want it done."

That made Lloyd nod. He chewed at a tag of skin on the side of his nail as he thought about it. "I'll start it tomorrow," he said finally. "If you want, I can get some real estate agents around to give you a quote?"

"That won't be necessary," he said. "I have someone in mind."

It turned out Tancredi's mother was a local realtor. Despite the issues with the property, and Bass, she'd agreed to take it on.

"I'll be back in a few days to check on your progress," Bass said. "Any problems, you have my number."

It was new. His old phone had been handed over to the FBI, where analysts would keep an eye on the text messages and DMs and generate appropriate responses. It was like a timeshare in him—his phone, his identity, even the words he used, and how he used them.

That probably should have bothered him, but it almost felt like a clean slate. And at least he knew Tag hadn't blocked this number.

Yet.

"Do you want to—" Lloyd trailed off and waved his hand at the dead square of lawn and broken windows. "Say goodbye to the old place or go in, get some sort of keepsake? Before we start work, I mean."

Bass gave the house that Shepherd bought one last look. For years he'd let it sit here and fester, so that every time he was sent a bill or a complaint, he'd remember he was angry. Now he'd gotten his revenge—Ville was in jail, Shepherd had been shipped to a prison hospital in Oregon for his recovery, and his dad had been dead for years—and it was time to let it go. He didn't think he'd ever muster forgiveness, although he'd tried, but he could maybe forget. Some of it.

"I already took what I needed," he said. "Thanks, though."

He left Lloyd to it and headed back to the car. Bass missed the bike, last seen on its way into the sheriff's department garage, but the cherry-red Mustang was a fair substitute. He ran his hand over the roof in an appreciative caress. The paintwork was smooth now that he'd buffed out the rust bubbles and repainted.

It turned out Tag had been right. He had stolen the Mustang a bit.

THE ONLY color about Kieran was his shock of red hair. He was nearly the same color as the sheets on the bed, as the bulky bandages over his chest and shoulder.

"I'm sorry," Tag said. He shifted uncomfortably in the molded plastic chair, his ribs still tender under his shirt. "This wouldn't have happened if I'd listened to you."

Kieran swallowed carefully and reached for the glass of water by the bedside.

"I *told* you not to get involved with that biker," he agreed. His voice sounded sticky, and he paused to take a drink. "I stand by that, and you should have listened to me. Maybe it would have been different if you hadn't gotten involved in that world."

"Maybe," Tag admitted stiffly, his throat thick as he choked back the urge to argue.

Kieran took the unusual step of not gloating. He touched his shoulder.

"But this? This happened because a child trafficker was angry that you'd helped a sick baby. We might not have ended things on a great note between us, and I feel no need to litigate whose fault that was, but I'm a doctor too. Do you really think I'd have told you to leave a child to suffer? Even if I knew I was going to get shot? I was never that much of a dick, was I?"

Tag laughed in surprise at the question and how relieved he was at being cut loose from the responsibility for this. He sat back and lied, "No, you weren't. But I don't think Freddie agrees that it wasn't my fault."

"Well, *he* can be a dick," Kieran said. His smile was tired but still had an edge of wonder about it. "He loves me, is all, and... he isn't going to go away, Tag, and you need to get used to that. We both made mistakes. We were both... careless. I cheated on you, and you got me shot. After this, I think whoever was to blame originally, we're even. Agreed?"

That didn't exactly sound fair.

Old habits made Tag bristle, ready to defend his status as the wronged party. Except it turned out it mattered less to Tag than he expected. It was over with Kieran. It would have been nice if they'd ended better. Maybe then they could have been friends or something. Now the best Tag could imagine was somewhere between polite and indifferent. It didn't really matter now, though.

They didn't matter anymore. The history was the history, but there was no future anymore. Not even in bad feelings.

"It was going to happen anyhow," Tag admitted for the first time. "We don't get along, do we?"

Kieran leaned his head back against the pillows. "No. Not for a while," he admitted. "But when they brought you into the hospital, back in New York, we all thought you were going to die. I guess I was so scared for you then that I figured I had to love you."

That stung Tag's ego a little, but only in principle. He knew what Kieran meant. That day in the street, when he'd seen Kieran's blood all over the wall, felt like the moment in a movie where people realized how they really felt—heightened, exaggerated. If nothing else traumatic had happened and Tag weren't fully committed to the bad idea that was Bass, maybe he would have thought it meant something more.

"What about you?" Kieran asked. "Are you okay?"

Tag shrugged. "Broken ribs, bruises." He lifted his hand, the cast so light that it was always a bit of a surprise when he saw it. "A few fractures. I'll live."

Kieran raised an eyebrow. "You'll live," he repeated with the professional edge to his voice that suggested he knew Tag better than Tag did. "Is that all you've got now? I understand your... biker friend...

was one of the men arrested. What does that mean for you? The hospital can't be thrilled that you got yourself involved in that."

That wasn't something he was supposed to talk about. The FBI had asked him to keep Bass's shock confession under wraps for now in case they needed to use him to draw out the remnants of the Brothers from wherever they'd gone to ground. But it wasn't easy.

The fact that your bad-news boyfriend being a secret undercover cop was the kind of thing you wanted to talk about, though? Did it mean he wasn't bad news after all, or worse? Should Tag be angry that Bass had lied to him, or let it go since Bass had told him directly that he was a liar?

"That's… complicated." Tag settled for the hedge that didn't break any confidentiality and didn't help him make any decisions either. "He's gone, though."

"I'm sorry," Kieran said. He didn't sound that convincing.

"Really?" Tag asked.

Kieran took another sip of water. "No," he said. "It's obviously for the best. But I'm sorry you didn't find the right person, the one who'll be there for you."

For a second Tag remembered the desperate edge in Bass's voice as he begged Shepherd to take him instead. The terrible, unconvincing lie of his over whether or not he cared.

"He was," Tag said. "When it mattered. He saved my life, Kieran."

"So did the dog, from what I hear," Kieran said acerbically. "And if you have to keep one of the two, dogs are probably easier on the furniture. Just because you can't have me, Tag, doesn't mean you burn your life down. You can do better. Find your own Freddie."

It wasn't funny, and Tag's ribs hurt too much to laugh. But Tag snorted a laugh between pained *ow*s as he hugged his ribs. By the time he could sit up straight again, Freddie had made it back, and between him and Kieran, it was obvious Tag had worn out his welcome. After a brief moment of confusion as he tried to work out how to say goodbye when they weren't together or at odds—a handshake was out since they'd both lost easy use of their right hands, a hug sounded godawful, and the go-to "fuck off" of the last few months didn't seem appropriate—he decided to just say goodbye.

He would have been disappointed if Freddie hadn't muttered, "And good riddance," as he walked away. One apology down and one to go. He took the elevator up to pediatrics.

Maria was there on her own rights. She was seventeen by a whole week. Ned told Tag the peds nurses got her cupcakes to celebrate. In her pale-blue smock and fluffy terrycloth slippers, she looked younger.

"She's going to testify," Deputy Tancredi told Tag as she walked him into the ward. "So once she leaves here, she'll go into crisis foster care. I think she's going to be okay."

It turned out she not only wasn't Ribka's mother, she was no relation to him at all. She had no idea who was either. Apparently she and Ville had gone down to Mexico for the weekend, and one night a man brought the baby to the door of their hotel room. After that she'd been left to take care of him while Shepherd arranged an adoption.

Tag sat down in his second uncomfortable chair of the day while Tancredi took up a station at the side of the room.

They had mirrored injuries—broken ribs, bruised ears, and a hand in plaster. Maria had a broken nose too and a foot encased in a blocky pink cast. Tag nodded to her hand as he sat down.

"Shepherd liked to stick to what he knew, huh?" he asked.

Maria nodded. Most of her long hair was gone, trimmed down to a pixie cut that tried, but failed, to hide the still-tender bald patches. She picked nervously at her fingernails, and Tag scratched under his cast.

"I'm sorry," they said at the same time.

Maria looked up and smiled. That might be the first time Tag had seen that. "I shouldn't have run away," she said. "I was scared they'd find me. They found me anyhow."

"I should have tried to help sooner," Tag countered. "I should have realized something was wrong."

She shrugged. "No one else did."

That probably wasn't true. Other people had heard the baby cry or watched Maria struggle with the stroller on the stairs, but they just went back to their own lives. Something was obviously wrong, but not in an easy-fix-and-walk-away way.

Tag rubbed his good hand over his jeans. "I just... wanted to make sure you were okay," he said. Then he gestured apologetically at her bruises. "As okay as possible."

She went to brush her hair back from her face and fumbled the gesture as she found none. Instead she rubbed her earlobe and looked around the small ward.

"I thought I would be buried by today," she said. "Dead. Instead I'm here. That's okay enough."

Tancredi caught Tag's eye and tilted her head in a done-here gesture. He acknowledged it and stood up. His ribs hated him.

"If you need anything—"

She shook her head and smoothed cotton down over her leg. "I take care of myself. You do the same."

Apparently, even without the threat of the Brothers, she wasn't that easy to help. Tag shrugged. "Even so," he said. "You know where I work."

She nodded her acceptance of that much, and then Tancredi ushered Tag back out into the hall.

"Sorry," she said. "Until she's out of here and settled somewhere, we don't want to risk anyone who says the wrong thing. For her sake as well as for the case."

Tag nodded. "I guess you'll get in touch with me when—"

"The DA will."

"Okay." Tag paused. He had tried, quite hard, not to care. It should have been easy. It wasn't as though there was a bedrock of foundation to even care about—a couple of dates, more sex, a phone full of dirty videos… and the fact that he suddenly couldn't sleep without the weighted blanket of another human being on him. "Have you heard anything from Bass? Nico, I mean."

"Detective Sebastiani?" Tancredi said. "I'm afraid I'm not at liberty to discuss that. It was always a risk to use his real identity and a fake history, but ideally no one in the Brothers would have ever realized that. Unfortunately Shepherd did, which means that, until the trial, Sebastiani's life is in danger."

Or, Tag translated for her, *it's your own fault.*

"You think I should have let Shepherd die?" he asked.

Tancredi glanced sideways at him. "You did what you thought was right," she said. "But it would have been easier if he died before the paramedics got there."

"First, do no harm," he said.

"You didn't shoot him," Tancredi pointed out. "You just could have not helped."

She wasn't wrong. It just didn't matter. Over the years Tag had treated plenty of people who didn't add much to the world with their existence. Some he'd been able to tell by the neo-Nazi ink on their skin or the bruises on their partner's, but some he'd probably thought were easy, pleasant patients. He treated them anyhow. No one would have blamed him if he hadn't done his best to save Shepherd's life—not even Tag, if he were honest—but what about the next asshole who beat his wife? Or threatened to attack one of the doctors who saved his life, because they were gay, or a woman, or a black woman? Would he be able to convince himself he had no choice but to treat them too?

"I'll bear that in mind next time," he said.

Tancredi tugged at her braid and snorted. "Fingers crossed there won't *be* a next time for you," she said. "It's my job, but local doctors shouldn't be taken hostage more than once a decade. Or, from what I hear, forced out of their home?"

"Annoyed out," Tag corrected with a shrug. "Eggs on the door, late-night calls, and a few anonymous letters."

Ten letters, all text speak and bluntly unimaginative threats. He'd refused to be scared off by someone who spelled *mutilate* as *mutl8*. It was the note on a scrap of lined paper that someone left on his pillow, with his bus number and time on it, that convinced him to go.

Bass had said his locks were shit.

"Apparently a lot of people around there liked the Brothers," he said, "or want the Brothers to think they did if this doesn't take."

"Look," Tancredi said as she fished in her pocket. "My mom's a real estate agent, and I know there's a couple of places she's struggled to get off the market this summer. If you drop me a line later, I can get you an address. She'll cut you a deal on rent, so it'll be cheaper than a hotel, and she'll be happy that the house isn't standing empty."

She handed him her card.

"I have about ten of these," he reminded her as he took it.

"Do you know where any of them are?" she asked. Tag couldn't argue with that, so he tucked the card into his jeans. "Seriously, check in later. You'd be doing her a favor."

"I can pay," he said.

Tancredi shrugged. "Iron the details out with her if you take it," she said. "You might see the neighborhood and decide you'd rather stick with the Super 8."

Tag scoffed at her. She'd obviously never spent the night there. It didn't have local color going for it, just toenails under the bed and a vague, greasy film on the shower curtain.

TWO DAYS later he got off the bus at the end of the street and wondered if she maybe had a point. A big brindle mastiff barked furiously from behind a not particularly sturdy picket fence, and there was a row of battered cars in various states of rust squeezed into the yard next door.

To be fair, it was probably a step up from the motel, and no one had thrown piss or warm water out of a window at him yet, so definitely better than his old apartment. Besides, he'd promised Tancredi's mother he wouldn't judge until he saw it, and in return, she agreed to let him pay his own utilities.

Apparently doctors who saved babies from biker gangs played well in the news. He must have looked less petrified and sick to his stomach than he felt in the news footage.

Faded chalk sketches were scrawled over the pavement. Whatever the powder had originally depicted had been scuffed underfoot until they were just pastel rainbow hues. Some of the houses had their windows papered over with scraps from local papers, newsprint pressed against the glass.

Tag checked his phone again for the address.

Number 82, Tancredi's email informed him, between the blue house and the one with a yellow truck. The truck didn't seem like a good choice of landmark since it could be driven away, but then he reached it. The pickup was propped up on blocks, the bed full of bundles of shrink-wrapped clothes.

Tag grimaced and almost turned around, but then he saw the house itself. The yard was just bare dirt and a concrete path, but the house was freshly painted white with a glossy blue door and oversized windows that were so clean they actually sparkled in the sunlight.

Okay. He could see why Tancredi's mother wanted him to see the house before he made a decision. He unhitched the gate, pushed it open, and headed up to the door. Tancredi said she'd have someone meet him here.

He knocked the door, and it swung open onto… nothing. The inside of the house was just bare walls and concrete floors. When Tag looked up, he could see the liner on the underside of the roof. Truncated pipes and wires jutted out of the walls, capped and looped together with wire, and the air smelled of dust and adhesive.

"What the hell?" Tag muttered. He started to text Tancredi but stalled when it came to what had actually happened. What was he supposed to say? That the house had been burgled? No, not the furniture. The actual house.

He stepped inside to have a look around. There wasn't much to see, but…. The door closed behind him with a sharp noise that made him jump and turn around. The panic that throbbed against his ears meant it took a moment for Tag to register that it wasn't one of the Brothers who'd trapped him.

Or it was, but… one he wanted to see.

"Bass," he said. Then he corrected himself. "Nico."

It didn't feel right.

Slouched against the door, hands in his pockets, Bass crooked up the corner of his mouth in a grin.

"I wanted you to see it when it was done," he said. "But apparently it's going to take weeks, and you know I'm not into delayed gratification."

Tag stared at him. Part of him had expected Bass to look different, to carry himself like a cop instead of a seedy asshole. Based on first impressions, though, the only thing that had changed was that he'd swapped his motorcycle boots for black chucks.

"You…."

Liar. Asshole. Manipulator. There were a lot of things Tag had called Bass in the two weeks since Merlo bundled him out of the SUV and they both disappeared. He'd come up with nearly as many questions—like what had been real and what had been part of the act.

Now he had his chance to say what he wanted.

Or… not.

Tag crossed the space between them in two long strides, pushed Bass back against the door, and kissed him. He buried his good fingers in Bass's curls and hungrily drank down the taste of him. Tongues tangled and teeth scraped over lips in rough, eager bites.

Bass gripped his hips and pulled him closer, until Tag's body pressed against long, lean muscle and bone. It didn't feel any different from when Bass was a criminal. Maybe there wasn't so much difference.

After a long, heady minute, Bass pulled back. He tilted his head against the door and gave Tag a curious look. The cut on his head had scabbed over and been picked off, but a tender swipe of pink scar tissue ran down from his curls to his eyebrow.

"Not going to deny I hoped we'd get around to this," Bass admitted. "But I didn't think it would be this easy."

Tag leaned in and rested his forehead against Bass's, breath mixed and warm between their lips. "Neither did I," he admitted. "You lied to me."

"I did."

"You were a cop," Tag pointed out as he traced the curve of Bass's mouth with soft, openmouthed kisses. "There's no way you should have called me to operate on Sonny that night. No way you should have gotten me involved."

"Merlo had officers outside," Bass mumbled. "If anything had happened, they were ready to get involved. But you're right. It was a shitty thing to do. Even if you had been just a hookup and not—"

"What."

"Fuck off," Bass said uncomfortably. He caught Tag's mouth with his and chewed gently on his lower lip. "I haven't been able to get you out my head since you turned up at my door in that tux, like Prince Charming on a promise. You... matter... a lot more than I planned. I should never have put you in that situation."

Tag stroked his thumb over Bass's jaw, stubble rough under his thumb. "No, you shouldn't have." He took a deep breath and tried to come up for air between the waves of anger, want, and relief that splashed over him. "I love you."

Amusement flashed across Bass's face, tangled through the arousal and caution. "Just had to one-up me, huh?"

"The bad-boy thing was hot," Tag said. "But I love you because you drove me to work, you sleep like a needy koala, you stole my car—"

Bass laughed and pushed himself off the door. "Your dirty talk still needs work. I didn't steal your car this time either. The Feds seized it with everything else at the garage, so I had to get it back. It's drivable now, so you're welcome."

"I don't like that you lied to me," Tag said. "I don't like that you were in danger and I didn't know. Do I even know who you are?"

"Better than anyone. And I'll never lie to you about anything like that again," Bass promised. "After this, no more undercover work for me. Between what happened with Shepherd, and you, I think I've already pushed my luck. So I've handed in my UC credentials, and, if everything works out, I'm going to transfer here full-time."

Tag spluttered. "Here? Is that safe? What about Shepherd? The Corpse Brothers weren't all arrested, and they have associates. Business partners. Tancredi made it sound like you'd have to lie low for the duration?"

Bass nodded slowly. "It was suggested," he said. "But I'm done lying about who I am. It's not going to be right away, not until after Shepherd's trial, but the Brothers who aren't dead are making deals, and Shepherd's friends are going to forget his number once the Feds make his money dry up. Once all that's done, it's going to be no more bad boy, just plain old Deputy Sebastiani. That be enough for you?"

Stupid question.

"I never loved you because you were a bad boy or a crook, any more than I love you because you're a cop," Tag said. "So… yeah, that's enough for me. I mean, don't get me wrong. I'm still pissed off at you for all of it. But I can be mad at you while you're in my bed, and I don't want to waste any more time."

Bass raised his eyebrows and smiled slowly. He turned and brushed a kiss over Tag's palm. "I know I don't want to waste any more," he said. "That's why I got Tancredi's mom to get you out here."

At the reminder, Tag finally peeled himself off Bass and stepped back. He waved his hand at the gutted space.

"Yeah, speaking of that, what is this?" he asked in confusion as he looked around. "I thought this was one of her rentals?"

Bass looked around, and an odd expression flitted over his face.

"It's mine. Bought and paid for," he said, a sliver of something dark in his voice. Then it faded away as Bass turned to smile at Tag. "I inherited it after my dad died, but that was a few years ago. So now that I want to fix it up, turns out it actually needs to be gutted and rebuilt from scratch—big windows, open plan, wet room, room for a dog… a small dog."

Tag snorted. "You stole that from my wish list when I was house hunting," he said. "So what, you thought if you came up with my dream house, I'd forgive you?"

"Yeah," Bass admitted. He slid around until he was in front of Tag and grinned up at him. "Did it work?"

"No," Tag said tartly. It wasn't quite a lie, but nearly. He knew he should be angry—he *was,* he *would* be for a while, when something reminded him—but Bass had saved his life, and he was here in front of Tag. Everything else seemed secondary to that right now. Tag grabbed a handful of Bass's shirt and pulled him closer until their bodies were pressed together. "But keep talking."

It was Tag's turn to get pressed back against the doorframe. Bass slid his hands around his waist and tucked his fingers into the back pockets of Tag's jeans.

"I just had a whole lot of bad memories ripped out of here, so I wanted to put some good ones back in," Bass said as he grazed a kiss over Tag's mouth, his lips warm and wet. "I want you to move in with me, Taggart Hayes, or I will once everything with Shepherd wraps up and the contractor is done with this place. You, me, and a dog. Try and one-up me on that, Doc."

TA MOORE is a Northern Irish writer of romantic suspense, urban fantasy, and contemporary romance novels. A childhood in a rural seaside town fostered a suspicious nature, a love of mystery, and a streak of black humour a mile wide. As her grandmother always said, "She'd laugh at a bad thing, that one," mind you, that was the pot calling the kettle black. TA studied history, Irish mythology, and English at University, mostly because she has always loved a good story. She has worked as a journalist, a finance manager, and in the arts sectors before she finally gave in to a lifelong desire to write.

Coffee, Doc Marten boots, and good friends are the essential things in life. Spiders, mayo, and heels are to be avoided.

Website: www.nevertobetold.co.uk
Facebook: www.facebook.com/TA.Moores
Twitter: @tammy_moore

BONE
TO PICK

TA MOORE

Digging Up Bones: Book One
A Novel from Plenty, California

Cloister Witte is a man with a dark past and a cute dog. He's happy to talk about the dog all day, but after growing up in the shadow of a missing brother, a deadbeat dad, and a criminal stepfather, he'd rather leave the past back in Montana. These days he's a K-9 officer in the San Diego County Sheriff's Department and pays a tithe to his ghosts by doing what no one was able to do for his brother—find the missing and bring them home.

He's good at solving difficult mysteries. The dog is even better.

This time the missing person is a ten-year-old boy who walked into the woods in the middle of the night and didn't come back. With the antagonistic help of distractingly handsome FBI agent Javi Merlo, it quickly becomes clear that Drew Hartley didn't run away. He was taken, and the evidence implies he's not the kidnapper's first victim. As the search intensifies, old grudges and tragedies are pulled into the light of day. But with each clue they uncover, it looks less and less likely that Drew will be found alive.

www.dreamspinnerpress.com

SKIN AND BONE

TA MOORE

Digging Up Bones: Book Two
A Novel from Plenty, California

Cloister Witte and his K-9 partner, Bourneville, find the lost and bring them home.

But the job doesn't always end there.

Janet Morrow, a young trans woman, lies in a coma after wandering away from her car during a storm. But just because Cloister found the young tourist doesn't mean she's home. What brought her to Plenty, California… and who didn't want her to leave?

With the help of Special Agent Javi Merlo, who continues to deny his growing feelings for the rough-edged deputy, Cloister unearths a ten-year-old conspiracy of silence that taps into Plenty's history of corruption.

Janet Morrow's old secrets aren't the only ones coming to light. Javi has tried to put his past behind him, but some people seem determined to pull his skeletons out of the closet. His dark history with a senior agent in Phoenix complicates not just the investigation but his relationship with Cloister.

And since when has he cared about that?

www.dreamspinnerpress.com

CPSIA information can be obtained
at www.ICGtesting.com
Printed in the USA
LVHW042048161219
640677LV00013B/1211/P